Berry on Top

Berry on Top

A Farm Fresh Romance

Book 6

Valerie Comer

Dedication

If your spiritual path has been full of pot-holes,
I dedicate this book to you.

Books by Valerie Comer

Farm Fresh Romance Novels

Raspberries and Vinegar
Wild Mint Tea
Sweetened with Honey
Dandelions for Dinner
Plum Upside Down
Berry on Top

Riverbend Romance Novellas

Secretly Yours
Pinky Promise
Sweet Serenade
Team Bride
Merry Kisses

Urban Farm Fresh Romance Novels

Secrets of Sunbeams

Snowflake Tiara Contemporary Series

More Than a Tiara

Fantasy Novel

Majai's Fury

Acknowledgments

Many thanks to Melanie, Donna, and Linda for being awesome beta readers on a quick turn-around. These gals *rock*! My entire street team is a constant source of encouragement. Thank you all!

Hugs and blessings to Nicole O'Dell. I'm so thankful for her, every single day. I'm also grateful to Ginger for talking me off the ledge and brainstorming with me when I needed a listening ear and a new perspective!

A huge shout-out to my fellow Christian contemporary romance authors at Inspy Romance and to my fellow travelers in the Christian Indie Authors Facebook group. What amazing folks to share the writing journey with.

I appreciate the readers and fans of my Farm Fresh Romance stories! I'm thankful for everyone who has posted reviews, liked my Facebook page, and especially to those who've joined my email list and written to tell me how much my stories mean to them. What an encouragement!

Thanks to my husband, Jim, who embodies romance in my life. I'm grateful... and very much in love! Thanks to my kids, their spouses, and their charming little daughters (my grandgirls), for being my inspiration, my support, and my delight.

I'm deeply thankful to Jesus, who makes all things new and sheds light and hope into dark corners. I write to honor Him.

Chapter 1 ---

*Y*ou have arrived at your destination."

"Come on, GPS," Liz Nemesek muttered. "At least pretend you're as nervous as I am."

She angled her car to the curb and stared at the trim house with its neatly shoveled sidewalk. Number 74. This was her parents' new home? The street hadn't even existed when she left Galena Landing.

She switched off the ignition and took a deep breath. Should she have called first? All she'd done was email from her friend's apartment in Fresno a few days ago, saying she was on her way.

The curtain beside the wrought-iron numbers twitched then fell. An instant later the front door swung open and a gray-haired woman ran toward her with outstretched arms.

Liz surged from the car. "Mom?"

She barely got the word out before she was rocked from side to side and squeezed breathless. Who knew her mother had so much strength in her?

"Liz. Oh, Lizzie, you've come home."

Liz's face was damp from either kisses or tears. Was Mom crying or was she? Likely both. She hadn't planned on getting emotional. Hadn't expected to be treated like a prodigal daughter. Would a reunion feast in her honor be next?

"Come inside, Liz. Your daddy can't wait to see you. How long are you staying? Please say you're home for good." Mom looped an arm around Liz's waist and tugged her up the sidewalk. "Let me call your brother. Maybe he and Jo and the kids can come for dinner."

Third millennium version of the fatted calf. Check.

Liz took a deep breath and allowed Mom to tow her into the house. She blinked, adjusting to the dimness after the bright December sun. Her vision narrowed to her father as he struggled to rise from a leather recliner across the room.

"Lizzie Rose?"

Her heart hiccuped. Sure, news of the illness that devastated him had reached her in Thailand over six years before. Six years. How could she — no. She wouldn't let the guilt get her.

Would. Not. Let it. She was here now, and it had to be soon enough.

Liz blinked back tears. "Hi, Daddy." She closed the distance and wrapped her arms around him. That horrid disease — Guillain-Barré — had done a number on him. He seemed frail. Much older than his sixty years. She should've...

No guilt, Liz. No guilt. She just couldn't go there.

He hugged her close. "Good to see you, Lizzie Rose. How long are you staying?"

That question again. She kissed his cheek. "Not sure, Dad. We'll see."

His brown eyes searched hers. "You're welcome as long as you can. We have room. Always for you."

Liz pushed out a smile. "Thanks." Where that space might be, she couldn't guess. If her parents extended the dining room table — about the only piece of furniture she recognized from her childhood — it would take up half the living room. A tiny hallway revealed three doorways and no stairs.

Yeah, she wouldn't be able to stay with them more than a day or two. Certainly not long enough to figure out her life. Oh, who was she kidding? She'd been trying for the last decade and more. Why think she might nail it this week... or next?

Mom set her cell phone down. "Zachary is stopping in on his way home from work. He says Madelynn was up all night sick, and he doesn't want to give us her germs, so they won't be coming for supper today."

Maddie. A niece Liz hadn't met yet. How old was she? Three? Four? "I'm sorry she's not feeling well." But it would be easier seeing her brother alone than with his happy little family around him. She'd never have guessed Zach would get his degree in veterinary medicine and return to northern Idaho to buy out the old vet clinic. He'd wanted out of Galena Landing as badly as she had.

Who else had come back? Hopefully she wouldn't run into anyone from her high school class.

"Would you like a cup of coffee? Or do you prefer tea?"

"Whichever you'd like. Really. I drink both."

"Or maybe hot apple cider. I know you used to like that."

Oh, man. Mom was fluttering. "It honestly doesn't matter."

"Or hot chocolate?"

"Mom..."

Mom dabbed her eyes. "I'm just so happy you're home. I can't believe you're really here. You look so nice. So tanned. Thailand must have agreed with you."

At times it had. Other times, not so much. Liz managed a smile. "It was a good place. A good job."

Dad shuffled over to the table and lowered himself into a seat. "Was? Are you home for good, then?"

Keep the smile on, Liz. "I'm moving back to the States permanently, yes, but I'm not sure exactly where I'll make my home. A recruiter in Vegas is putting together some leads."

Biting her lip, Mom stared at her a moment before turning to put the kettle on.

"Galena Landing has really grown in the past eleven years." Dad folded his hands on the table. "You might find a good opportunity right here."

Trust Dad to have kept track of the exact amount of time. "I'll see." She might have to. The opportunity she'd returned to interview for in Fresno had been offered to someone else. Life wasn't fair. It never had been and apparently wasn't starting now.

The kettle whistled, and Mom poured hot water into the teapot. At least that was still the same one Liz remembered from her childhood. Why couldn't her parents have kept the old Formica kitchen table and padded vinyl chairs instead of the formal dining table and wooden chairs? They just ditched everything when they moved to town?

Of course, she'd ditched everything when she moved to Thailand.

Not going there. She'd had good reasons, and one of them was the guy she'd convinced herself she was in love with back then. She'd managed to block him out of her mind, sometimes for weeks at a time. When she'd been in Fresno, she'd asked Kara for news, but her friend hadn't kept up with many of their high school friends. Being back in the USA brought so many memories surging to the surface.

She didn't need a better reason to look for a job far from Idaho. Mason would return to visit his parents, at least occasionally. Because everybody did that, except her. She'd poke around a bit, discover where he lived now, and find herself a new job somewhere across the country. The continent was big enough for both of them.

"Here you go, Liz. Cream? Sugar? Or maybe honey. We get buckets of it from Green Acres."

"Green Acres?"

"Where Grandma used to live. We sold the farm to three young ladies back before your dad got sick. Then your brother married one of them." Mom smiled. "It's like we gained three daughters at once."

Right. One daughter had run away, but no big deal. Three random strangers could take her place. They were probably good Christian girls like Liz's older sisters. She'd never figured out how to measure up. "That's nice. I can't wait to meet everyone." It might not be exactly true, but it was appropriate. At least meeting her niece and nephew would be a good thing. She liked kids.

Picturing her big brother as a husband and father, though? That took a ton of imagination.

Mom removed a package of meat from the freezer and put it in the microwave.

"What kind of work are you looking for?" asked Dad.

The million-dollar question. How did a one-month course on how to teach English and a decade of experience in a foreign culture translate into a job back home? "I'm not entirely sure."

Dad nodded. "The feed store is looking for someone, or there's always Super One. Or you might be able to find a spot at Green Acres."

Her brother's commune? Not likely. "I'll see what's available." Somewhere else. Liz rose. "If you're certain you have room for me for a few nights, I'll get my bags in from the car."

Mom turned, flapping her hands. "Oh, leave them. Zachary will be here in a minute. I know he won't mind getting them for you."

15

Liz opened her mouth, shut it again, and sat back down. Mom was probably trying to ram a decade of lost hovering into one day.

A truck rumbled to a stop outside the house and a couple of doors slammed.

Mom rushed over to the door and opened it. The winter wind whistled in. "There's your brother now."

Liz took a deep breath. She could do this. She stood and took two steps closer before Zach stomped in wearing a down parka, knit cap, and mitts. Another man, equally bundled up, followed him and shut the door.

Liz reached for Zach, and he wrapped her against his cold coat. "Lizzie! Good to see you." He released her and smiled into her eyes for a second before turning. "You remember Mason Waterman?"

No. Couldn't be.

The other man pulled off his knit cap, revealing the blond hair and square jaw of someone she used to know far too well. His blue eyes warmed. "Hi, Liz. Welcome back to Galena Landing."

Not Mason. Anyone but him. The room swam, and she grabbed Zach to stay upright.

o0o

Mason Waterman glanced at Steve, Rosemary, and Zach. They were all staring at Liz, who looked about to faint dead away.

Not the response he'd been going for, but perhaps not unexpected. He reached for the doorknob behind him. "I, uh, I'll just wait out in the truck."

That snapped Rosemary out of it. "No, Mason. It's too cold out there."

It wasn't all that cozy in here, either. At least not when Liz's narrowed eyes met his again. Her set jaw told him she remembered every minute that had passed between them that spring. He had plenty of regrets, but maybe this wasn't the right moment for apologies. After all, what did her family know about their past? By everyone's current confused response, he'd bet the answer was *nothing.*

"I just put on a pot of tea." Rosemary pointed back at the kitchen. "And I baked chocolate chip cookies. Please don't rush off."

Zach shrugged out of his parka and kicked off his boots while Liz backed away. "We can stay a few minutes. Can't turn down homemade cookies, can we, Mason?"

At this moment, he'd have no trouble doing so.

Liz gripped the back of a dining chair with enough intensity to turn her knuckles white. There were no rings on her left hand. That was good, right? Or, no. It might have been better if she'd found some other guy. Gotten married. Had a few kids. That would've proven he hadn't hurt her too deeply.

Mason had skipped the wedding part and gone directly to having kids. A family hadn't been enough to keep him and Erin together, though. Man. Where would he even start explaining — let alone apologizing — to Liz? Erin certainly hadn't been open to hearing any of it.

Please, God. You've forgiven me for all the messes I've made. Is it too much to hope that Liz might, too?

By the look on her face, he'd better not hold his breath.

Mason slowly peeled off his coat and hung it in the nearby closet before removing his boots. Zach had already taken a seat at the table with a mug of tea in front of him. Liz still stood, her hands clenched on the chair between her father and brother.

Keeping a buffer. He couldn't blame her. How could she have guessed he'd follow Zach in the door? She couldn't. Likely no one had even thought to tell her he and the twins had moved back to Galena landing. Their old crowd had dispersed long ago. No one knew or cared anymore about what happened way back then.

Except Liz.

And him.

Mason took the chair on the other side of Zach and smiled at Rosemary. "Thanks for the tea."

"You're very welcome. What brings you along with Zach?"

He shrugged. "I dropped my car off at the shop to get a new transmission installed this morning. He offered me a ride for the next couple of days until it's ready."

"Handy you live so close then." Steve reached for a cookie then nudged the plate over to Mason.

Liz's head came up and she glanced sharply from one to the other. She knew as well as he did that the Waterman farm was across the valley from her childhood home.

Steve turned toward Liz. "Mason's renting our old farmhouse from Green Acres. Did your mother tell you your brother and his group bought the home place?"

Her nod seemed a bit jerky, but her gaze flicked back to him. "That's nice." Not at all what her eyes said.

"Come out to the farm tomorrow for supper?" Zach asked Liz.

"Mom said your daughter was sick."

Zach chuckled. "Nothing keeps Maddie down for long. We do, however, try to remember that Dad has a compromised immune system, so we give him a buffer of a few days to make sure."

"You'll want to meet Jo and the children." Rosemary's voice held a hint of hope. Meet Jo and the kids? Wow. How long had it been since Liz had been home? She'd taken her retreat to the Far East more seriously than Mason had realized.

She took a deep breath. "I, um, I could probably do that."

"And the rest of the gang," Steve put in. "Busy place they have out there."

"Th-the gang?" Liz's eyes flicked to Mason's then away.

"The other members of their community," Rosemary said.

18

"Um…"

Liz probably wanted to know if he'd be there for dinner. If he was part of the gang. Then she could find a way out. He wasn't going to make it that easy. Not until he'd found ten minutes of privacy to let her know how sorry he was. Then he'd leave her alone.

He hadn't received an invite for tomorrow's meal yet, but it wouldn't be hard to wrangle one. He nudged the plate closer to her. "Want a cookie? Your mom hasn't lost her touch."

She shook her head. "No, thanks."

Rosemary jumped to her feet. "So sweet of you to say that, Mason. Let me send a few home for the twins."

Once again Liz's eyes snapped to meet his. "Twins?" The word came out more a breath than audible.

Mason tried to hold her gaze with sheer force of will. "Avery and Christopher. They're not quite six."

A smile that didn't reach her eyes pushed at the corners of her mouth. "Well, congratulations to you and the missus."

Not what he wanted to get into in front of her family. "There is no Mrs. Waterman, Liz. Besides my mother."

"I'm sorry."

He was sorry, too, but the loss likely wasn't what Liz expected. "I've never been married."

"Then—" She clamped her mouth closed.

Mason took a deep breath. "My life didn't exactly turn out the way I'd intended when I was a teenager. Did yours?"

Twin red dots rose high in her cheeks. "That is none of your business, Mason Waterman. Excuse me, please. I need to get my things in from the car before it turns pitch dark."

"Let me do that." Zach pushed back his chair, glancing from one to the other as he snagged another cookie. "Staying in town long, Liz?"

Her eyes shot fiery darts at Mason. "Two or three days. Tops."

She wasn't going to make this easy, was she? But he'd do what it took to grab a few minutes. She had to hear him out. She might never forgive him, but maybe he could finally forgive himself.

Chapter 2 --

*D*id you sleep well?" A smile wreathed Mom's face.

How to answer? Liz made a show of rubbing her eyes.

Mom's smile faded. "That inflatable mattress probably isn't the best. We got it for when Madelynn stays over."

Better to just say it. "Mom, it leaks." Not that the mattress was all that kept her awake. Mason's piercing eyes hadn't helped.

"Oh, no." Mom's hand covered her mouth. "I'm so sorry. We'll find something else for tonight."

Like a hotel? Driving into town, Liz hadn't seen anything besides the old Landing Pad. She'd only be in town a few days, so it wouldn't burn too much of her savings. "Don't worry about it. I've slept on worse."

Her mom glanced at the clock, but whatever. She'd gone back in time ten time zones. Or ahead fourteen, depending which way you looked at it.

"What would you like to eat? Bacon and eggs? Pancakes? Waffles?"

Liz closed her eyes and silently counted to ten. "No need to go crazy. Mind if I have a quick shower? Then I'll get some toast and coffee, if that's okay."

"But—"

"I don't need a big breakfast. I never did."

"I don't mind…"

"Mom, please."

Her mother blinked back tears and her jaw trembled.

Good job, Liz. Back for less than a day, and Mom's crying. That's got to be a record, even for you. But what could she say to smooth things over?

"I'll just be a few minutes." She bolted into the bathroom and turned on the shower. A minute later, water sluiced over her body. *Get it together, Liz. Other people have normal conversations with their parents all the time.* Yeah, but they didn't usually leave an eleven-year gap. She shouldn't have returned until she had her life together. Or she should've come much sooner. One or the other.

She'd make some small talk over coffee then go online to see if the placement company in Las Vegas had news for her. Her hands stilled from massaging shampoo into her scalp. Surely they had faster Internet here in town than the dial-up they'd had on the farm?

A few minutes later she peered at herself in the steamed-up mirror. Just a bit of makeup. Dry and style her hair. Nothing to do with the possibility of running into Mason. She had to look together. No one needed to know how fragmented she was inside. She could pretend for a few days.

Mason.

Imagine him a father. Imagine him a nice guy. A friend of her brother's.

Imagine the impossible.

Today was all about her parents. She'd drive out to the farm and deal with all that later. One thing at a time.

"Ready?" she asked her reflection.

There was no reply.

oOo

Mason stared out the big windows of the straw bale house to the children having a snowball fight beside the driveway in the dusk. He wasn't watching for Liz. Not at all. Simply keeping an eye on the twins and hoping Christopher didn't pelt Maddie Nemesek in the face again.

Christopher and Finnley, Brent's son, had ganged up on the two girls. Avery was the same age as the boys and could hold her own, or at least close enough. Maddie, on the other hand, flung handfuls like a three-year-old and whined if any snow hit her. Not that he could blame her. Christopher had developed a strong throwing arm with little accuracy to go with it. Mason had felt the sting more than once with a few bruises to prove it.

Headlights crept down Thompson Road in the gathering gloom, falling snow angling across the beams.

His heart sped up. Liz. What a shock to see her yesterday. She looked good. Glimpses of the teen girl remained, but she'd become a beautiful woman. Strong. Wary.

The car turned in the driveway and parked beyond Noel's truck.

Jo came up beside Mason. "She's here?"

He nodded. "Looks like."

Zach stepped out onto the deck as Liz exited her car. A snowball sailed over the truck and splattered on Liz's head. She whirled. Christopher's hand came over his mouth then he shoved at Finnley and the two boys wrestled in the snow, Zach's Border collie joining in the melee.

Mason strode to the door and shoved his feet into boots. Did he have to admit the young hoodlum was his? What a way to make an impression. He opened the door and stepped into the icy dusk. "Christopher!"

No response, other than the muffled sound of wrestling and a few grunts.

Face flaming, Mason forged across the driveway and pulled his son up by the hood of his parka. "Christopher."

The little boy's jaw set as he glared up.

"You will come with me, and you will tell the lady you're sorry."

Christopher shot a sidelong glance toward the parking area, where Zach and Liz spoke quietly. "Don't wanna."

"I'm not asking you, son. You don't even know her, and you hit her right on the head. Do you think that was very nice?" Not that it would be better to bean someone he knew.

"Wasn't on purpose."

"It was still your hand that threw the snowball. Which you need to learn to control." He gave Christopher's shoulder a little nudge. "Move it."

"Yeah, Christopher," taunted Avery. "Go say *sorry*."

Christopher whirled out of Mason's grasp and glared at his twin. "Shut up."

"Dad! He said—"

"I heard him. Christopher. Now."

How could such a small body give such a deep sigh? Mason set his arm across Christopher's shoulders and urged the reluctant boy forward.

Zach lifted Maddie in his arms to meet her Aunt Liz as Mason approached. Liz's gaze narrowed as she caught sight of him behind her brother.

She was going to be *so* impressed to find out who'd hit her.

Mason steered his son beside Zach and squeezed the boy's shoulder. "Liz, I'd like you to meet my son, Christopher. He has something to say to you."

"Sorry," his son mumbled sullenly to his scuffing boot.

"Christopher."

The boy sighed and glanced up at him before looking at Liz, who was finger-combing snow out of her shoulder-length blond hair. "I'm sorry for hitting you with a snowball, Miss Liz." He glared up at Mason. "Happy?"

Uh. Not really. Mason became aware of Avery sidling up on his other side. Might as well get it all over with at once. "Liz, this is my daughter, Avery."

Liz's eyes warmed as she glanced from Avery to Christopher. "Nice to meet you two. Apology accepted." The darts returned to her eyes when she focused back on him. She might forgive his son, but Mason wouldn't be so lucky any time soon.

"Well, let's get inside." Zach turned toward the house. "Come on, Finnley. I know you're out here somewhere."

The other boy ran toward the house, and Christopher wrenched free and chased after him. Both slid on the packed path then scrambled up the steps, across the deck, and past Jo through the open door.

Liz turned toward her brother as the little girls ran after the boys. "So this is your house?"

"Nope, Jo and I live in a log cabin at the foot of the hill." He pointed up the path lit by solar lanterns.

"Then..."

"We eat most of our meals here, though. This was the first house built after Jo and her friends bought the property. Come back in daylight, and we'll give you the full tour."

"What's the big building at the end of the driveway? It looks like a hotel or something."

"A school, to teach people how to live sustainably."

Liz shook her head. They were at the base of the steps to the house, and Mason hung back to let Liz and Zach go first. By the time he got inside, the sounds of childish laughter and running water intermingled from down the hallway. Somebody had sent the kids to wash up. Good call.

Mason caught Liz's coat as she shrugged out of it and met her eyes as they narrowed. He smiled and hung her jacket with his.

The great room stretched to the right. Flames flickered in the fireplace, casting a welcoming glow to the seating areas. A tall, glittering Christmas tree stood in the corner. To the left, the farmhouse table.

Liz stared at the long table. "How many people live here, anyway?"

Zach tucked another log in the fireplace, so Liz must be speaking to Mason. "Uh, five families? Or six. But some of them have gone to Portland for Christmas."

"You don't know how many?" Liz's plucked eyebrows tented above her blue eyes.

He could lose himself there. "Depends on if you count me and the twins or not."

She shook her head and turned away.

Guess that meant Liz didn't think he counted. Surprise.

o0o

A petite woman with a toddler wedged on her hip and a big smile on her face bustled toward Liz. "Liz! I'm Jo. I've heard so much about you."

Liz smiled. Her sister-in-law looked just like the photos. "Nice to meet you."

Jo held out her free arm, and Liz leaned in for a quick hug.

"This is our son, John. He's thirteen months old."

The little guy looked just like Zach's baby pictures. Zachary. A dad. But that wasn't as weird as Mason with kids.

What was he doing here, anyway? Hadn't Mom said he lived next door at the old farmhouse? Now he and Zach shepherded the children to the table. Another baby banged a spoon on a highchair tray, and Jo deftly strapped John into a second one.

Liz looked past Jo into the kitchen, where four people worked together. "Who's that?"

Jo handed a strip of yellow pepper to her son and another to the other child. "Come, let me introduce you to everyone."

Deep breath. More people meant she had to pay less attention to Mason. The diversion could only be good. She allowed her sister-in-law to link their arms and pull her to the kitchen.

"This is Zach's sister Liz," Jo announced. "This is Claire and her husband, Noel. Claire is a chef, and I'm a lousy one, so I'm glad I was smart enough to latch onto her friendship back in our college days."

A woman with short brown hair smiled at Liz. "Pleased to meet you. The little guy in the high chair is our ten-month-old son, Ash."

Her husband nodded at Liz, a dimple deepening his scruffy cheek. "Welcome." He turned back to scooping chicken into a large pottery bowl. It smelled amazing.

"It's good to be here." It was even kind of true. Her curiosity about the group was getting the best of her.

"I'm Allison," said the other woman. Tall and thin, her long dark hair swung nearly to her waist. "And my husband, Brent. I take it you've met our little guy, Finnley?"

Finnley. The shadow that disappeared after Mason's kid nailed her with a snowball. She nodded. "Nice to meet you. Are you a chef, too?"

Allison chuckled. "Not so much. I can cook well enough to keep folks from starving, and that's about it. My main job here is running our school."

"Oh." The school Dad had mentioned? "That's nice."

Allison glanced at her husband. "Brent is a contractor. He's just finished up a couple of big houses in the area and will be renovating your childhood home soon."

"Oh?" Liz turned to the man with an Asian cast to his features. Definitely not Thai. Korean, maybe. "Like what?" It was hard to imagine the farmhouse any different, but it had needed updating when she was a kid. If nothing had been done in the meanwhile, it no doubt could use a facelift.

"We'll be taking it apart, room by room, adding insulation and updating wiring before adding new sheet rock and flooring."

"They put a new roof on the house in October," said Jo from behind Liz.

A baby yelled from over at the table.

"Everyone ready to eat?" Claire set a bowl of vegetables on the table. "We can fill Liz in on the details over dinner."

Liz turned and rammed straight into Mason, who caught her arms to steady her. She jerked away, not meeting his gaze, and edged past him as the others set bowls and platters on the table.

Where would they want her to sit? Better not be anywhere near Mason Waterman.

Christopher glared at her from across the table as she approached. No problem. She'd keep her distance.

"Here, Liz. Have a seat." Jo indicated a chair beside Zach, who was bent over, listening to whatever his daughter whispered in his ear.

Liz slid into the chair, trying not to notice Mason round the table and sit between his children. At least he wasn't directly across from her but down a bit. She could live with the arrangement just this once.

"Who wants to say grace?" asked Noel from the end of the table.

Maddie's hand shot up. "Me!" The little girl ducked her head. "God is great. God is good, and we thank Him for this food. Amen."

Looked like Liz's brother and sister-in-law were busy brainwashing the next generation. Before Liz could do more than reach for her napkin, she realized everyone's heads were still bowed.

Noel's voice continued, "Thank You, Father, for all Your

28

blessings to us. We thank You for bringing Liz home and ask that You'll guide her path. We love You. In the name of Your son, Jesus, amen."

If God were guiding her path — which was pretty much laughable — He'd better start with guiding her away from Idaho. This was not a place she wanted to stay.

Chapter 3 --

*T*his chicken is yummy, Mr. Noel." Avery batted her eyelashes as she looked at Noel. "Thank you for dinner."

Mason slid his arm across the back of his daughter's chair. Now that was more like it. Liz would see at least one of his kids had some manners.

"You're welcome, Avery. We're always glad to have your family over."

He didn't miss the sharp glance Liz shot him, but there was no need to meet her gaze. All through dinner he'd remained acutely aware of every movement she'd made and every word she'd spoken, all while never looking directly at her. His presence made her uncomfortable, but it was hard to know how much of her discomfort was about him and how much from returning to Galena Landing at all after such a long absence.

Mason was pretty sure both sources of angst could be laid directly at his feet. He owed it to her to apologize and do what he could to put the past where it belonged. He'd moved on, albeit in fits and starts, but it didn't look like she had. God's grace had—

"Mason?" Allison's voice.

He blinked. "Sorry, yes?"

She chuckled. "What shifts are you working across the holidays? Have your parents said what days they can keep the twins?"

School vacation. The bane of single parents. "I work my

regular shifts, other than Christmas Day and New Year's Day. Mom can do Mondays and Tuesdays. Dad can manage a day here and there in a pinch."

Dad had flat out told Mason he didn't know how he did it. Dad couldn't have raised kids by himself. Well, Mason hadn't planned to. Who did? Life, lemons, and lemonade. A guy did what he had to.

Thank You, God, for strength for every day.

Not that Mason would be against marrying. Where had that thought come from? It's not what he told his mother every time she brought up the subject or introduced him to the daughter of another long-lost friend.

But Liz... now where had that thought come from?

"Brent and I need to go to Coeur d'Alene for a couple of days after Christmas." Allison sighed. "It's been so busy with the farm school we haven't gotten away in forever."

"You're taking the same break as the public schools?"

"Longer. We'll reconvene in mid-February and teach greenhouse maintenance before starting the planting season. Also animal husbandry with lambs and calves starting to pop."

"The break will do you all good."

Several farm members worked at the school, which had finally become established with fifteen to twenty students per term.

Brent turned to Mason. "Allison and I are snagging a week away in late January. I got a great deal on a four-star on the beach in Thailand." He grinned at Liz. "I should get some tips from you before our trip."

The old restlessness shifted in Mason's gut. Someday he'd get a chance to travel. Someday his life wouldn't revolve around a dead-end job and two small children in a rural backwater. But the future stretched out before him bleakly. The only spark was Liz, and she hated him.

So did Erin, for that matter.

He deserved the hate in both cases, and more.

But God had forgiven him. Mason shouldn't have moved back to Galena Landing, even though Liz hadn't returned in more than a decade. Even though Mom and Dad had agreed it was the only thing that made sense after Erin moved out. Even though he'd made better, closer friends in this group than he'd ever had in his life.

He was still a guy alone. A single dad. Who would want to take him on, him with all his baggage?

Certainly not Liz.

Even the thought was crazy. Why think of her that way? Why allow a crack in his facade?

Her voice caught his attention as she spoke to Brent. Mason's mind strove to catch up as she talked about how the tsunami had devastated the coastline and traumatized Thailand not long before she'd moved there, and how the country had recovered.

"We'd love to see some of your photos." Allison's eyes shone. "We're really looking forward to the trip."

Zach glanced at Liz. "We can either plug a flash drive into the TV or hook your laptop up to it. I'd love to see your pictures, too."

"Oh, I don't know..." Liz's voice petered out as she glanced at Mason.

"Sounds good." He looked straight at her. "I'm interested, too."

Bright dots rode high on her cheeks as she swept a lock of blond hair behind her ear. "I didn't bring my laptop tonight."

"Maybe Sunday after church?" suggested Jo. "We can invite your parents for lunch and the afternoon."

Liz concentrated on moving her fork around her plate. She hadn't eaten much of the fabulous dinner Claire and Noel had created. "I guess," she said at last.

"How long are you in town, Liz?" Jo scooped two more pieces

of broccoli on the highchair tray, and John attacked them. She glanced at her sister-in-law. "Rosemary didn't say."

Liz fired another glance at Mason. "Not long. Just a few days."

Jo tilted her head. "Why so short? That isn't enough time to catch up with them. And besides, Chri—"

"It's long enough. I'm waiting to hear about a possible job from a company in Las Vegas."

"Over Christmas?" Zach dropped his elbows on the table and peered at his sister. "Not much happens this time of year in the corporate world. Life should resume after the new year."

"You can't be alone in a strange city over Christmas," said Jo. "Not when you have family and friends here who want to spend time with you."

Mason would have to be the stupidest man on the planet to miss the pointed barbs Liz shot him. So... she might have considered staying longer if it weren't for him? Half of him rebelled against making it easier for her, but the other half reminded him that if she bolted before he'd said his piece, he might never get another chance.

Suddenly that was the most important thing in the world. To make her understand the sincere depth of his apology.

"Dad." Christopher tugged at his arm. "Dad, can I go play?"

Mason glanced at his son's plate. "Eat your veggies first."

Christopher slumped. "But I don't like broccoli."

"Broccoli is little trees," Maddie announced. "They're yummy." She popped one in her mouth, chewed a couple of times, then opened her mouth to prove her point. Or something.

Zach tapped on her plate. "Maddie, shut your mouth when you have food in it. No one wants to see half-chewed broccoli."

Mason nudged Christopher's shoulder. "Eat 'em up, buddy. See? Finnley is all done."

His son scowled as he speared a piece and put it in his mouth.

Mason leaned closer. "Eat nicely or we will go straight home after dinner and you won't have more time to play with Finnley. And no dessert."

Christopher glared at him as though sizing up Mason's resolve. Evidently the boy was satisfied and swallowed the bite before stabbing a second piece of broccoli.

Good. Because Mason didn't want to leave without catching a moment with Liz. Still, he'd been learning the importance of consistency with the twins, especially Christopher. It was taking time to overcome the early years when he hadn't known how to stick to his guns, but the few glimmers of positive results reminded him he was on the right track.

Like now. Christopher wasn't happy, but he was listening. For once.

oOo

As soon as the meal was over, Liz jumped up to help clear the table.

"Hey, you're a guest." Claire thumbed over at Liz's chair. "Relax. We've got this."

She didn't want to relax. Didn't know how. It was bad enough being back in the US at all, but sitting across the table from Mason made it a thousand times harder.

Why did the man have to look so amazing? The wiry teen she'd once known now had clearly defined biceps rippling beneath a navy Henley-style shirt. He'd never been tall, but his boyish frame had filled out with broader shoulders and not an ounce of fat. What did he do for a living?

She'd listened carefully but caught no hints. All she'd gathered was he didn't work here at the farm but in Galena Landing. And he lived in her childhood home, which was all kinds of wrong.

34

He was the one who'd walked into her family and made himself at home. Had she really expected everything to be the same? She'd known better. Known about Dad's close call. Known about her brother's marriage and kids, to say nothing of the fact that her perrfect older sisters' lives had gone on, too.

It was just her. She'd lived in a time warp, pretending she was still eighteen, but thirty wasn't that far away. Most people her age had settled down long ago or were well on their way.

She offered her small niece a smile.

Maddie beamed at her. "It's gonna be Christmas soon." But the little girl said it more like Kwithmith.

A tiny piece of ice inside of Liz melted. "It is."

"That's when Jesus was a baby. Littler than John or Ash."

Liz nodded.

"Jesus loves everyone and wants us to be good. Did you know that?"

Anyone else, and Liz would have snubbed them, but a small child not quite four who looked at her with adoration? She couldn't do it. "I've heard that before."

Maddie leaned back against her chair. "Christmas is pretty and it is presents."

Good to know there was some kind of normal in that curly little head. "I like your Christmas tree." Liz pointed down the length of the table to the tree at the far end of the great room. "Did you help decorate it?"

Maddie nodded. "Me and Finnley and Avery and Christopher. But John and Ash are too little. See, Daddy put a fence around the tree to keep the babies out."

Liz smiled. She'd seen the linked baby gates with stacks of gifts behind it. Must be easier than saying *no* a thousand times.

"I made a Christmas present for you, Auntie Liz."

"You did?" Liz felt the eyes of others at the table burning into her head. Like Mason's. "That's very sweet of you." The chasm in front of her grew. How could she keep from falling in? Yet she had to.

"But we can't give presents until Christmas. Mama said so." Maddie shook her head, her brown eyes focused on Liz's. "And we can't tell secrets, either."

Jo reached past Maddie to pick up plates. "So Auntie Liz needs to come for Christmas, right, sweetie? So she can get her present?" Jo winked at Liz.

Maddie nodded, eyes shining as brown curls tumbled around her head.

Liz bit her lip. "We'll see what happens." Christmas was only a week away. It might be rude to leave before the twenty-fourth. Oh, who was she kidding? She *knew* it was, especially as she had no place to go. Sitting in a Vegas hotel room by herself held no appeal. She wasn't close enough to her older sisters to invite herself to either Cindy's or Heather's house.

Trapped.

She'd done it to herself, coming back in mid-December. Had her subconscious been planning on a cozy family time all along? Had her subconscious known Mason lived here?

Liz leaned closer to her little niece. "I'm not sure your Grandma and Grandpa can put up with me that long."

"Don't be silly, Liz," said Zach. "You know they've missed you like crazy all these years."

She looked over at her brother. Trust him to be listening. "It's not like they have room for me. A leaky air mattress in the middle of Mom's sewing room isn't all that inviting."

Zach shrugged. "They don't get much company. Those who come stay out here at the farm. Between all of us, there are several vacant guest rooms. You're welcome to stay here, too."

Liz's mind raced. It sounded like a leap from the frying pan to the fire, but it might be worth it to sleep in a real bed. Her hip had pressed against the wood floor most of the night while the thick air mattress cradled her, nearly suffocating her in its embrace. She shuddered involuntarily.

Zach chuckled. "Promise we don't bite."

He'd misunderstood, but whatever. "You have room at your house?" she asked. She wanted to see the home he'd made with Jo.

"On the sofa." He grimaced. "Which is more comfortable than that air mattress. I told Mom to get a foamie instead, but she said it would take up too much room in her fabric cupboard. It's just for Maddie the rare time she stays there overnight."

Leaky air mattress at her folks'. A sofa at her brother's. Neither sounded like a great option.

"We have a spare room just down the hall." Claire set a slice of warm cake in front of her, the fragrance of apples and cinnamon filling Liz's senses. "You're welcome to it. Ash usually sleeps through the night, but he's been teething, so I can't guarantee it."

Delightful.

"There's my old apartment," Allison said. "Furnished but unoccupied. It would only take an hour or so to get the chill out of the air."

"Great idea." Brent pushed back from the table. "I'll run over and turn up the heat right now."

"But..."

Brent paused with one hand stretched toward his coat.

Why was she hesitating? It sounded like the next best thing to heaven. Or it would if it weren't Idaho, and Mason didn't live next door. Liz glanced around the table. "Are you sure I wouldn't be intruding? It's only for a few days."

Jo's eyes twinkled. "We'll make you stay through New Year's. That's the price you have to pay for a two-bedroom apartment all to yourself, meals provided."

Tempting. "I wouldn't be putting anyone out?"

"Not at all," said Allison. "I lived there while Brent was building our house, then Chelsea did until she and Keanan were married. It's been vacant since summer."

Thoughts of the air mattress surfaced. "If you're sure Mom and Dad won't be offended..." she said to Zach.

He shook his head. "They'll be happy you're nearby and not disappearing so quickly. They come by often, and town's not far. I'll even drive you in after dinner to grab your bags."

Liz let out a breath. "If you're sure."

Brent slipped his arms into the sleeves of his jacket. "Be right back. Don't eat my apple cake, you hear?" He winked at Finnley before disappearing out into the cold.

She met Mason's gaze across the table for a quick second. His blue eyes warmed slightly before she ducked her head.

An error in judgment.

But she seemed doomed to make mistakes. What was one more?

Chapter 4 --

*M*ason managed to breathe. Liz had committed to staying at Green Acres Farm for two weeks. Hadn't she? That would likely be long enough for him to have the talk with her he knew must happen. Of course, during those two weeks the twins would spend a lot of time at the farm because they were out of school, and he still had to work. He could only hope Christopher and Avery wouldn't turn her off so completely she'd manage to keep avoiding him.

Christopher had finally eaten his broccoli then made short work of a piece of apple cake. He and Finnley now built a train track clear across the great room floor, but Avery leaned against Mason's chest, listening to the adult conversation over tea.

What would he have done without this group of friends over the past year and a half? He wasn't sure Galena Landing could've held him if not for this bunch. Yeah, Mom and Dad asked him to move back and offered to help with the kids, but, on a day-in-day-out basis, that wouldn't have been enough. Neither of them seemed to connect with the twins. They hadn't known how to treat him as a child, either.

He couldn't blame them for how he'd turned out, though.

Ash began to wail just as John fell asleep with his forehead in his dessert.

"Excuse me." Claire reached for her baby. "Time to nurse him and tuck him in for the night." With Ash settled on her hip, she turned to Liz. "Everyone just comes in here in the morning when they're ready for breakfast. There's bacon and eggs in the fridge and pans handy. Bread for toast, honey in the cupboard, and blackberry jelly in the fridge. Canned fruit in the larder. Feel free to scrounge for something else, if you like. Either way, I hope you'll make yourself at home."

Liz bit her lip. "Thank you. You're too kind."

"Not at all. It's how we operate."

Noel chuckled. "You've got two weeks, and then we'll put you on meal rotation. Enjoy it while you can."

Had Liz's gaze snuck to Mason's again? She seemed as hypersensitive to him as he was to her. Better not let anyone clue in to that, because this was a bloodthirsty bunch. Only Zach had witnessed the awkwardness when Mason and Liz had met for the first time since high school, and Zach was as dumb as an ox. He hadn't noticed a thing.

"Miss Liz is so pretty," Avery whispered into Mason's ear.

He smoothed his daughter's back. Funny how even a child could see that. "She is," he whispered back.

"Is she your friend? She doesn't talk to you."

"Shh." He held Avery tighter. "We knew each other a long time ago."

It wasn't his imagination. Liz's gaze angled between him and Avery. Guess they hadn't been as quiet as he thought. "Scoot, Avery. Go play with the boys." She clambered down.

"It's snowing out there," announced Zach. "Want me to run you into town for your stuff now? Jo will want me back soon to read bedtime stories to Maddie."

Liz stood. "Um, okay. Now is good, I guess. If you're sure I'm not putting anyone out."

"Not at all. Brent and I will pop over and make up the bed now, if it's okay to leave Finnley here a few minutes?" Allison

40

turned to Mason.

"Sure, go for it. I'll give Noel a hand in the kitchen."

First things first, though. He lifted Liz's coat off the hook by the door and held it for her as Zach shrugged into his own. By the set angle of Liz's jaw, his overture wasn't welcome, but what else was a guy supposed to do to snag a quick minute? He adjusted the collar across her shoulders as Zach slipped out into the night air.

"Liz. We need to talk," he said in a low voice as he nudged the door closed with his foot.

She turned so quickly his hands dropped to his sides. "I don't think we have anything to talk about, Mason Waterman."

He tried to capture her gaze, but she was intent on the door-knob. He blocked her escape route. That would work for about another minute until Zach had the truck started and Allison found the bedding in the hall closet. "Liz."

She bit her lip and held her head high. "Excuse me, please."

"I am sorry for my actions toward you in the past. I've asked God's forgiveness, and now I'm asking yours. I treated you horribly. I know that, and I'm sorrier than you can imagine. Can you forgive me?"

"Do you know what I want?"

She hadn't said *no*. Did he dare relax his guard? "What?"

"I'd like to never see you again as long as I live. I'd like to never talk to you again or hear your voice. Do you think that could be arranged?"

Mason shifted closer by half a step. She smelled of spring flowers and cinnamon. "I don't think so."

Her gaze narrowed and she stared straight at him for a few seconds. "You don't deserve forgiveness."

Allison's and Brent's voices grew louder as they came back to the great room. Outside, Zach's truck rumbled to life.

"I know I don't," Mason said simply. "But I *am* sorry."

"Just stay out of my way, okay? I'll be gone before you know it, and you can carry on doing whatever it is you do best." She reached for the door handle. "So long as you're not hurting anyone else."

Mason wasn't ready to let her get away. "You need to hear me out before you leave again."

She made a sound of disbelief. "Or what? You've already done it all to me."

"Liz, I wronged you. I know I did. But if you don't allow me this conversation, I'll follow you, whether it's to Thailand or Timbuktu. I won't let you leave for eleven years and ignore me. Never again."

"Sounds like an idle threat, Mason. Please move so I can join my brother."

He opened the door and watched her flounce out as the brisk wind blew in. Yeah. This wasn't going to be easy.

oOo

"Mom, it's not that I don't love you. It's that the air mattress leaks. Plus, you'll see more of me if I stay out at the farm for two weeks than if I leave for Vegas tomorrow."

Her mother glanced between Liz and Zach. "But we only just got you back."

Liz bit back the words that wanted out. She'd stuffed them down the whole drive into town after Mason had forced her to listen before letting her past him. Now she wanted to scream and run, in either order and in any direction.

Instead she managed a smile of sorts. "You can't tell me you won't be glad to have your sewing space back. I saw the stack of quilt blocks you've been piecing tucked behind your machine."

"But—"

"No buts, Mom. I'll take you out for lunch tomorrow. How's that? We can spend time catching up." Hopefully she could keep the conversation steered to gossip about the neighbors so her mother wouldn't delve too deeply.

Mom bit her lip.

Zach shifted from one foot to the other. "You and Dad should come out for Sunday lunch. Liz is going to show us pictures of Thailand on the big screen."

Had she really agreed to do that? She'd need to find time to filter through her digital albums. Not everything in them was suitable for family entertainment. Not *her* family, anyway.

"Okay, I guess it's all right." Mom swooped in to give Liz a hug. "I just hate to share you when you've been away so long."

Liz set her bags on the tile by the door. "I'll see you tomorrow. I hope it doesn't snow a lot more. I'm not used to driving in this stuff."

"I'll come get you if you want. Doing lunch was your idea, and I'm not giving it up."

"Okay." Liz pecked her mom's cheek. "Give Daddy a kiss for me." She followed Zach out the door and climbed into his truck while he lifted her bags into the back seat.

Zach turned the truck toward the farm and glanced at her. "So, Lizzie..."

Uh oh. What was that tone all about? "Hmm?"

"How well did you know Mason when you guys were in high school? You must've been in the same class or close to it."

No way. She wasn't going anywhere near that topic with her brother. *Please, if there's a God.*

But the silence was expectant, and Zach kept glancing her way even when he should be watching the slippery road.

"Same class," she said at last. "We knew each other some."

"Define *some.*"

Nope. "Who all do you keep track of from your class? Gabe and who else?"

"Liz. How well did you know Mason?"

"It's kind of not any of your business."

He chuckled, but it sounded a bit harsh. "You hit upon the very reason it might *be* my business, little sister. I could've cut the tension between you with a knife, and that's not even including when Mason and I came in at the folks' place yesterday. You looked like you'd seen a ghost."

And she'd thought he hadn't noticed. "We didn't part on the best of terms back then, okay? But it's all fine now." Liar. "A lot of water has gone under the bridge."

"Is he the reason you went to Thailand and never came back?"

"Hey!" She poked Zach in the arm. "I came back. I'm right here."

"You're trying really hard, Liz, but you're not fooling me. Could you just answer a straight question?"

No?

The truck trundled across the bridge. Snow swirled toward the headlights in a mesmerizing way. Why had she returned to Idaho in winter? But she'd loved the snow as a child. Loved building snowmen and making snow angels. She hadn't had to drive in it.

"I'm waiting, Lizzie."

"Zachary, in case you hadn't figured it out, I don't want to talk about Mason or about high school. I'm an adult, and I don't have to if I don't want to. So can you just drop it already?"

"Did he hurt you?"

Like nothing in her life before or since. She stared out the passenger window.

"Sis, I didn't know you had a history with him. He asked to rent the farmhouse. He seems like a good dad, but I know he had a bit of a reputation back then. I know from personal experience that a guy can go astray, and God can forgive him and restore him."

She managed to get the words out without spitting. "I didn't say we had a history."

44

Zach sighed. "Just because I'm male doesn't mean I'm blind or stupid. I won't push you, since you obviously have no intention of telling me anything. Combine a good memory with a good imagination, and I can add up the parts you're not saying."

Protesting now would get her exactly nowhere. And silence was no better an option.

"I need you to know a few things, Lizzie. One, I believe Mason is a changed man. Two, I think God brought you home for a reason and, three, if you ever decide you need someone to talk to, try me or Jo, okay? We're here for you."

Tears stung Liz's eyelids and she blinked them away even as the snow-covered fields outside the vehicle blurred. "I'll keep that in mind," she choked out.

"That's all I'm asking of you. I'm making the rest of my requests to God."

Wasn't that the way it had always been? Her brother had been a steady force in the church youth group all through school. Would he really understand if she dumped the whole sordid tale on him? Not likely, but it was nice that he noticed and cared enough to try.

Changing the subject would be good. "So tell me about the Border collie I saw. Is he from Mom's dogs?"

Her brother's face brightened. "Yes, Domino is from Sadie's last litter. He's such a good dog, great with the kids and helpful with the stock."

Good. Let him talk dogs for the rest of the way back to the farm.

Chapter 5 ---

*L*iz sat across from her mother in The Sizzling Skillet. The atmosphere hadn't changed a bit since last time she'd been here, but the food was better than she remembered. There were only so many times she could mention that, though, and they'd already exhausted discussing Dad's struggles with Guillain-Barré Syndrome. There were some things she just didn't want to know about how her parents had dealt with things.

"I'm so glad you're home." Mom reached across the table and captured Liz's hand before she could pull it away. "I only wish you were staying."

Liz forced a smile. "Do you say the same thing to Heather and Cindy when they visit?"

Mom let out a little sigh. "Sometimes. We enjoy having Maddie and John close by so much it's hard to think what all we miss in our other grandchildren's lives when they live so far away."

Liz had missed everything since Heather's daughter had been a baby. All her nephews had been born while she was in Thailand. When she thought about Heather's son and Cindy's stair-step boys, pangs of regret dug deeply. It had been easier not to think of them often. Now, seeing Zach with his children reminded her of all she'd missed.

The choice seemed the only option at the time. Maybe it

hadn't been, but it was too late to redo those years.

With a start, she realized her mother was still talking. "Cindy said she wished they could come for Christmas to see you, but they were just here at Thanksgiving, and Tom is preaching at their church that weekend. It's not easy for them to get away."

The perfect family and in ministry, too. Her parents' sun had always risen and set around their eldest child. "I understand."

"She asked for your new cell number, and I gave it to her. She wants to invite you to visit them in Denver sometime soon. Maybe she can help you find a job."

"That would be nice." Yeah, right. Denver wasn't on her short list of places to visit, let alone relocate. All she needed was to be reminded every day about all the ways she didn't measure up.

"So, tell me what kind of position you're looking for, Lizzie." Mom stirred honey into her tea.

"I still love teaching ESL, but I've taken all my courses for a Bachelor of Education online. Getting a practicum is a bit trickier because I was overseas."

Mom stared at her. "I didn't know that."

Liz shrugged. There was plenty her parents didn't know. "Then I'd like to get my master's and teach at the college level. But first things first."

"That's what Allison has."

"Allison?" Oh, right, the tall, thin woman who'd made up her bed last night.

"She heads up the school at the farm." Mom's eyes widened. "Maybe you could teach there."

As if. "I'm not credentialed."

"Neither is Sierra, although I suppose she has some degrees." Mom brushed that aside with her hand. "The thing is, I know they're looking to expand, and their courses don't all require a ton of experience."

"Who is Sierra?"

"Oh, I suppose you haven't met her. She married Gabe Rubachuk after Bethany died. You remember Gabe, don't you?"

Liz nodded. Her brother's best friend since she could remember, Gabe had been in and out of the farmhouse practically daily. She'd had a crush on him as a preteen, but even then she'd known it was no use. Liz had been way too young for him, and he'd only had eyes for Bethany, anyway. "It must have broken his heart when she was killed."

Mom nodded. "He went off to Romania to work in the orphanage at the same time as Dad and I went."

Right. They'd gone to Eastern Europe when Dad was convalescing, not to the Far East where their youngest daughter lived. Liz had no one to blame but herself. She'd done a really good job of pushing her family away.

"When he came back, he and Sierra got together."

"And she teaches at the school." Was that where this conversation had started?

"Yes, and Gabe administers it. They've gone to Portland to spend the holidays with Sierra's family. Chelsea and Keanan went, too."

If Mom had mentioned these people in her emails, Liz didn't recall much. She'd been guilty of a lot of skimming, but she supposed she'd better get up to speed now that she was home, at least for a while. "And who are they?"

"Oh, I'm sorry. Chelsea is Sierra's sister. She is an event planner and keeps other farm activities organized. They cater weddings and the like." Mom's hand swept those details aside, as well. "Her husband does a lot of the farm labor, along with Noel, whom I'm sure you've met."

"Claire's husband." The good-looking man with the tousled brown hair who'd looked as at home in the kitchen as his wife, the chef. Liz had always gone for the blonds. Gabe. Mason.

She refocused on her mother, trying to get all the farm

inhabitants straight. That didn't include thinking about Mason. He lived next door. In the house where she'd grown up. Maybe one of his kids slept in her old room, but probably not. It was the smallest of the four bedrooms.

"Anyway, Allison was saying they could use another teacher next term," Mom said triumphantly. She'd finally brought the conversation back around. "You should talk to her about it."

Liz let her eyebrows rise. "And teach farming? An instructor should be at least a half step ahead of her students."

"You grew up on the farm. You know more than you think you do."

Still wasn't happening. "I was thinking more of an immigrant-rich city, where I could put my cross-cultural skills to use."

Mom bit her lip. "I understand, though it's not as different as you might think. Many of the students at the farm are from inner cities. They've come to understand how vital food security is, but the realities of the physical labor and the mental adjustments aren't easy."

Liz stared at her mother. Those words didn't sound like the woman who'd been a farm wife all Liz's growing-up years.

"Why, Rosemary! How good to see you."

Liz glanced up at the woman who'd appeared at the end of their table. She caught her breath as she locked gazes with Mason's mother.

Emma Waterman frowned. "Liz?"

"Yes, Lizzie is home for a visit." Beaming, Mom leaned across the table. "Isn't that wonderful?"

Liz managed a smile, but no words came out.

Emma gave her a once-over.

What was she thinking? Mason's parents had attended Galena Gospel Church back then, though Mason had rebelled and quit going as a young teen.

"So you're back and ready to settle down?"

The words *it's about time* hung silently in the air, or maybe Liz's over-active imagination added them. And what business was it of Emma's?

"I'd love to hear all about Thailand sometime, and what your plans are for the future."

If Liz knew, she wouldn't mind telling everyone. As it was, she forced a smile to her lips. "Thank you."

Questions flickered in the older woman's eyes as she glanced between Liz and her mom. "I look forward to it."

What was all that about? Did Emma Waterman know? Liz's gut plummeted. There was no way Mason had told his parents. He wouldn't have.

o0o

Mason settled into a chair about as far as he could get from the big screen TV, but close enough to see and hear. He needed to know what Liz's life had been like in the intervening years. He needed it with desperation.

Allison found the HDMI connector, enabling Liz to plug her laptop into the screen. For someone who stood in front of classrooms on a daily basis, she looked pretty nervous. Maybe it was because he was present. But, no, her unease wasn't limited to him. Zach had said emails from her had been few and far between, even to their parents.

If only he could go back and do it all over again. The pang in his heart stabbed him anew. *If only.*

"So, I lived in Bangkok for the first few years, teaching at a British academy. Here's a picture of that."

A beautiful Oriental building flashed onto the screen, and Mason focused on the display.

"This is my apartment."

"Looks pretty nice," said Jo. "Did you have a roommate, or did you have it to yourself?"

Mason doubted anyone else would notice the twin pink dots high on Liz's cheeks.

"They came and went." She shot him a glance so short he almost missed it. So. Male roommates? Lovers? Why should it even bother him, with the life he'd lived?

He knew. Because she hadn't been that kind of girl before. It had been his life during high school and for years afterward, but not hers. It was his fault she'd walked away from everything she'd ever known. Ever believed. He'd found his way back to faith, but she hadn't. Not yet.

Mason breathed a prayer, one of thousands. Perhaps millions.

Liz showed image after image of Thailand's capital city, its beaches and surrounding countryside before detailing her move to Chiang Mai, further north. Had anyone besides him noticed that her photos were devoid of people? Oh, there were plenty that contained hurrying crowds, but none of friends smiling into the camera. None of her.

Had she been that alone? Or had she carefully sorted out which parts of her life to share with those on the farm? He'd bet there were thousands of other image files on her laptop. Of course, there wasn't time to run through them all in a couple of hours. He got that.

Allison and Brent asked more questions than anyone else, in preparation for their upcoming trip.

A glance around the room showed Liz's dad with tears in his eyes. The Guillain-Barré had brought Steve's emotions closer to the surface, but Mason didn't know what the tears meant. Joy at his daughter's return? Sadness for the years lost? Or had he sensed some of the same things Mason had?

A snowball slammed the window with a loud splat, and Mason headed to the door, Brent right behind him. Those boys were going to wreck something yet.

oOo

"Christopher!" hollered Mason from outside just as Brent yelled, "Finnley!"

Allison and Jo surged for the window, Maddie and Avery crowding beside them.

Whew. Liz glanced at the few photos she'd copied to this folder but still not shown. They didn't matter. She shrugged. "That's about it, anyway."

"Thank you, Lizzie Rose." Dad's gaze met hers. "You've had so many adventures."

And she'd only displayed the family-friendly version. Dad didn't need to know about all the relationships, all the men who'd gone through her apartment. About Sanun, who'd lasted the longest, but of course had to marry a Thai woman in the end. That had been the last straw.

"I think I'll make hot cocoa for the kids." Jo turned away from the window. "Anyone else want some? Or hot apple cider?"

The sweet treat from her childhood sounded appealing. "Cider sounds good."

Claire hopped out of the love seat, where Noel sat cradling their sleeping son. "There's a gallon of juice that should be thawed by now. I'll come give you a hand, Jo."

How long had it been since Liz had really belonged to anything? Even her family hadn't been like this when she was a kid. Cindy and Heather had been a team, always older and always making sure Liz knew she wasn't wanted. Zach had been the typical rough-and-tumble boy, climbing trees and playing hard with Gabe. Had the tree house the boys built disintegrated over the years?

They'd all left tail-end Liz to fend for herself, and she'd been doing it ever since. But a place — a group — like this, where a bunch of friends lived and worked together? It could almost be tempting.

Almost.

Boots stomped on the deck outside before the door opened and the men and boys came in. Mason unzipped his son's jacket as Christopher kicked his boots into the corner. Then the boy pulled off his snow pants while Finnley did the same. Both boys' cheeks were rosy, their hair tousled, and their eyes bright.

Wintertime on the farm was good for kids.

His father pointed at Christopher's boots, and the boy straightened them, sighing. Then he and Finnley dashed down the corridor to the bathroom, where splashing sounds soon ensued.

Mason glanced up and caught her staring. A slow smile creased his cheeks below those intense blue eyes.

Liz's cheeks flushed as she turned her attention back to her laptop. She might have been tempted to put action to her mother's idea about teaching at the farm school, but Mason had arrived first. This was his community, not hers, no matter that it was her family involved. She'd abdicated, and he'd stepped in.

No, she'd email the recruiter in Vegas again tomorrow, and be out of Galena Landing as early in the new year as possible.

Chapter 6 --

"Thanks for inviting us to dinner, Mom." Mason shrugged out of his jacket in the farmhouse entry.

Christopher parked both fists on his hips, blocking the doorway. "I want to play with Finnley."

Nudging him out of the way, Mason tousled his son's hair. "Tomorrow, buddy. Aunt Allison said you can come play all day."

Avery looked up from the kitchen table, where she had colored pencils and markers spread across the surface. "Hi, Daddy."

"Hi, princess." He leaned over her. "What are you making?"

The paper in front of her had a man and two children that likely represented him and the twins. But she was busy coloring another figure off at the edge of the paper. This one appeared to be female, but had blond hair like the others.

Avery ran her fingers over the drawing. "Why don't I have a mommy?"

There wasn't much Mason could say to that. "I'm sorry, princess." And he was. Sorry for so many things he'd helped set in motion and then couldn't control.

Dishes clattered a few feet away as Mom unloaded the dishwasher. "Have you heard from Erin lately?"

Mason straightened, rubbing his daughter's shoulder. "Not for a couple of months." He tried to catch Mom's eye, but she wasn't looking at him. Did they have to talk about Erin in front of the children?

Avery sighed. "Maybe you could get us a new mommy."

He narrowed his gaze at the drawing. The woman off to the side had straight blond hair. She also wore navy pants and a blue top. Wasn't that what Liz had been wearing the other day?

A sucker punch landed in his gut. Avery hadn't drawn Erin. He took a deep breath and let it out slowly. "Maybe someday," he said lightly. "Jesus knows you want a mommy." And that Mason wanted a wife. A woman who loved him and cared for the twins like they were her own. It wasn't likely to be Erin, that was for sure. "Now it's time to clean up the art supplies so we can set the table."

Avery gathered a handful of pencils and dropped them into the tin. "Can I take my picture home, Nana?"

"Sure, sweetie. You made a nice one for me yesterday. See? It's on the fridge."

"Here, Daddy. You put it somewhere safe, okay?" Avery glanced at Christopher.

That was a kid who had no patience for doing anything sitting at a table. The kindergarten teacher despaired of him. Mason had been much the same. He hadn't gotten along particularly well with formal education all the way through school.

Mason rolled the drawing and stuck the tube in his coat sleeve while Mom sent the twins to wash up. He swung open the door at the sound of Dad's boots clomping up the walkway outside. "Hey, Dad."

"Hey yourself, son."

"Need any help with the chores before I head home?"

Dad shot him a sharp glance. "You're staying for supper, aren't you? Your mother was counting on it."

"Yes, but Christopher and I could help you after if you like."

Dad shrugged. "I've got it."

Mason turned back to the kitchen. If his father only welcomed the little boy outside on days like this, Christopher wouldn't get so stir crazy. But Dad had done the same to Mason, not letting him help until he was physically able to do a man's job. By then, it had been too late to build a relationship between them. Not that Mason could claim to be perfect in the parenting department.

"We're ready to eat when you've washed up, Gary." Mom set a bowl of mashed potatoes on the table.

"Smells good, Emma. Be right with you." Dad marched off down the hallway and came back in a minute.

Mason helped his kids dish up potatoes, gravy, and slices of roast beef. And — oh, great — broccoli. Christopher's nose was already curling. Mason scooped several limp pieces onto his son's plate. At least Claire didn't cook the stuff to death.

Christopher stabbed both elbows on the table and scowled. "I don't like broccoli."

"It's good for you," Mom said. "And there's cheese sauce."

Mason didn't like it so well himself. He took a larger scoop than he'd given his son before adding some to Avery's plate. Being a dad — a role model — gave him responsibilities. He lifted a smaller bowl and looked at Christopher. "Want cheese sauce?"

Christopher heaved a mighty sigh. "I guess."

"Yes, please, Daddy." Avery made a face at Christopher.

Mason ladled some on the broccoli on all three plates then passed it to his father.

"How was work today?" asked Dad.

"All right. I spend too much time inside this time of year."

"You could've been a farmer. Office hours are minimal."

Mason forced a grin. "The ideal would be somewhere in between." He half-suspected that his father spent more time than necessary in the barn, just to stay out of Mom's space.

Dad cut up his roast beef. "The new transmission running well?"

"The car has never run better."

"Good, good."

Christopher stirred gravy all over his plate, mixing it with cheese sauce until everything took a blended, rather disgusting hue.

"Eat up," Mason said quietly.

The boy sighed and put a small bite in his mouth. Potatoes only. What a surprise.

Mom swirled a piece of broccoli in cheese sauce and made a show of popping it in her mouth and smiling at Christopher.

Like that was going to make a difference.

"Mason says he hasn't heard from Erin in a while," she said to Dad.

Did she really have to bring this topic up again, especially in front of the twins?

Dad grunted. "It's not normal for a woman to abandon her children."

"But Erin was never—"

"Can we not talk about this right here, right now?" Mason gave each parent a pointed look.

"Little pitchers have big ears," Dad commented, buttering a slice of bread.

"What's that mean?" Christopher glanced around the table.

Mason sighed. "Eat your supper, buddy."

"Funny way to say that," mumbled his son, stabbing a piece of broccoli with his fork.

"I see Liz Nemesek is back in town," Mom said. "Have you run into her?"

Mason's dinner turned to sawdust. Nothing was casual with Mom. "She's staying out at the farm, so I've seen her a couple of times. Avery, do you need me to cut up your meat?"

She shook her head, eyes wide. "Miss Liz is very pretty."

Mason turned to the other side. "How about you, Christopher?" If he could even find the beef under all that cheese and gravy.

"No thanks, Dad."

"Okay, well, eat up then. We need to get going pretty quickly here." Mason gave his mother another pointed look. Whatever she thought she remembered from years back was best forgotten, and whatever she thought about the situation today was best not mentioned in front of the twins. Thankfully she was working at the feed store for the rest of the week, and the kids would go next door to the farm.

The questions there would be easier to handle.

o0o

Liz headed over to the straw bale house mid-morning. After a few days of overcast skies and snow, the sun blazed from intensely blue skies with only a few puffy white clouds. Sunlight glittered on the gentle curves of the unmarred snow. She took a deep breath and released it, a puff of condensation floating briefly in front of her face.

Yes, she'd missed winter. Maybe one of the women would like to go for a walk. Liz eyed the snow banks. Maybe snowshoeing up the mountain road. Now that would be a treat.

She blinked as her eyes adjusted to the interior of the house, dim even with wide windows welcoming the brightness in through crystal clear panels. "It's gorgeous out there," she announced, unwinding the scarf from around her collar. "How I've missed winter!"

From behind the kitchen peninsula came Claire's chuckle. "If a few days of snow puts this much sparkle on your cheeks, how did you ever survive ten years in Thailand?"

"Necessity." Liz hung her coat and lined her boots up on the drip tray. "But I know one thing. That company had better find me a position in the northern half of the USA. California or Florida is not going to cut it."

Allison appeared beside Claire. "Looking for food? I can fix you something if you like. And coffee's on."

Liz padded over to the kitchen on sock feet. "I'll just make a couple of pieces of toast, if that's okay. And yes to the coffee."

Allison chuckled as Avery ran in from the great room. "Miss Liz! You look pretty today."

It wasn't the child's fault she had Mason for a father, and she looked a bit less like him than her brother did. Liz smiled at her. "Thank you, Avery."

"The boys are playing outside," the girl informed her. "Aunt Allison said maybe we'd bake Christmas cookies today. Do you like cookies?"

Aromas of molasses and cinnamon wafted through Liz's memories. Mom had wrapped her in an oversized apron, and she'd helped mix, roll, cut, and decorate gingerbread men. "I love cookies."

"Goody. Maybe you can help us. Let's have a cookie-making party." Avery looked from one adult to another, eyes bright. "Can we?"

Allison reached over and smoothed Avery's short thick hair. "I think we can do that. We're going caroling tomorrow evening, and it would be fun to give people a plate of treats." She looked up at Liz with a smile. "I hope you can come, too."

"Maybe." She hadn't specified if Mason would be going. "But either way, I'm happy to bake."

"Sounds good." Claire slid a mug of coffee across the peninsula to Liz. "It's not like we haven't made any yet, but these starving children inhale them as fast as we allow it."

Allison chuckled. "Sure, blame the children. I've seen the

guys' hands in the cookie jar more often. Brent insists he's eaten only half a dozen. At a time, that is."

Liz peered into the toaster. "How does this thing keep up with so many people? It only makes four slices."

"Well, for starters, we don't serve a lot of toast. We already go through a couple of loaves of bread a day without making it central."

Liz's cheeks flushed. "I'm sorry. I should have asked if it was okay. I can buy my own bread." In fact, she should've already been doing that.

"Oh, don't worry about it. You asked, and I'm answering. When we make toast for the crew, we broil it by the sheet. We thought about getting one of those big rotating toasters like institutional kitchens have, but decided against it."

"I can't imagine how much of everything you must go through." Liz smeared butter on the hot toast and then a drizzle of honey.

Claire pointed at the pantry door. The entire surface was a dry erase board with charts. "We didn't start out cooking for a dozen or more. At first it was just Jo, Sierra, and me. As the crew grew, we adapted. There have been all kinds of tipping points."

"Tell me about Jo."

"She'll be over in a bit. Why not ask her?"

Because it still felt so weird to think of having a sister-in-law? To realize her brother was a dad? And not only Zach. She caught a glimpse of Avery's bright eyes across the counter, and her gut soured. Mason, too. All these people thought marriage and kids were normal.

Liz was dying of curiosity at what happened to Erin. Had Erin been smart enough to dump Mason before he made her the laughing stock of their social scene? But still, they'd had children together. They must have had some good years in there. Hopefully.

No way was she going to ask. And, even if it was part of what Mason wanted to tell her, that didn't mean she was ready to hear about it from him. If he was ready to apologize for past wrongs, she'd make him grovel... and then she'd tell him no. She wouldn't help him clear his conscience.

Some vague memory of a Bible verse from when she was a kid surfaced. Something about forgiving someone seventy times seven. It wasn't like she was on speaking terms with God, though, so she didn't need to listen. A bit of Bible would do Mason a world of good. Her? She didn't need it.

Chapter 7 --

Mason was a sucker for, "Please, Daddy?" It didn't matter which child. He was pretty sure his parents had said no to him a whole lot more often than he could bring himself to with the twins.

Which is how he found himself at Green Acres Thursday evening. He'd been trying to stay away and give Liz some space. Probably didn't count when his kids spent all day there while he was at work.

He couldn't convince himself that the caroling evening was going to be a good time to talk to Liz. He'd have to catch her one-on-one sometime, away from the team and definitely very far away from his inquisitive children. And with their history, he couldn't exactly blame Liz for making sure they were never alone, even for a minute.

Even now, as the group wound up an early supper of thick, rich, stew and bundled into parkas, she stuck to Jo or Zach like glue. She'd chosen wisely. Mason had no intention of delving into the past with anyone else present but, next to Steve and Rosemary, Liz's brother and his wife were the last people he'd pick as bystanders. Zach was one concerned-looking big brother.

"I want to ride with Maddie." Avery crossed her arms over her chest and glared at Mason.

"You can't. Kids have to ride in their own seats. It's a law in

Idaho." Okay, his daughter couldn't push him over in *every* circumstance. Good to know.

"But you can put my seat in Mr. Zach's truck."

"Sorry, princess. Miss Liz is their guest. I think she's going to ride with them."

"Or Miss Liz could ride with us. Then it would be okay not to ride with Maddie."

Mason stared down the pint-sized girl. "Nope. Not happening."

Her lower lip jutted.

"Can you stick it out further?" Allison patted Avery's shoulder as she walked by. "There's almost enough room for a bird to land."

Avery scowled.

Mason nudged her. "Finish getting ready, princess. You'll have lots of time with Maddie. You can stand beside her and sing."

Man, he'd never gone caroling in his life. He could carry a tune okay, but didn't sing out in church. The things he did for his kids.

And to see Liz.

o0o

The families piled out of their vehicles in front of a detached home in an older neighborhood. Liz didn't bother asking whose house it was. Galena Landing had doubled in size since she'd left, so odds were she wouldn't know the inhabitants, anyway.

She joined as the troupe made their way up the drive, covered with a few inches of fresh snow. More was falling, flakes glittering in the glow from the street lamps. Liz inhaled deeply, the brisk air filling her, cleansing her.

Noel began singing *Silent Night,* and everyone joined in by the second word. As they built in volume, a drapery at the front window twitched as someone peered out. Before the group launched into *O Little Town of Bethlehem,* an elderly couple stood in the doorway, framed in the light behind them.

When they paused at the end of the fourth carol, the man beckoned. "Come in. Come in! You must be freezing. Let us fix you some cocoa."

"No, thanks." Jo laughed as she pressed a tin into the woman's hands. "We've just begun. We wanted to wish you a Merry Christmas."

Behind her, Liz heard a scraping sound. She turned to see all four guys moving snow with big shovels.

"But—" The man stepped out onto the cement landing and holding out his hand as though to stop them.

"No *buts,* Ed."

Liz peered closer. Ed Graysen? Wow, he'd aged since her high school days. He looked old. Bent over. Decrepit.

"Well, thank you." Ed looked out at the group. "You children did a fine job singing." Then his gaze settled on her. "Liz? Is that you? I heard a rumor you were home."

Home. What a strange word. Home... and yet not, at all. "Hi, Mr. Graysen. Yes, it's me."

He held out both arms. "Well, come here, and let us give you a hug."

Oh man. She hated being pushed into the limelight, but Jo and Claire made room, and it would be rude not to. She mounted the few steps and found herself enveloped in the old man's arms and, a moment later, Mrs. Graysen's as well.

"We've been praying for you, Lizzie," the woman whispered. "Every single day. It's so good to see you home."

Tears stung Liz's eyes, and she blinked them back. "Thank you." Even though it didn't seem likely that God was in the business of answering anyone's prayers, it didn't hurt for this old couple to believe they'd had a part in her return. They didn't know she blamed it on Sanun. Or had it just been time?

Mrs. Graysen patted Liz's arm. "Do come visit us sometime. Bring your mother, maybe. We'd like to hear all about Thailand. We've never gone anywhere like that."

Liz managed a smile as she disengaged. "I'm not sure how long I'll be here but, if I get a chance, I'll come by."

"Please do."

Behind her, Liz heard the muffled clang of shovels landing in the back of Zach's pickup. "I need to go. Merry Christmas."

"Merry Christmas, Liz." Mr. Graysen's large hand rested on her shoulder. "Remember the reason for the season."

Liz turned for the vehicles, where parents already helped kids buckle in. *The reason for the season.* That had always sounded like such a cliché. Maybe it was to some people, but she was pretty sure Ed Graysen hadn't meant it that way.

A dozen old people's houses and nearly as many shoveled driveways later, the group assembled in the lounge of the Galena Hills Care Facility. Avery and Maddie, clutching each other's hands, stood in front of a bent-over elderly woman, who stroked Maddie's brown curls and murmured nonsense to them.

Jo leaned closer to Liz. "This is where your grandmother lived out her final years."

Unexpected tears prickled Liz's eyes. "Did you know her?"

"I did. I worked here as nutritionist. She was very sweet."

Memories of sitting on a stool in the trailer kitchen, short legs swinging, surrounded Liz. Grandma Humbert had always been good for homemade cookies and a listening ear but, round about puberty, Liz stopped going next door. She and her friends had been too busy trying to catch the eye of the boys to hang out with old women in polyester pants and permed hair.

Lousy choice. One of many.

She would not glance at Mason Waterman to confirm the

stupidity and pain behind her teen fantasies.

"I don't know if anyone told you, but your grandmother gave Zach her wedding rings for me." Jo lifted her left hand. "Told him to ask me to marry him when we were still busy being antagonistic to each other."

Liz raised her eyebrows. "It wasn't love at first sight?"

"It rarely is, from what I hear." Jo looked around the group.

Liz's glance took in the Green Acres adults as they chatted with the old people. Even Mason crouched beside some old man's wheelchair while the senior mumbled something to Christopher and Finnley.

If she didn't know Mason as well as she did, she could be attracted to a man like him. He seemed so nice. So normal. She choked back a derisive snort.

"You and Mason knew each other in high school? Zach says you were in the same class."

"I knew him." Liz kept her voice low and steady. This was hardly the place for this conversation. "He was a jerk."

Jo's hand — the one with antique rings on it — rested on Liz's arm. "He's changed. Grown up, if you will."

Oh, he'd grown up, all right. Devastatingly so.

"Most important, he's put his faith in Jesus and become a new creature. He said that though his parents dragged him to church as a child, he never really understood or cared at the time."

Show no emotion. "Sounds about right."

"I'm probably meddling." Jo's voice was just above a whisper. "But I've seen him watching you. After watching the entire gang at Green Acres fall in love, I'm pretty sure I recognize the signs, and yet you—"

"Yes, you are meddling." Liz jerked away from her sister-in-law's hand. "You have no idea what happened, and it isn't any of your business. He may have you fooled with those soulful eyes, but you're completely wrong. So don't even start matchmaking because I know things you don't know." She stared into Jo's brown eyes. "Things you will never know."

Trembling, she took a step away, trying to feel the ambience of the lounge again. Trying to find joy in the old peoples' faces. A good many of them stared vacantly. She knew what that felt like, and she was at least fifty years younger than any of them.

She needed air.

Liz grabbed her parka from the stack of coats by the door and punched in the escape code she'd heard the director give Jo upon arrival. The door crawled open as though pushed by snails, and Liz edged through the gap long before it was fully open.

"Liz!"

Zach. But she was in no mood to go back in and have a nice little conversation with her brother. She strode down the sidewalk toward the waiting vehicles. If only she'd driven herself, she could hop in and leave. Either stop at the farm and grab her stuff or not. Just get as far away from Idaho as she could.

But no. She was stuck where everything reminded her of the past. Where she was not a full adult who'd been on her own for a decade, deciding where to live, where to work, and whom to date. No, here she had to put up with a sister-in-law she'd barely met — a woman who thought she knew all about who was in love with whom — telling her Mason was changed. That he'd become a Christian and was in love with her.

As if.

The automatic door rumbled behind her, letting out the sound of the children's high voices and the adults' lower ones. Heavy footsteps came toward her. Why couldn't her brother leave her alone?

"Liz."

It wasn't Zach. It was Mason, and there was no place to flee.

Chapter 8 --

*L*iz pivoted in the glow of a streetlamp. "Don't come one step closer, or I'll scream bloody murder."

The welcome he'd expected, if not hoped for. Mason held up both hands. "I have no intention of manhandling you."

The unspoken word *again* hung in the snow-spangled air.

"Just go back inside. Or get in your car and drive away. Leave me alone."

"I need to talk to you, Liz."

"No, you don't. We have nothing to say to each other. Nothing. Do you hear me?" She backed away, her gaze fixed on him as she reached Zach's pickup on the circle drive then edged around it.

He could still get to her if he wanted, but that was no way to win her over. "I hear you, and I don't blame you. But that doesn't stop the need."

Her eyes narrowed.

Bad word choice, Waterman. "That's not what I meant."

"Sure."

"Please listen, Liz. I was a jerk. An idiot. A predator."

"Yes, you were." She rested her arms on the edge of the truck box. "And, so help me, God, you will never have a chance to treat me like that again."

He closed his eyes for a second, absorbing the verbal blow. "That's the thing. God *has* helped me. He showed me the mess I was. The horrible, egotistical, cruel guy."

She nodded. "That about sums you up." Her words were bitter, and he absorbed them, too.

"God whacked me upside the head, Liz. He got my attention, and He showed me He loved me anyway. That Jesus died for me so that I could have a relationship with Him."

"That's nice. God doesn't have very good taste in friends, does He?"

Mason shifted from one foot to the other. "You could say that. But that's the business He's in. The Bible says Jesus didn't come to heal the well, but the sick. Those who needed it most."

"Don't bother quoting Scripture at me. I've heard it all."

Was he responsible for her rejection of her childhood faith? She'd been on her way before that night, but he'd certainly helped.

"I've repented before God, Liz. I begged for His forgiveness." He took a deep breath. "Not just for what I did to you. There were others."

If she twitched a muscle, he couldn't tell. "I need you to know that I'm sorry to the core of my being. I'd do anything to undo that night, to make it up to you in some way. I don't deserve your forgiveness, but I'm asking for it, anyway."

"No, Mason. I will not forgive you."

He reeled from the venom in her voice.

"You took more than my virginity. You made me the laughing stock of Galena High. I trusted you. I thought you loved me, and you shattered me."

"I know," he said quietly. "I'm sorry."

"*You're* sorry? You have no idea. You made me think you cared about me when it was nothing but a game, and I was too stupid to know until everyone laughed at me at school the next day. You'd taken bets you could make the good little girl fall like everyone else. Don't come to me all pious and expect *I'm sorry* to mean anything to me now. There is no forgiveness, Mason

Waterman. Do you hear me? There. Is. No. Forgiveness."

"There's forgiveness in Jesus, Liz. He's wiped my slate clean."

"Well, I haven't."

"I've prayed for you every single day since I met Jesus. Not just that you'd find your way back to Him. Not just that you'd forgive me, but that He'd heal you." He took a few steps closer and noted her wince. Two steps more and he leaned against the truck bed across from her.

"Go away, Mason." The fire had gone out of her voice, and only the ice remained. "You've said your piece. Now you can stop praying for me and get on with your life. Must be nice."

He regarded her steadily. "I won't stop praying for you, and my life hasn't been exactly nice."

Her jaw tensed, but she said nothing.

"I slept with a lot of girls, Liz. A lot of drunken one-night stands, and a few longer relationships of a few weeks." He grimaced. "When Erin informed me she was pregnant, I told her to get an abortion and get out of my life, but she said no on both counts. I still don't know why, but I'm thankful."

Liz stared at him.

"By the time the twins were born, I'd kept a job for nearly a year. I was trying to be a good guy."

Telling this story would be easier if Liz gave any response at all. But at least she was listening.

"We thought we could have it all back then. We stuck together for the sake of the kids. When Erin started going out with other guys and leaving me with the babies, I retaliated in kind."

Liz straightened, her head slowly shaking. "I don't want to hear this."

He didn't want to relive it. He'd been the worst kind of fool. "Off and on we actually tried to make it work between us, but we had so much baggage and didn't have a clue where to begin. And then we'd fight and push away again." He took a deep breath. "There was a lot of fighting."

"If we're quoting the Bible, I think that's called reaping what's been sowed."

Mason forced a laugh. "Something like that. But I knew there had to be more. Nearly everyone we hung out with was in a similar open relationship, but that's not what I'd been raised with. Not what my parents had. Or yours."

Back to no response, but at least she hadn't run. Maybe he could get it all said tonight before everyone else came out. The twins didn't need to hear this, for sure. Not until they were older. Much older.

"A guy I worked with invited me to some meetings at his church. I didn't plan to attend, but the girl I was supposed to go out with that night stood me up, and the church was just around the corner. I didn't want to go home to Erin, so I went in. I went every night for a week, and at the end of it, I gave my life to Jesus."

"Well, if anyone needed saving, it was you. Congratulations."

"Erin was livid, but I tried to help her understand." Much like he was trying to explain to Liz, now. "It took me another year or more to come to grips with how God viewed my lifestyle. Oh, I'd quit the party scene and going out with other girls, but Erin and I weren't married. I asked her to marry me for the sake of the twins and told her no more sex until we'd tied the knot. I started sleeping on the sofa."

Liz snorted.

"She didn't care. She was getting all she wanted elsewhere." Sometimes at home, too, while he and their toddlers were in the other room. He'd deserved all the pain Erin had inflicted on him. Mason looked across the truck at Liz. So much pain, from so many angles. If only God had rescued him sooner, but Mason hadn't been listening.

"And then one day she just left. I didn't hear from her for weeks and, when I did, she said she'd moved on, and I should do the same."

"But what about the children?"

Ah. Liz had been listening, after all. "She left them behind. They were holding her back, she said."

"But..."

Mason sighed. "I know. But that's Erin. She emails or calls occasionally. Sends them a card on their birthday and sometimes a gift. That's about it."

"Those poor kids."

Was she softening?

"You have sure left a trail behind you, haven't you? It's not much comfort to know I'm not your only victim."

He accepted those words, too. "After a year or two, I realized Erin wasn't coming back. I was working a dead-end job, paying for childcare, and barely keeping us fed. Without help from that church in Billings, I don't know what would have happened. So I decided to swallow my pride and come back to Galena Landing. I found a job, my parents helped with the kids, and the crew at Green Acres has become my extended family."

"Yes, I've noticed how you took over not only my childhood home but my family. Nice work."

"Don't be bitter, Liz. Your family and their friends — they are wonderful people who are trying to live as light to the world around them, not only environmentally but spiritually."

"Don't worry. I'll leave them to you. I'll be out of everyone's way in a week or two, and you all can just keep on doing what you're doing. Far be it from me to unbalance things."

"Or you could stay."

When her eyes widened, he realized he'd said those words out loud. They hung in the air like a snowflake caught in a cross breeze.

"Not happening. I'm not falling under your charm again. I'm not talking to a God who didn't protect me when I was seventeen and could've used some help. I'm not cozying up to a family who could never, ever understand what I've been through and why I've made the choices I have." Liz pushed back from the truck and waved her hands. "You came back first. Fine. It's all yours. No contest."

The knife seared through him yet again. Sure, he wanted her forgiveness. In the past few days, he'd even found himself attracted to her. Like, really attracted, and not just because of their shared history. But she needed to forgive him for her own sake more than for his. He had the peace of knowing he'd done what he could, that God had removed his guilt. Hard to remember, when Liz's presence brought it all back, but some time on his knees tonight when the twins were in bed would soothe his soul again.

But Liz. How long would she be tormented?

The whoosh of the nursing home door warned him this conversation was coming to a close. Voices and laughter spilled out, including his children's. Footsteps crunched on the sidewalk behind him.

He lowered his voice. "Liz, you can't stop me from praying for you. Whatever you think of me for the rest of your life, you owe it to yourself to find your way back to God. He's waiting for you."

"I don't care. Don't you understand? It's too late, and it's all your fault."

Mason bowed his head. It was only too late if she held firm. But that it was his fault was undeniable.

Chapter 9 --

*B*ut you shouldn't have." Liz held up the soft coral-toned sweater and looked from Claire to Allison. "I don't have anything for you."

The other two women exchanged a smile, and Claire reached over with a hug. "We didn't get it for you expecting something in return. That's not what Christmas is all about."

Liz couldn't remember what Christmas was supposed to be all about. She hadn't bothered celebrating in Thailand. Some years she'd forgotten to send even a card or email to her parents. Then she'd felt massively guilty when they phoned her. She hadn't always answered those calls.

"Thank you, Auntie Liz!" Maddie bounced in front of her, clutching her stuffed tiger. "He's so soft."

At least she'd brought gifts for her family this year. Little John toddled around with his elephant, righting himself as often as he tripped over packaging on the floor.

Ash wailed as John trundled by. Claire and Noel's baby pulled himself to standing beside anything that held still long enough, including Domino, who was usually smart enough to evade the clutching fingers.

John crouched and offered the elephant to Ash, who stopped crying long enough to stuff a tusk into his mouth. Then John was on his way again, elephant under his arm, leaving Ash with fresh tears.

"We're all going to be in trouble once Ash can keep up with John." Allison laughed. "Those two are going to make Finnley and Christopher look tame, I think."

Did she have to bring up Mason's child? Liz had been enjoying the fact that Mason and the twins were at his parents' house for Christmas Eve. She'd had trouble blocking the memory of his words from two nights ago. They'd sounded so sincere, and his facial expression had matched them.

But she'd sincerely believed he loved her in the spring of their senior year, too, and he'd used and abused her. He was a master of deception. She'd fallen for him in high school — hard — and she'd never gotten over what had happened as a result. She wasn't going anywhere near that situation again. Wasn't going near him.

"Thank you, Lizzie Rose."

She blinked back into the great room of the straw bale house and focused on her father, who held up the rattan ball she'd given him. "You're welcome, Daddy." She hadn't figured out how to talk to him again, either. He seemed as sharp as ever, though his body wasn't much ahead of the residents at the nursing home.

The recruiters hadn't answered her email yesterday other than an auto-responder saying their offices were closed over the holidays. They had to find her something. Anything. The sooner the better. Whoever coined the phrase *you can't go home again* was onto something, because nothing about Galena Landing or the farm where she'd grown up remained the same.

Mason Waterman lived there. How much more messed up could life be than that? She desperately wanted to see the house. To walk through the rooms, to climb the stairs and maybe slide down the rail as she often had as a child. To see if her bedroom was really as tiny as she remembered. No way she could go through it with Mason living there.

"Bedtime for John." Jo scooped him up. "Give me a few minutes to tuck him in, then how about a game of Blackout or something? It's too early to call it a night." She glanced over to where Maddie and Finnley chugged a train around a track with many more sections than it'd had before the gifting.

"Good idea." Claire got to her feet. "I'll get Ash settled, too."

The little guy rubbed his eyes and reached for his mom.

Noel flicked his chin toward the kitchen, his eyes on Zach. "That leaves you and me on snacks, bro."

Zach looked between their parents. "Want to stay for a while longer?"

"Sure," said Dad. "Pretty sure I've still got what it takes." He smiled at Liz.

She jumped up. "Can I help you guys with food?" She certainly couldn't help with nursing babies, though she could probably get the hang of cloth diapers if needed.

"Oh, that's okay." Zach pointed back at her chair. "We laid out everything earlier, so it won't take Noel and me long. Go ahead and visit with the folks."

Protesting would get her nowhere. A minute later she was alone — at least if she didn't count the children off in the corner — with her parents. She'd been avoiding that as much as she could. Probably they were smart enough to recognize the signs. She slumped back into the armchair.

"We haven't seen much of you, Lizzie." Dad's voice was mild.

Because someone had offered her a two-bedroom duplex all to herself, and she'd come out as little as possible?

She shrugged, not quite meeting his gaze. "I've been online a lot, looking for a job. Plus I'm not used to driving in snow anymore."

"We've sure had a lot of that this week," Mom put in. "I can't remember when we've had this much before Christmas. Often we get most of it in January."

"The almanac says we're in for tons then, too," said Dad.

"That will build up a good pack in the high country and lower the risk of forest fires next summer."

Mom nodded. "Always a good thing."

Silence. Guess that subject was about exhausted. "Thanks for the sweater. You guessed correctly that I don't have a lot of warm clothes."

"That's what I said to Jo and Allison when they asked. You always liked to be fashionable."

Which had been a source of contention between her and her parents when she was a teen. She'd begged for the latest everything. Didn't look like that attitude afflicted Jo, Allison, or Claire. Around here everyone seemed to go for comfy, but she had a reputation to protect. There must be a teaching job for her somewhere. Something worth dressing up for.

Liz stroked the three sweaters on her lap. Coral, teal, and a fuzzy one in lavender. "These are all great. Thanks for putting in a good word."

Behind her, the guys set dishes on the plank farmhouse table with gentle thunks. Chairs scraped lightly on the etched concrete floor.

She'd been told to stay put, so she stared into the crackling fire. Warm, mesmerizing.

"Liz, I wish you'd let us in," Mom said quietly. "What is going on in your pretty head? Do you miss Thailand so much? What brought you home?"

Liz shot a glance at her mother. If she confided, would her parents kick Mason out of their house? Wait, no. They didn't even own it anymore. This whole outfit belonged to her brother and all his friends. Besides, no one would believe her. She should've come back before he had if she wanted to stake a claim.

Easy, then. She'd been on her own for over a decade, and she'd keep it up. Lots of people had minimal contact with their parents and childhood friends and survived just fine. Still, seeing the many interconnections at play in this group tugged at something inside her. It would be nice if...

But *if* didn't exist. There was no time machine. No way to go back to before the senior class party, before she'd fancied herself in love with Mason. This was her reality. She had to play the cards she'd been dealt.

Jo and Claire entered from the bedroom wing. "Ready for Blackout?" Jo rubbed her hands together. "Where are the cards, Zach?"

Maybe Liz would do better with a game where the outcome of her played cards wouldn't derail her entire future.

o0o

Mason's cell phone rang as he pulled into the driveway after Christmas dinner with his parents. He froze at the ringtone, one that rarely occurred, but one he always needed to be braced for.

Erin.

"Into the house, kids. Get your jammies on and we'll have some stories by the tree before bed."

The phone rang again.

"Aren't you going to answer that, Daddy?" asked Avery.

"In a minute, princess. You guys scoot inside, okay? I'll be there before you know it."

Christopher grumbled as he shoved the car door open. Avery followed suit, and the two of them trundled up the back steps to the veranda before disappearing into the house. The kitchen light flicked on through the window.

Silence.

Mason stared at the phone. He breathed a prayer as he tapped Erin's number to return the call.

"Hi, Erin."

"Screening your calls, Mason?" Shrill voices and laughter sounded in the background.

Caught redhanded. "I was busy with the kids. They've gone to get ready for bed now."

"But I wanted to talk to them."

Was her voice slurred, or was she just putting on a big pout? Hard to tell without seeing her face. "I'm not sure that's a good idea."

"Oh, don't be such a spoilsport. I thought they'd like to come spend some time with me."

What did *some time* mean? Mason's fingers tightened around his phone. "They've just got a few more days off before school starts again." Over a week, but hopefully she wouldn't think of that.

"Oh, Mason. Don't be silly. They're in kindergarten, right? It's not that important."

"Stability is important."

"I'm their mother."

A mother who rarely remembered. "You're the one who left us. You're the one who never calls or visits. You're the one who forgot to acknowledge their last birthday. You think I'm just going to stick them on a plane and believe you'll take good care of them? That's not how parenting works, Erin."

"Well, trust you to be the expert."

He ground his teeth together. "It's not like I had much choice. Did you think I'd just turn them over to the state foster care system? They're my children, Erin. My flesh and blood." He'd doubted that a time or two, given Erin's propensities, but Christopher especially was too much like him in both looks and personality to believe it for long. "As their father, it's my responsibility to keep them safe. To take care of their needs."

"Honestly, Mason. They're my children, too."

"What made you remember?"

She was silent for a moment as the background noises dimmed. He heard a door shut, and then quiet.

"I never forgot."

No one but him sat in the car to see his eyebrows go up. "You signed away all rights to them." After he'd tracked her down.

She sighed. "Maybe I wish I hadn't."

That was a new twist. "Not good enough, Erin. There's no way I'm sending them to you." It was true, but guilt remained. Sure, Erin had been more messed up when he met her than Liz had been, so maybe he wasn't as responsible for her downward spiral. He'd help her if he could, but not at the expense of the twins. He'd accepted responsibility for them, and he wasn't abdicating.

"I just need to see them. Spend some time with them."

"Why?"

Mason could hear music and laughter in the background as she paused. "I just do."

The quiet simplicity in her words tugged at him. He'd been needy once, and his buddy had introduced him to Jesus. Erin hadn't been ready then. Was she now? Could he deny her the chance?

"Hey, Erin?" He spoke quickly, before he lost his nerve.

"What?"

"I don't feel good about sending the kids to you, but why don't you come visit for a bit? Their birthday is coming up." Mid-February would give him time to brace himself and the twins for the visit.

Her voice turned coy. "Are you inviting me back, Mason?"

"Uh, not that way. A visit for the sake of the twins. My friends next door have a spare bedroom."

Liz.

Oh, no. He shouldn't have invited Erin. This was a disaster in the making. But Liz would be long gone by then. She could hardly wait. He didn't stand a chance with her, even without adding Erin to the mix, live and in person.

His one responsibility was to his children. Was it right to keep Avery, especially, from her mother? Christopher probably wouldn't care.

Christopher. Uh oh. That boy had been inside without supervision for long enough to get into trouble. "I need to go, Erin. It's time for bedtime stories."

"Man, you've gone the whole nine yards, haven't you? Bedtime stories." But she sounded more wistful than mocking this time.

He pushed the car open and got out. The temperature in the vehicle had chilled to match the outside air. "I helped create these children, Erin. It's not their fault we were such a mess back then. But yes, God is giving me strength every single day to be the best dad I can for them. It's not easy parenting alone. I won't pretend it is. But they mean everything to me." He climbed the back steps. "Think about it. Come for their birthday, and let me tell you how God has changed my life."

"Maybe."

"Good night, Erin. Jesus loves you."

Chapter 10 --

*T*he brilliant blue sky beckoned Liz through the window a few days later. A thick layer of glittering hoar frost coated every twig on every branch of every tree. It outlined the few grasses and shrubs tall enough to poke through the two feet of snow or more that had fallen in the past week.

How had she spent a decade away from winter? She'd missed snow, missed the lung-clearing air, missed the purity of the whole experience.

Though your sins be as scarlet, they shall be as white as snow.

The memory verse from her childhood streamed through her mind. What did that mean, anyhow? What was a scarlet sin? She remembered *black as sin*, but wasn't red supposed to represent the blood of Jesus that washed someone clean?

Liz turned from the window to put on her parka and mitts. Enough of that line of thought. She obviously needed to get away from Galena Landing and its reminders of her Christian upbringing.

The cold air swarmed her as she left the duplex. Wow, it must be pushing thirty below. Maybe she didn't need a job in the north, after all. Cities rarely looked this sparkling in winter but got dirty and gray quickly from all the exhaust fumes and trampling.

Well, she'd have to wait and see what the recruiting company found for her before she could make a firm decision.

The deck to the main house was a skating rink from the layer of ice. Liz slid cautiously across the shimmering wood.

"Dad, I'm cold."

Liz's hand stilled on the door handle. Christopher's voice. She shouldn't be able to hear them so clearly across the field.

"Then hurry it up. We'll get you two warmed up in a minute. Come on, Avery."

Liz turned slowly.

Mason and his children trudged down the well-worn path between the two farms. One snowsuit leg bulged above Avery's boot, while the other had been tugged overtop. Christopher looked even more askew than his sister, his blond hair sticking out from beneath his knitted hat.

Man, those kids needed a mother.

Her gut tinged at the memory of how Mason's eyes softened when he looked at her. Wasn't going to be her, though, mothering Erin's kids. She'd fallen for Mason's baby blues once before, and it had scarred her for life.

"Miss Liz!" called Avery. "It's c-c-cold at our house."

And Liz had somehow been caught standing outside. She shouldn't have paused at the voices. "Oh, is it? I'm sorry to hear that."

"Power's out from all that ice," Mason said matter-of-factly.

It had seemed so warm in the duplex, though. Was it residual heat? Or maybe it had been colder than she'd noticed. Though it was nothing like some childhood mornings, when she could see her breath in her little bedroom under the eaves.

Christopher slid across the deck. "Whee, this is fun!"

Avery inched her way to Liz then wrapped both arms around Liz's middle. Liz patted the child on the back.

"Brent planned to help me rig up solar panels and battery systems for a backup." Mason reached past Liz and opened the door. "But things got busy through the fall and we didn't get to it yet. Inside, kids." Mason looked at Liz. "Were you coming or going?"

Caught. Both in transition and by those blue eyes. She could retreat, but why let him win? Besides, she had nothing for breakfast in her little place. She tipped her head at him and entered the straw bale house in front of him. Warmth immediately enveloped her, warmth that had nothing to do with Mason's close proximity.

Claire appeared beyond the peninsula dividing the kitchen from the dining room. "Hi, guys. Anyone hungry?" Then her eyes seemed to notice Liz in the midst of the Watermans, and her eyebrows rose.

"Breakfast is exactly why I came over." Liz bent to unzip her boots. "Just happened to get here at the same time. Can I help?"

"Me, too!" Avery shed her snowsuit in short order, eyes bright. "I want to help."

Noel, holding Ash, stepped into view beside Claire. "You called North Idaho Power? Any idea how soon they'll get electricity back up?"

In Liz's periphery, Mason shook his head. "Ice froze on lines all over the valley. Half the town is blacked out, so technicians need to start there, where the nursing home and other vital services are running off generators."

Half the town? She shot a questioning look at Mason.

"The downtown and the north side. Your folks are in that new subdivision. From what the woman on the phone said, that area is unaffected."

Whew. Dad wasn't able to get around as he used to, and loss of electricity would really affect him.

"Glad to hear that." Noel nodded.

Mason shrugged out of his parka. "Trees are down across power lines, across roads. The whole thing is a mess out there. It's going to take N.I.P. time to get everything running again."

"It's a good thing you were on the same side of the problem as your family when it happened," said Noel. "I imagine there are folks who can't get where they need to go."

"The tire shop has no power, so I'm off today." Mason hung up his coat then his kids' snowsuits. He straightened their boots on the mat. "The house is the same temperature as outside, give or take a couple of degrees and, of course, the waterlines are frozen solid."

Noel set Ash down, and the little guy pulled to standing against a dining room chair, watching them all with a big grin on his round face.

Liz ruffled his curly head as she passed him on her way into the kitchen. Sounded like Mason would be here for the duration. Well, she'd head back to her private space as soon as she'd eaten and helped clean up. Or she'd climb the hill and visit Jo and the children. Maybe Zach was home, too, if roads were closed and power out at his veterinary clinic. She didn't need to spend one extra minute around Mason or his children.

o0o

Mason settled on a tall stool on the dining room side of the peninsula where he could keep an eye on Christopher, who was running and sliding on the etched concrete floor.

Ash crawled after Christopher, chortling happily. When Christopher paused for a moment, the baby practiced his new skill of standing without holding onto anything. He stood, slightly hunched over with hands outstretched, a look of pure concentration on his face. Christopher flew past, and the little guy wobbled.

"Careful of Ash!"

"He should stay out of my way."

"Christopher."

"Aw, Dad. He's just a boring baby. Where's Finnley? Can I go to his house?"

"No, they went to Coeur d'Alene yesterday for a few days. Remember?"

Christopher's shoulders slumped. "There's no one to play with. There's nothing to do."

"We'll find something." No idea what. Ash seemed safe for the moment, so Mason turned his attention into the kitchen where Liz and Claire chopped vegetables at the butcher block island, his daughter standing on a stool beside them.

"I don't like mushrooms," Avery announced, her lower lip jutting out.

Claire chuckled. "And yet you seem to like everything I cook. I bet if you pretend to not know there are mushrooms in your scrambled eggs, you won't even notice them."

Avery scowled.

Mason let out a long slow breath. Being around the Green Acres bunch had opened his eyes to what healthy family meals could look like, but what single father had time or energy for all the extra work to cook from scratch? His kids were way too used to takeout from the diner.

"Here you go, Noel." Liz scooped a mound of chopped zucchini into a bowl. "How many eggs do you want cracked?"

"Might as well go with an even dozen. Which reminds me, I need to check how the chickens fared in the cold last night. If it affected their laying, we may have to cut back on eggs for breakfast, but we're good for now."

Liz reached into the commercial double-door refrigerator and pulled out a carton of eggs. She started breaking them into another bowl.

Ash wailed from behind Mason, who whirled on the chair to see the baby lying on his back.

Christopher stood a few feet away, both hands in the air. "I didn't touch him. Promise."

Mason shook his head and scooped the baby into his arms.

Memories of juggling two assaulted him. It was way easier now that the twins were in kindergarten compared to the first few years. He'd barely slept, barely functioned. He'd never planned to have kids. Definitely he'd never foreseen being a single father. If he could, would he go back and change anything?

His gaze caught on Liz, bent over the bowl so her hair fell forward, partially hiding her face.

He'd definitely go back and be a different teenager. One who respected others, who wasn't so full of himself. One who hadn't robbed Liz of her virginity and tainted ten years of her life.

As hard as parenting alone was, as painful as the path from his teen years to the present, it had taken the twins to shove him out of the mess his life had spiraled into. Without them, would he have ever found his way back to Galena Landing? Back to God?

Noel turned to the stove and scraped a blob of bacon fat into each of two large cast iron skillets. A moment later he divided the bowl containing onions, mushrooms, and zucchini between the sizzling pans.

Mason jiggled Ash on his knee. The baby quieted and stretched for papers on the tile peninsula. Mason pushed them out of reach.

"He okay?" asked Claire.

"Seems to be. Just took a tumble." Ash twisted and shoved his finger up Mason's nose. "Hey, stop that." Mason pushed Ash's hand away.

Claire laughed. "Thanks for getting him. Breakfast in a minute. That will cure what ails him."

Liz glanced over. Her gaze seemed trapped on Mason's so he barely dared breathe. What was she thinking? Might she consider forgiving him for ruining her life? How would things be different if he'd valued her when they were teens? Would they have ended up together in a happy, godly home with a kid or two of their own?

His knee jiggled out of control, and Ash bounced along with a chortle. Mason couldn't help grinning at the happy baby sound any more than he could break eye contact with Liz.

Christopher climbed onto the other counter stool. "I'm hungry, Dad. That smells good."

Avery turned, narrowing her gaze at her twin. "You won't like it. It has mushrooms."

Christopher shrugged. "Maybe they're okay."

"Are your hands clean, Christopher?" asked Claire. "Mason, would you mind washing Ash and strapping him into his high chair? We're nearly ready here."

"I can do that." Mason tucked the wiggling baby under his arm like a football and herded Christopher toward the bathroom.

Behind him, he heard Claire's voice. "Avery, would you help Miss Liz set the table?"

"I like helping Miss Liz."

Of course she did.

A few minutes later, Mason found himself sitting across the plank table from Liz while Noel asked the blessing and Ash banged his spoon against the wooden tray.

"I want toast," Christopher whined as Mason scooped eggs onto his plate then turned to do the same for Avery.

"There isn't any bread," Claire informed him. "Somebody needs to bake a few loaves today. I started the sourdough last night." She glanced at Liz sitting beside her. "Did your mom teach you to make bread?"

"It was one of my Saturday jobs all through high school." Liz spooned a small helping of scrambled eggs onto her plate. "I'm not sure I remember how. It's been a long time."

Noel chuckled. "It's probably like riding a bike. Once you know how, muscle memory never forgets."

"If you're asking me to help with it today, I'm willing." Liz passed the eggs to Claire. "Not without supervision, though. Mom didn't do sourdough."

"Can I help?" asked Avery.

"Sure you can, sweetie." Claire poured milk into a metal tumbler and handed it to Ash. "You're never too young to learn."

Too bad his parents didn't treat the twins like that. No helping until they were old enough to actually do the job properly. By then, Mason doubted the kids would be interested. He needed to pull his parenting role models from Green Acres instead.

"Yay." Avery shot a triumphant look at her twin. "I get to help."

"So?" Christopher scowled back. "It's sissy stuff."

Noel reached across the corner of the table and tousled Christopher's hair. "A man who likes to eat should learn to cook and bake. It's definitely not sissy stuff."

"Thanks," Mason mouthed at his friend as his son stared quizzically at Noel.

"Maybe if the girls are baking bread, we guys can make dessert for later. Looks like we'll be spending most of the day inside anyway." Noel tilted his head at Christopher. "You up for that, buddy?"

"Cookies?"

"I was thinking more of a huckleberry platz, but we can probably squeeze in a few dozen cookies. Good thing we have two ovens."

"I like peanut butter." Christopher crossed his arms.

"We can do that."

"Peanut butter?" Mason raised his eyebrows at Noel. "Doesn't sound very local."

Noel grinned. "And you'd be right, but we can't get enough local hazelnuts to make our own nut butter yet. Our trees have just started producing, and we seem to have plenty of uses for the few we've got so far without grinding them."

"Well, that's cool." Mason nudged Christopher's shoulder.

"My son got his love of peanut butter cookies from me. I'm definitely in, if only to justify eating all the ones I plan to."

Liz glanced up from poking her eggs around her plate. She didn't seem to have much of an appetite.

Just the thought of spending part of the day in the kitchen with Liz roused Mason's hunger, and he dug into his breakfast. It wasn't hard to be thankful his electricity was out next door.

Chapter 11 --

*L*iz kneaded a six-loaf batch of sourdough bread, giving the large aluminum bowl a quarter spin with each push. "A little more flour."

Avery had the system down pat with a quarter-cup measure. She sprinkled flour along the edge of the dough as Liz held it back.

Noel had been right. Her hands remembered how to knead. She glanced at Claire. "Is this usually your job?"

"Oh, not at all. Several of us rotate, so my turn only comes up every two weeks or so. Sierra, Gabe, Chelsea, and Keanan are also on regular rotation, but they're in Portland right now. They were thinking of driving back today, but with so much ice on the highways, they're waiting until tomorrow. Anyway, Noel pitches in sometimes on bread, and so does Jo."

Curiosity got the better of Liz. "How do you decide who does what chore?"

Claire stood across the island, chopping vegetables for stew. "At first we rotated everything evenly no matter what, but Gabe came up with a new system when he married Sierra and joined the team. He made a detailed list of all the daily and weekly chores

91

from dishwashing to feeding the animals then assigned everyone a number of chores. Some were assigned a smaller number, like Allison, Brent, and Zach, since they work full-time. We each volunteered for the ones we wanted and did some shuffling to cover the remainder. It's worked out pretty well."

"I can't imagine what it takes to run a place like this." Especially when extra people showed up, like Mason and the twins. As far as she'd observed, he didn't have a regular assignment. But then, he wasn't really part of Green Acres. He just rented the old farmhouse and invited himself over a lot.

Wearing an apron with *Stand Clear: Man Cooking* blazoned across the front, Mason ran the big Bosch mixer while Christopher dumped in flour from a pre-measured container.

She'd never seen the day coming when Mason would be so domesticated. There were a lot of things about him she didn't know. She'd assumed too much. Could a guy change as much as he seemed to have?

Knead. Spin. Knead. Spin.

Adoring blue eyes gazed at her from just beyond the bowl's rim. Avery had a serious case of hero worship for Liz. What had she done to deserve that?

Liz lifted the elastic dough into a second large bowl that Claire had greased for her. She covered it with a damp towel. "Where does this rise?"

"The shelf above the cook stove."

After she set the bowl in the alcove, she turned back to Claire. "Want help with the stew?"

"Sure. You can scrub and peel the parsnips in the sink."

"I'll help!" Avery scooted the stool over to the sink.

Liz sighed. The child was sweet, and the circumstances of her birth weren't her fault. But she obviously had designs on finding a new mother, and Liz hated to see her crushed. Liz was definitely not volunteering for the job.

She peeled parsnips and a turnip while Avery ran each vegetable over to Claire for chopping. Behind her, Noel explained to Christopher how to mound dough on the cookie sheet.

"Excuse me."

Liz jumped at Mason's voice right beside her.

"Mind if I wash this out in the second sink?" He held up the bowl for the Bosch. "Noel needs it for the dough for dessert."

"Um, go ahead." Liz scooted over as far as she could and still reach the remaining carrots. She couldn't very well leave the kitchen just because Mason stood next to her, heat from his arm warming hers.

He turned the tap his direction, letting it run until the water warmed while he squirted detergent into the bowl.

Liz held her breath and waited.

Mason glanced at her. "Sorry." When his bowl was half full of water, he turned off the faucet and swiveled it back to her. He picked up a scrubby and swished it around. "Thanks for letting Avery help," he said quietly.

Liz lifted a shoulder. "It's okay."

"No, really. She craves normal, and she doesn't get enough of it."

"I noticed."

He winced. "I know you hate me, and I can't say that I blame you. Thanks for not taking it out on my kids."

She'd been tempted, a time or two, but she'd been raised better than that. "It's not their fault."

Mason glanced her direction, pursing his lips. "Thanks for noticing."

"Quit thanking me. I haven't done anything to deserve it."

"Sorry."

He could stop saying that, too. Liz glanced behind her to see Avery cutting up a parsnip under Claire's close supervision. The little girl bit her lip in concentration. "I'm sure you'll soon find the perfect woman for you and the twins, and your daughter will get all the affirmation she needs."

Wonder what Mason's perfect woman would look like.

He watched her, but she didn't turn to meet his gaze. "I haven't been looking for anyone since Erin left us." His voice was so quiet she could barely hear him. "Until recently."

Liz swung to face him. "I'm not sure what you're saying." She had some guesses, and didn't like the direction of them.

Both kids looked over from their tasks. Great. All Liz needed was to interest everyone else in this conversation. She turned back to the sink and picked up another carrot.

Mason twisted the faucet to rinse his bowl. He glanced over his shoulder then leaned closer to her. "I'm saying I'm really glad to see you again, Liz. I'm thankful God brought you home to Galena Landing."

"That's got nothing to do with your kids. I'm leaving as soon as I can, and you can get right back to doing whatever it is you do. Don't let me interfere with your life, and don't get any thoughts about permanence."

"I'm praying for you, Liz."

Great. Just what she needed. She jerked the tap back to her side of the sink. "Don't bother."

"That's the thing, Liz. You can't stop someone from praying for you. You can't stop God from pursuing you. Trust me, I know. He keeps at it."

She shifted further from him. This was why she needed out of Galena Landing as soon as possible. The recruiting office didn't open for another week, but surely there was someplace she could go in between. Cindy's or Heather's? Like either would be an improvement. Their God-talk would make Mason's sound like he was an amateur. Because he was.

If there were any justice in this world, Mason wouldn't be all cozy with Jesus. Any God who'd forgive Mason was not a God she wanted to be close to. If He even existed.

Something panged inside. She could question that all she wanted, but deep down inside, she knew God was real.

o0o

Mason and Christopher joined Zach and Noel in tossing hay to the Percherons as well as the cows and sheep. Christopher gathered eggs while Noel added a second heater to the chicken barn. With all of them working together, it didn't take long to see to the animals' needs.

Noel peeked into the greenhouse as they walked back to the house and grimaced. "That's it for anything fresh out of there for a couple of months. I'll come out tomorrow and grab those frozen cabbages. Maybe we'll have a cabbage-roll-making day."

Christopher's nose wrinkled.

Noel clapped him on the shoulder. "Have you ever had them?"

The boy shook his head. "Cabbage is yucky."

"And that's where you'd be wrong." Noel chuckled. "I'll see what's on the menu for tomorrow, but with the Portlanders still away, I'm pretty sure Claire and I get kitchen duty."

"You might still be stuck with us." Spending the day around Liz, though she'd barely spoken to him, had made today one of the best Mason had had in recent memory, but the thought of returning to the farmhouse in its sub-zero condition was out of the question.

"You can't sleep over there in that cold," Zach put in.

"There's a spare room in our house." Noel blew out a breath that froze in the cold air. "While we're bundled up, why don't we all go and help you bring back what you and the kids will need overnight?"

"Are you sure?" Mason hadn't wanted to assume.

Noel swung his head to look at Mason, his eyebrows drawn

95

together. "Of course. You think we'd put you out in this weather?"

He'd done some winter camping as a teen, but his five-year-olds weren't up for that. "Thanks. You're right. This is as good a time as any to get some toothbrushes, pajamas, and clothes for tomorrow."

They tromped down the trail between the two farms single file, the chill deepening as the sun touched the far horizon.

"I hope those frozen water pipes don't burst," Zach said as they entered the house.

The temperature wasn't a noticeable improvement from outside. "Yeah, could be a mess if they do. Christopher, get your backpack and put some clean clothes in it, okay?" Thankfully Mason had done the laundry just before Christmas. Stuff wasn't folded, but the children's baskets were back in their rooms.

"Do I have to take my boots off?"

Mason shook his head. "Keep them on and go for it."

Christopher's eyes brightened, and he headed for the staircase.

Zach chuckled. "What kid doesn't want to get away with wearing boots inside? Noel, want to come have a look at the pipes in the basement with me?" Noel nodded and the two men tromped down the steep steps to the lower level.

Mason followed his son up, found his and Avery's backpacks, and stuffed both with essentials. He crammed Avery's favorite teddy bear into the top of hers then zipped it. "Ready, buddy?"

"It's c-cold in here." Christopher stood in the doorway, shrugging his Batman pack over his shoulders.

"Yep. Sure is."

"Dad, why can't we live at Noel and Claire's house all the time? Their house is warm and they have cookies and good food."

Mason grinned at his son. "They do, but we're not part of their family. We are our own family."

"But we don't have a mom. I've been thinking about what

96

Avery said, that she wants a mom. I do, too."

This wasn't the time to let his son know that Erin wanted to visit. "I'd like you to have one, too, but it's not quite that simple."

"What about Miss Liz? I don't think she already has kids. She could be our mom. She seems kind of nice, and I think she can cook."

"You telling me I can't?"

Christopher rolled his eyes. "You're a man, Dad. Cooking is a job for a woman."

"Haven't you ever noticed that Noel cooks more often than anyone else at that house? That all the men cook sometimes?"

"Well, I guess..." His puffed breath froze in the air.

"It's not a woman's job, son. It's how things in families often land up, especially if the dad has a job in town like Zach and Brent do. In real families like over at Green Acres, everyone does whatever jobs need doing. If they're especially good at cooking, like Noel and Claire, then they do that job oftener than some other people do."

"Anyway, me and Avery want a mom. Partly because you're not really good at cooking and because we want someone to hug us and love us."

Mason crouched in front of his son. "Don't I hug you and love you?"

Christopher stepped into his open arms. "Yeah, but a mom could do it better."

Tears prickled the corners of Mason's eyes and froze in place. "You know we can ask God for anything when we pray, right? So if we ask God to give you a mom, maybe He will say yes."

The serious blue eyes looked deep into Mason's own. "Do you think so?"

"God says in the Bible that sometimes we don't have things because we don't ask. He wants to hear our requests. He wants us to tell Him the things we need."

And if God were listening, He'd been hearing a lot from Mason lately on the same topic. He usually framed the request differently, though. When Mason asked, it was more like, "Please, Lord, let Liz forgive me and love me enough to marry me."

Chapter 12 --

*G*reat bread, sis." Zach reached for another piece.

"Very good." Mason nodded in Liz's direction as he buttered a steaming slice for Christopher.

"I had a good helper." Liz smiled at Avery, and the little girl beamed back.

"You guys had a crazy kitchen day." Jo added a few pieces of carrot and parsnip to John's highchair tray then turned to Maddie. "Eat three more bites and you can have a cookie for dessert."

Noel chuckled. "If you finish *every* bite, you can have a cookie and some huckleberry platz. How's that for a deal?"

Maddie nodded and dug her fork into her bowl, coming up with a piece of beef. "It's yummy."

Liz had been on her own for so many years she'd never wondered what living in a community would be like. The thought had never crossed her radar. Even having Mason and his kids in and out hadn't fazed her today. The bright sunshine streaming in the windows had helped, but so had the realization she could retreat to the little duplex across the yard. No one had made her be sociable. She'd actually wanted to.

The rise and fall of chatter around the table cocooned her. She felt welcomed here. No pressure, just family and friendship.

Mason looked up and caught her gaze, his blue eyes warming.

Time held still for a long moment then Christopher tugged on his arm, and Mason bent to hear his son's words.

Liz pushed stew around her bowl with a crust of warm, fragrant sourdough bread. Hadn't eleven years been long enough

99

to get Mason Waterman out of her head? She'd had such a crush on him as a teenager. Nearly all the girls had. He dated frequently. Liz knew he was bad news, but her infatuation had seemed harmless. After all, the other girls were prettier. Sexier. More his type. Compared to them, she was a little country mouse. A farm girl. And even a Christian.

Late in their senior year, he seemed to notice her for the first time. He'd invited her to the class party, and that night he'd taken from her what she'd been all too willing to give up.

And the news had spread through Galena High like wildfire. The good little Christian girl had fallen. Everyone mocked her, even Mason.

She'd spent years hating him — despising him — only to find he'd changed. Now he was the believer and she the one who had no use for the God who'd failed her.

Maybe she'd failed God first. She'd known Mason was fire, and yet she'd played with matches until she'd gotten burned. She'd done it to herself. Yes, Mason had helped. Yes, God had allowed it, but she had no one to blame but herself.

Liz squirmed in her chair. Accepting the guilt was new and roused feelings of vulnerability. Could everyone see it on her face?

Jo and Claire were each focused on their little ones while the three men discussed the problem of Mason's frozen waterlines and what it would take to get them thawed once power was restored. Only Avery seemed to notice Liz. The little girl smiled at her with something akin to hero worship.

Forgiving Mason opened up too much. More than Liz was prepared for, really, but the venom that had poisoned her thoughts all these years had dissipated. She couldn't bring it back any more than she could command vapor.

oOo

"Can I help, Dad? I helped make it." His son's blue eyes begged.

"Sure, Christopher. Let me carry the tray, and you can set down the dishes, okay?"

"Okay." Christopher bit his lip as he lifted a dessert dish of huckleberry platz and set it in front of Liz.

Liz examined the dish then smiled at the boy. "Hey, that looks great! Thank you."

Mason wasn't immune to the puff of pride in his son's chest.

"You're welcome. See? We put whipped cream on top. And a berry."

"I see that. The berry on top is the perfect finishing touch."

Liz hadn't said that many words to Christopher in one go before. Just the fact she'd taken a moment to praise his son put the berry on top of Mason's day... and the day had been pretty good, all things considered.

"It looks berry yummy," said Avery. "Get it? Berry? Very?"

Noel groaned. "Good one, Avery."

"It was berry funny." Maddie giggled.

Mason couldn't help chuckling.

Christopher focused on setting down several more dishes. "That's a rhyming word, right, Dad? Berry and very."

"Yes, it is. Can you think of other words that rhyme with those?"

"Carry," said Avery promptly. "And cherry."

"Good ones. Now let your brother think of some."

Christopher offloaded the last two bowls, and Mason set the empty tray back on the peninsula. Everyone stayed silent, waiting for Christopher's rhyme.

"Merry?" he asked, slipping back into his seat. "Like when we say Merry Christmas."

Mason nodded.

"That's not all it means." Avery nudged Mason with her

elbow. "It means to have a wedding, right?"

"That's another meaning." He felt a flush burning up his cheeks and encasing his ears. He'd been the one to suggest the game. Should've known better.

"I think we should have a wedding, Dad."

Zach laughed.

Thanks, friend. "Maybe someday, princess. Now eat up your dessert." Definitely not looking at Liz after that one.

Avery slumped into her seat. "Can we do more rhymes?"

"Maddie paddy," announced Maddie.

"Ash flash," returned Avery.

"Have some berry platz," interrupted Jo. "You can practice rhyming later."

Avery sighed and had a bite of dessert. "This is berry good," she said, looking around as though to gauge reactions.

Mason nudged her. "That's enough for now." He glanced over at Liz.

She quickly averted her gaze, poking her fork into the dessert.

"Avery made me wonder something," Zach said half an hour later as Mason carried plates into the kitchen.

"Hmm?" Mason raised his eyebrows at his friend.

"If you've dated since moving back to Galena Landing, I haven't heard the rumor."

Thankfully Liz had excused herself for the evening, and Jo and Claire were making up beds for the twins on the spare room floor, leaving the guys on cleanup. "No rumors have been missed."

"Any particular reason?"

"It hasn't been for lack of my mom trying to set me up with someone."

Zach chuckled. "Mothers think they need to help with everything. Are you hoping to reconnect with the twins' mom?"

"Erin?" Mason reared back, shaking his head. "No. That'll never happen. Though I did hear from her on Christmas Day."

"Oh?"

"I invited her for the kids' birthday in February. I can't believe I did that. It will be a disaster for sure."

Zach scrubbed a baking pan. "Might not be so bad."

"Might not. If you're willing to pray about it, I'd be grateful."

"Jo and I pray for you every day."

Unexpected emotion prickled Mason's eyes. "Really? Thank you. God knows we can sure use them."

"Well, I admire you. I doubt I could do as well as you if I had to raise Maddie and John alone."

Mason swallowed hard as he slotted plates into the dishwasher. "Don't admire me. I'm not worthy of that."

"It's not about being worthy, Waterman. I know you've had a rough go, and you brought a lot of it on yourself, but since Jesus saved you, you've turned your back on your old life and focused forward. That's the part I admire."

Clearly Zach had no idea what Mason had done to his sister. It was nothing short of a miracle the gossip hadn't blown out of the high school and flooded the entire town back then. And now wasn't the time to own up. Not when Liz was back on the farm, with her own reasons for silence.

"Who's your mom trying to set you up with?"

Mason exhaled. "This week? The daughter of some friend of hers. I told her we couldn't come for dinner tonight like she wanted us to. Never thought I'd be so grateful for closed roads and no power."

"I'm guessing she just wants you to be happy."

"And to babysit the kids less."

Zach glanced over. "You think?"

"I don't know what to think. They're not the same kind of hands-on grandparents your parents are, that's for sure."

"I'm sorry. Sometimes I forget how good I have it."

Mason arranged glasses in the dishwasher's top rack. From the other part of the house, he could hear the kids' voices and Ash's cry mixed with lower-pitched adult voices. Would living on the edge of this community be as close as he got to a real family of his own? No, he and the twins were a real family, even without a woman. A mom. A wife.

He shoved the dishwasher door closed and turned the machine on. Crossing his arms, he leaned against it as the water began to gurgle. "May I ask you something?"

Zach rinsed the last pot and set it upside down in the drain rack. "Yeah?"

"How did you know God's will for your life?"

"What do you mean?" Zach quirked an eyebrow.

Good question. "I still feel so new to this whole faith thing. I wasted so much time, but I'm really trying to do the right thing now."

Zach nodded, giving Mason his full attention.

"So I don't know if I'm doing what God wants me to. I didn't really ask Him if I should come back to Galena Landing. I was struggling. Desperate for help, if you will. And when my mom suggested I try for that farm extension agent job when Harry Rigger retired, it seemed I had nothing to lose."

"And then the county closed the office." Zach harrumphed in sympathy. "You'd been there what, six months?"

"Not even. And now the tire shop. I can do the work all right, and I know people need good tires." Mason forced a laugh. "Especially when the highways are a mess, like this week. But it feels pointless."

Zach chuckled. "Old King Solomon said everything was empty and meaningless."

At Mason's raised eyebrows, Zach continued. "Read Ecclesiastes sometime if you want a jaded king's perspective. He was one of the wealthiest men who ever lived, but it didn't satisfy him."

Mason shook his head. "I'm not talking about money. I don't have a lot of it, true, but it's... everything else. Sorry, I'm not good at talking about this stuff."

"No, you're doing fine. A man needs someone to talk to sometimes. I've always had Gabe, and these other guys have become like brothers to me in the past few years. Noel. Brent. Keanan." Zach regarded Mason steadily. "Always room for one more."

He wouldn't say that if he knew Mason's history. It would almost be a relief to have that out in the open. Then he'd know if Zach's offer of friendship — brotherhood — was real. It wouldn't be, though. If Liz couldn't forgive him, why would her protective brother? He could barely forgive himself.

And yet God had. God was all-knowing, yet had promised to forget Mason's sin. That didn't even make sense, but he'd take it.

"Want to talk about it?"

So tempting, but he couldn't go there and risk losing Zach's friendship. Or everyone at Green Acres, really. He owed it to the twins to keep a good relationship here. Everyone helped keep a semblance of normal for the kids. Christopher needed Finnley's friendship. Avery practically worshiped all the women. She'd colored what could only be Liz on the side of that drawing the other day.

"No. Not tonight, anyway." He grabbed the dishcloth and brushed past Zach to wipe the dining room table.

Liz's new teal sweater — the one that looked amazing on her — disappeared down the corridor beyond the fireplace.

He froze in place, hand poised over the table, staring at the now-empty hallway. She'd left the house half an hour ago, hadn't she? When had she returned, and what had she overheard?

Whew for not spilling his guts to her brother.

Chapter 13 --

Tere. Now you have a place to sleep." Jo hugged Avery to her side while Maddie bounced on the bed. "Madelynn Grace, stop that."

The little girl jumped to the floor nearly on top of her brother, knocking him to his diapered bottom. He began to wail.

Liz scooped up her nephew. Here was her escape. "Want a hand taking the kids up to your place? Sounds like it must be bedtime."

Jo peered past her toward the hallway. "The guys still cleaning up? You're welcome, of course, but Zach promised Maddie some extra time tonight."

"He and Mason were still busy in the kitchen a minute ago." And Liz needed to process what she'd heard. The vulnerability in Mason's voice had driven straight to her soul. And Zach had almost sounded wise. Her brother as a grownup never ceased to amaze her.

It wasn't high school any more. She was the only one stuck there.

She jiggled John and he tucked his head against her shoulder, thumb in his mouth. Her heart turned to off-the-chart mush.

"We're done now."

Liz whirled at the sound of her brother's voice.

Maddie flung herself at Zach's knees, and John stretched his arms. Zach bent to scoop his daughter then settled John on his other arm. "Ready to go?" he asked Jo.

Behind Zach, Mason leaned against the doorframe, his blue eyes locked on Liz.

Breath fled her lungs, and she couldn't tear her gaze away. Did he know she'd overheard?

The Mason she'd loved to hate for a full decade was gone. He was as hot as he'd ever been, but the selfish boy had turned into an adult. A strong man. A good father... yeah, she hated to admit that even to herself. Mason was everything she'd ever wanted in a man. He'd been the high school bad boy. The dangerous guy that made her crazy for him. And then angry at him, but in the light of the changed man in front of her, the anger and bitterness she'd clung to like a comforting blanket had floated away.

That didn't mean she could fall under his charm again. Her chin tipped up a little, and she realized she was still staring at him like they were locked in some kind of private world. The blue in his eyes warmed slightly.

"Liz?"

With a start, she turned to her sister-in-law. "Yes?" Did her voice sound breathless to anyone else?

"Want to come to town with me tomorrow if the roads are clear? I haven't seen your folks since Christmas."

"Um, sure. We could do that."

"See you in the morning, then."

"Good night, Auntie Liz," came Maddie's sweet voice as Zach turned with his double burden.

"Good night, sweetie."

Mason stepped into the room, making way for the family to leave. "Avery, take your jammies down to the bathroom and get changed. Brush your teeth while you're there."

Liz gauged the distance to freedom while Avery reached for her backpack.

"Christopher, get your pajamas on."

"But, Da—"

Mason held up his hand. "Liz and I are leaving the room. You have five minutes."

Christopher slumped.

Liz eyed the gap at the door. Yes, she was leaving. Mason had shifted enough that she could get past without brushing against him. The thought of touching him sent squiggles down her back. *Stop it, Liz. Get out while the getting's good.*

She was halfway through the opening when a touch halted her. She stared at Mason's warm hand on her arm. A working man's hand, with scars and scrapes. Tingles spread from the spot.

"Liz?"

She wouldn't look up. Wouldn't meet his eyes. Too late. Some magnetic force pulled him square into her line of vision. Liz swallowed hard.

"Can we talk? Out in the great room?"

She didn't have to agree. She could gather her pain and bitterness around her like a cloak and stride across the yard in the crisp night. Alone. But they weren't as comforting as they'd once been.

Somehow her head nodded. "I can make tea."

His fingers slid a few inches on her arm, sending shock waves through her body. "Thanks. That sounds good."

"Okay. I'll go make some while you tuck your kids in." It took physical effort to break eye contact.

"I'll be out in five. Ten tops."

Liz escaped down the corridor and into the darkened kitchen. She leaned against the counter, trying to gather her wits. Why had she agreed?

Because two weeks of being around Mason had convinced her

he wasn't the same guy she'd once known all too well. How could he be so different and yet have the same pull he'd ever had?

She lifted the kettle with shaking hands and filled it with water.

oOo

"God bless Daddy and Grandma and Grandpa and Maddie and John and Jo and Zach and Ash and Claire and Noel and Finnley and Allison and Brent—" Avery came up for air "—and take care of my mommy." She tugged at Mason's arm. "Does God remember I want a new mommy or do I have to tell Him again?"

Sitting on the other side of Mason on the edge of the bed, Christopher crossed his arms. "God remembers everything. I don't know why we have to keep saying the same stuff."

Mason tightened his arms around both kids. "Do you like it when I tell you I love you, even though I said it before? I told you once when you were a baby, so I shouldn't have to keep saying it."

Christopher squinted up at him. "That's different."

"Not really. God is happy when we love Him so much we want to keep telling Him. It's good manners to say please and thank you to people. God likes to hear those things as much as we do."

"But we keep asking God for a new mom, and He hasn't sent one."

Mason felt the same way. A bit impatient. Would Liz have the tea made by now? Would she tire of waiting for him or think he'd changed his mind? "Is it my turn to pray now?"

Both kids nodded, and Mason prayed a blessing over them. He tucked them into the sleeping bags on the floor, kissed their cheeks, and switched off the light. "Sleep tight."

Two sleepy voices murmured, "Good night, Daddy," as he

slipped out the door.

For a moment he leaned his forehead against the hallway wall and breathed his own grownup prayer before entering the great room. Liz sat in one of the armchairs, her feet tucked up under her and two cups of tea on the end table beside her, an invitation to take the chair on the other side. He drank in the sight of her in the soft light, her blond hair swishing against her shoulders, the teal sweater hugging her curves. She met his gaze.

She was beautiful.

He had no right to think there could ever be more than an uneasy truce. No, that was Satan whispering. In Jesus, he was new. He wasn't worthy. Who ever was? But he was a child of the one true King, and that counted for a lot. For everything worthwhile.

"Hi, Liz."

"I made tea. I hope chamomile is okay. I wasn't sure if you liked it with honey and cream, but I did put a bit of both in. I can make another cup if you'd rather." She looked away and picked up her cup.

"It will be perfect." Mason lowered himself into the easy chair angled near hers and had a sip of the tea. How did he start this conversation?

"Your daughter is very sweet."

Okay, that worked. "Yes, she is. I know she gets kind of clingy, too."

"I guess that's understandable."

"She feels a hole in her life and tries to fill it. Christopher acts out instead." He took a deep breath. "More like I did."

Brows raised, Liz eyed him over the top of her mug.

"All of us have a hole in our lives, Liz. I tried to fill it with stuff that made me feel important. Being popular. Being dangerous." A sharp laugh erupted. "Good thing we didn't have gangs here. I'd have been a candidate."

"I had a hole, too."

Her voice was so quiet he could barely hear her.

"I don't know why. My sisters — even Zach — were such good little church kids. I'm sure they weren't perfect, but I couldn't tell you any tales of wild rebellion. I don't know why it wasn't enough for me. I was raised the same."

"Zach had his moments, I hear. When he was in veterinary college."

Liz shrugged. "I wasn't around to see it. And he is a model husband and father now."

"He's one of the good ones. All the guys here challenge me constantly, just by the godly lives they lead."

"You're trying to tell me it's all God." Her voice took on a singsong quality. "There's a God-shaped hole inside every one of us." She shook her head. "If I heard it once, I heard it a thousand times. I don't really buy into it."

Mason tightened his grip on his cup. "Yet you agree everyone has that empty spot."

She pursed her lips for a moment and stared at some spot beyond his head. "I'm not sure. Maybe. It's not as obvious with some people as others."

"Some do seem to have it all together, but if you get talking to them, there always seems to be a longing for more."

Liz shifted on the chair. "Well, we're human. Never satisfied with what we've got. That drive creates progress in the human race."

Mason grinned. "I think that lack of satisfaction might be the hole inside us."

"Maybe."

"What have you tried to fill that hole with, Liz?" he asked quietly.

She narrowed her gaze at him. "It isn't any of your business."

"More to the point, did it work?"

No reply. If she bit her lip any harder, there'd be blood.

"Me, I tried to fill it with popularity. With sex. With recreational drugs and partying. No matter what I poured in, I was still empty. I think what they told you is true. I wish I'd seen earlier that it was God I needed." He shook his head. "But I wasn't ready, I guess. I had to bang my head against a jagged rock until it bled before I got to the end of my own ideas and realized there was more."

She said nothing, but she didn't jerk out of the chair and leave the room, so he pushed on. "I suspect you've tried many of the same things I did. Maybe to a different degree. I need you to know, Liz, that God really wants to be part of your life. You'll never be satisfied until He is… because He won't stop nudging you and reminding you."

"I never thought I'd hear you preach a sermon at me. Like, for real."

There was no venom in her voice.

"I know. Sometimes it still surprises me, too. As you can see, accepting Jesus didn't solve all my problems. It's still hard being a single parent. Still hard making ends meet. But you know? The emptiness inside is gone, and that makes dealing with the rest possible."

"I had it all when I was a kid, Mason. I'd been brainwashed with the whole Jesus thing. So, if God is the answer, how do you explain that there was still emptiness?"

Give me words, Lord. "Brainwashed isn't the same as having a relationship. It takes spending time together and two-way communication. My guess is that you thought it was automatic because it looked so easy for others."

Liz nodded slowly. "Makes sense. I remember Heather and Cindy discussing what they'd read in their devotions. I didn't get it even then. I'd read the assigned verses, spit out a prayer, and move on to other things."

Mason leaned back in his chair. This amount of vulnerability he hadn't expected when he'd asked her to stay, but it was obvious God was exposing her sore spots in a healing effort. "I didn't even have that. My parents went to church, but we didn't really talk about God at home. I saw my mom read her Bible once in a while. We said grace at meals. That was about it."

He didn't feel the need to fill the quiet moment that followed. It was almost companionable. Did he dare let himself dream of a home, a marriage with Liz? More evenings like this, just sharing their hearts after the children crawled in bed?

"You said something about us never being satisfied, and that keeps humanity progressing." No. He hadn't meant to go back there.

Her eyebrows rose. "Right. Doesn't matter whether people are Christians or Buddhists or atheists."

"Oh, it matters a great deal, in the end. But I hear what you're saying. Humans were made to reach." He was here now. "While God definitely turned my entire life around and gave me reason to wake up every morning and be the best dad I could be any given day, you're right that we have other needs." One or two had come to his attention more in the past few weeks since Liz had returned.

"Maslow's hierarchy."

He blinked. "The what?"

"Let me see what I remember about it." She pursed her lips. "It's like there's some kind of pyramid of human need. Different levels, but if one level isn't met, like food and water, for instance, the other levels fade into lack of importance. I mean, if we can't breathe, the need for dinner has little meaning."

"I see what you mean, I think. So when our need for God is met, we can feel the other needs and deal with them."

"That's not what I said. People everywhere need to breathe. That's more fundamental than God."

"Except that God created the atmosphere, so without Him, we

wouldn't breathe."

Liz rolled her eyes. "They've brainwashed you, too."

"Do you have a better explanation?"

"No, actually, I don't. For all I've gone my own way, I still believe in God. Nothing else makes sense to me. It's the personal part I have trouble with." She raised a hand. "And don't bother quoting John three sixteen at me. I remember them all."

He met her eyes for a long moment. "And yet there's a hole."

Chapter 14 --

*L*iz looked around the kitchen the next morning. "Where is everyone?"

Claire, wearing Ash in a carrier on her back, glanced up from helping Avery chop a carrot. "If by everyone you mean the guys, Noel and Zach are next door trying to get the water pipes thawed. Mason is at work."

"The power came back on?" And of course, the emptiness was only Mason's absence. And Noel's. It wasn't like twenty people had gone missing.

"Mason got a text a couple of hours ago. The power company restored town last evening and worked through the night in this part of the grid."

Liz should be thrilled that he and the kids would soon be off Green Acres, even if next door wasn't that far away. After the heart-to-heart she and Mason had last night, much of the venom was gone.

"I slept on the floor, Miss Liz." Avery beamed at her. "It was almost as comfy as my bed. Did you sleep good?"

Liz shook her head. "No, I had a hard time sleeping. Some nights are just like that, you know?"

Avery nodded in sympathy, but Claire's eyebrows rose. "How late did you stay up talking?"

So it wasn't coincidence that neither Claire nor Noel had come back out of their room last evening. They'd known what was happening. Had Mason told them everything? But only curiosity gleamed in Claire's eyes, not pity.

"It was after one." Nearly two, if she were being completely honest. Every word they'd spoken had replayed in her mind during her sleepless hours. Even though there had been more tense moments, especially when he talked easily of his new faith, over all she'd been surprised how pleasant it had been to talk to him. How comfortable it had seemed.

She'd never dreamed she'd think of Mason and comfort in the same sentence.

"Sounds like you had a lot to catch up on. Mason mentioned you'd known each other in high school."

In the biblical sense of the word. But if he hadn't given details to his friends, she could only sigh with relief. "Yes, we were in the same grad year. He's kept up with some of our classmates that I didn't." Only Kara had remained her true friend.

Liz set two slices of bread in the toaster and pushed the button down. Hey, she'd baked it. She deserved the treat. "So what is the plan for today?"

"Aren't you going into town with Jo?"

Oh. Right. She'd forgotten. That meant she wouldn't be seeing Mason this morning. Who would have guessed there might be a twinge of disappointment at that thought? "Yes. Not sure what time."

Claire glanced at the clock. "She'll probably be down here in the next half hour. She's never been much of a morning person."

Liz poured a cup of coffee before reaching for the toast. She slathered butter on both pieces then drizzled honey over top. Plate and cup in hand, she rounded the peninsula and perched on one of the counter stools. "And you? Are we leaving you in the lurch?" She grinned. "Or maybe giving you some much-needed quiet time."

Claire rubbed a hand over Avery's shoulder. "My right-hand girl and I will keep busy. The gang is all due back by suppertime."

"I shouldn't have said I'd go to town. You need help."

"We're good. I've cooked for more people with less help." Claire's eyebrows rose as her brown eyes stared unflinchingly at Liz. "Besides, I know your mom is really looking forward to spending more time with you."

Busted. "I guess." Liz glanced at Avery. How much would the child pick up? "Mom and I have never been really close. She always favored Cindy and Heather. And Zach was the only boy. He could do no wrong."

"She's talked about you more than your sisters combined since I met her."

Huh. That was a surprise. "The prodigal child."

"Not just that, I'm pretty sure. She ached with missing you."

Liz took a sip of coffee. Avery seemed to overlook nothing, her gaze ping-ponging with the conversation. "Are you close with your mom?"

Claire grimaced. "Touché. She hasn't been here since Noel's and my wedding, but we did go to Denver with Ash last summer for a few days. It was... awkward. I'm glad Ash has one set of grandparents who love him and dote on him."

"Where do Noel's parents live?"

"Missoula. They remarried last year. His dad had been a wandering alcoholic for over twenty years. Then God got hold of his life and he's been sober four years now."

Huh. Other people had skeletons in their closets, too. "I can't believe she trusted him enough to marry him again."

Claire shook her head, smiling. "It was all God, for sure."

God again. Liz pushed her plate away, the toast half eaten. What was with everyone here? To be fair, she hadn't been able to get away from God in Thailand, either. There'd been those missionaries and the small church down the street, where everyone went around with glowing faces.

God couldn't be trusted. She'd tried to be a good Christian girl growing up, even when other kids teased her. And that made her a target for Mason to gloat when she proved to be no different from the others.

She was halfway to forgiving Mason. Could she forgive him without forgiving God? Maybe. Mason had been a kid, too focused on maintaining his popularity to worry about the long-term results of what he'd done to her. He'd changed. She could see that. He was stable now and had made a home for himself and his children.

God, on the other hand, was all-powerful if her parents were to be believed. That meant He could have met her halfway or even more. He could've heard her cries and rescued her. He could even have kept her from being infatuated with Mason in the first place.

But He hadn't. He'd ignored her pleas. Turned His back and left her to suffer. Why would He treat her any differently now?

The biblical story of the prodigal son flashed in her mind. The guy's father had seen him returning and ran to meet him. Hugged him. Thrown a big party for the neighborhood.

It would be nice if it were a true story. Instead, God would watch her return from a high-up window, and He'd smile in smug satisfaction. "Nice, she's back. She can hang out with all the other workers in my kingdom. Now, what was I doing?" And He'd turn back to His desk or His crystal ball or whatever.

Yeah, that personal hug and party would never happen. She wouldn't give God a chance to snub her again.

oOo

Cacophony greeted Mason as he entered the straw bale house after a long day at the tire shop. Claire had texted him to invite him for supper again tonight what with all the travelers home. Besides, she'd said, Avery had been such a big help with the meal it was only fair the little girl got to share in the eating of it.

If this kept up, Mason was going to have to add himself to the cooking rotation. Not that he deserved to be part of them. He was only a renter, a neighbor, a friend. One who depended on the community next door to help with his kids when needed.

Avery catapulted against his legs and he scooped her up. "Oomph. You're getting heavy."

She giggled against his neck. "I'm growing."

"Yes, you are." He squeezed her and nuzzled her cheeks with his stubble.

"Ooh, that tickles. Do you smell the yummy supper, Daddy?"

"I do. Claire said you helped. What did you make?"

"It's ribs. They've been cooking in the oven for a really long time. And Claire let me measure the rice and water. Did you know you put salt in rice when it cooks, Daddy?"

He wracked his brain. "No, I didn't know that."

She nodded, peering straight into his eyes. "Well, you do."

"Good to know." Mason hugged her tight then set her down. "Let me get my coat and boots off, princess."

Avery scampered off to a corner of the great room where she and Maddie had set up an entire orphanage of dolls, by the looks of it.

"Hey, Waterman." Zach came out of the kitchen carrying a large bowl of coleslaw. "We're going to have to replace some of the waterlines at the farmhouse, or at least some of the fittings. Noel got it thawed out but there's a leak somewhere."

Brent came in from the great room. "Did you call Ed's Plumbing?"

Zach nodded. "We're on a wait list. A lot of people had trouble with their pipes with those nasty temperatures."

Allison sidled up beside Brent. "What did people do in the old days? Surely it's been this cold in Idaho before."

Zach chuckled. "Yep, this isn't all that unusual, really. We get a week or two of this type of temperatures several times a winter.

If the power stays on, all is well. I mean, we had wrapped the pipes in a heat tape in the basement where they're most vulnerable. But with the power out—" he snapped his fingers "—they froze solid."

"I'll have a look tomorrow." Brent looked thoughtful. "I might be able to find a plumber more quickly than Ed can come."

Mason shook his head. These guys took such good care of him. Of the kids. "Too bad it isn't really Ed Graysen who still owns that shop. He would've worked around the clock to get everyone going again, and not even charged overtime."

Zach grinned. "He's one of the good ones, all right. But he's gotten so decrepit in the past few years that I hesitate to even hint to him that we've got a problem. I wouldn't want to be responsible for him wielding a propane torch down there. It's all copper."

"Yeah, I get that." Mason bit his lip.

"Not a big problem, though. They'll get to it soon." Zach punched Mason lightly in the shoulder. "At least you have got a warm place to sleep over here in the meanwhile."

"About that. I don't mean to impose..."

Zach shook his head. "You're not imposing. Not in the least. We're your landlords, remember? It's our job to take care of you."

And his meals and babysitting and everything? Mason caught a glimpse of Liz on the other side of the peninsula. More time here meant more time with Liz, though long talks like last night might not be as easy to restage with the Portlanders and everyone home. "If you're sure."

"Hey, it's not my house you're invading. It's Noel and Claire's, but I know for a fact they don't mind. For one thing, Avery has been packing Ash around and keeping him happy." Zach twitched his head toward the great room. "Not that he and John play their role as orphans the way Avery and Maddie want them to."

Mason laughed. "I bet."

"Chow's up!" called Claire as Noel carried a deep roasting pan to the table. "Come on, everyone. Let's not let this get cold."

Gabe, Sierra, Keanan, and Chelsea herded the children to the table and into their seats. Mason took his place between Avery and Christopher, and Brent prayed the blessing over their meal.

"Nice to have Finnley back?" Mason asked his son as he passed the bowl of rice.

Christopher's face brightened. "Aunt Allison let us build a fort in Finnley's loft. She said it was too cold to play outside."

Mason ruffled his son's hair. "She's right, but it's supposed to start warming up tomorrow."

"Do we have to move back to our house? I'd rather keep living here."

Avery pressed against his other arm. "Me, too."

"Then you're in luck that it will be another day or more before someone can fix the water pipes."

"Yay!" Both kids cheered.

Mason shook his head, grinning, and caught Liz's gaze from across the table. Hopefully, that meant another evening or more of visiting with Liz. Because now that he'd seen her again and gotten to know the mature, adult Liz, he couldn't get enough.

Was there any chance she'd not only welcome Jesus back into her life, but him?

He allowed a smile just for her to lift his cheeks as he looked into her eyes. She bit her lip pensively and glanced between him and the children. When she met his eyes again, she gave him a small smile back.

He'd take it.

Chapter 15 --

B riiing.

Liz glanced at her cell. Her heart stilled as she recognized the number she'd been waiting to see. She lifted the phone with shaking hands and swiped it on to receive the call.

"Hello?"

"This is Glenda from Recruiters International. Am I speaking with Elizabeth Nemesek?"

"Good morning, Glenda. Yes, this is Elizabeth."

After four evenings in a row staying up late with Mason — plus everyone hanging out on New Year's Eve, so that made five — she wasn't sure what she wanted anymore. They'd caught up on what mutual friends were doing, eaten popcorn, watched a few movies, and played endless checkers.

"I have good news for you. I have three companies interested in interviewing you for upcoming openings."

Her heart skipped a beat. "For teaching ESL?"

"They're companies that work with immigrants and offer some language classes. As they are all based in Las Vegas, I'd like to request that you come and do these interviews in person rather than via Skype. Would it be possible for you to be at our offices at nine a.m. Monday? I'd like to meet you and go over protocol in advance. I'll set up one interview for Monday afternoon and the other two for Tuesday, if that meets with your approval."

It was Friday. Surely she could get a flight tomorrow or Sunday? Sunday would be better to prevent hotel costs from dipping unnecessarily into her savings. "I'm sure that won't be a problem."

"Excellent. If you have any questions, feel free to call. I check for messages periodically over the weekend."

"Thank you. Sounds good."

Liz stared at the phone for a long time after ending the call. This was what she wanted, right? An opportunity to get into a big company where she could teach.

Oh, she was so confused. Were she and Mason building anything? He'd kept it very casual except for the intensity in his eyes and the occasional electricity when they touched accidentally. No kisses. No caresses. No words of enduring passion.

He'd be smart enough not to push her, right? The least bit over the line, and she'd know he was the same guy he'd been a decade before. But she didn't believe that. She'd seen the changes. They had to be real. He wasn't that talented an actor to fool everyone, especially her. Plus his kids worshiped the ground he walked on. The old Mason wouldn't have had that adoration. Wouldn't have deserved it.

What was holding him back from saying what was obviously in his eyes? Sure, she'd only been back for three weeks, but since she'd offered her forgiveness, he hadn't said one word to move their relationship forward. So maybe all he wanted was friendship.

She wanted more.

Liz rocked back in her chair.

Yes, she wanted more. The realization seeped through her and into her soul. All her life she'd been the one on the outside, peering in through a window. She'd never felt like the wanted child in her family. With the four years between Zach and her, it didn't take a genius to figure out she hadn't been planned. After all, her parents already had two perfect little girls. Maybe if she'd been another boy...?

She shook her head. It wasn't just her family. She'd felt just as outside at church. At school. She'd always been on the fringes, never the center. For a brief week or two she'd thought she'd achieved that when Mason — the most popular guy in Galena High — invited her to the party.

And look how that had turned out.

In Thailand, she really had been the outsider. Sanun had been the last to enjoy a fling with the foreigner before settling down with a Thai woman. Liz would never have been accepted long term. Why had it taken her so long to realize she'd never fully be at home there?

She paced the small duplex. Maybe she was destined to be alone. To never have that kind of love. She wouldn't be the first woman to stay single yet carve out a full life.

But how to make it full without a husband and family?

Snow glistened outside the window, and moisture dripped from the roof. The nasty cold snap had broken. With power and water restored, Mason and the kids had moved back to the farmhouse yesterday. She'd missed their visit last night, but he had a life to get back to.

And she had a life to move forward to. The phone call with Glenda was just the first step.

oOo

A text buzzed on Mason's phone, distracting him from sorting the pile of laundry the kids had accumulated in the past week.

Claire. *Did you know Liz was leaving tomorrow for interviews in Vegas?*

His gut twisted. So soon? But it was January, and the business world was once again on track. Her dream lay elsewhere, and she'd be following it away from northern Idaho.

Leaving him behind.

The phone buzzed again. *Want to come for supper?*

He shook his head but couldn't stop the grin. He'd figured Claire and Noel knew he and Liz had been in the great room so many evenings this past week. It was kind of shocking, really, that the Kenzies had never stayed up late or needed a drink of water after they retired. And now Claire was blatantly matchmaking.

But should he go? Everyone would be there, so the odds of snagging a few minutes alone with her were slim. He couldn't stay past the twins' bedtime like when they'd been tucked in just down the hall.

And besides, hadn't he worn out his welcome yet?

Finnley adds his invitation.

Mason grinned at that. Christopher and Avery were moping today, too, after so many days of having Finnley and Maddie there to play with anytime they wanted.

It wasn't all about him. He had the kids to think about, too.

He texted back. *Only if you put me on cleanup. Trust me, you don't want me cooking.*

But it's Liz's night on cleanup.

He shook his head and chuckled. *If you think you're being subtle, it's not working.*

Who, me?

Fine, I accept. It will make the twins happy.

How about you?

Mason stared at the phone and bit his lip. *I guess that's up to Liz. And God.*

Had he just admitted to Claire that he had a thing for Liz? And by text, no less. Not that she would spread it around or make him uncomfortable.

I get it. Supper at 5:30. Jo and Zach are cooking.

Thanks. See you then.

"Daddy?" Avery came down the basement stairs just far

enough to see him.

"Yes?" Still kneeling in front of the washer, he pocketed his phone.

"Why doesn't my mommy love me?"

Ouch. Wasn't that heavy for a Saturday morning? He could demur and say of course Erin loved Avery, but the little girl wouldn't be fooled. She'd seen so little evidence of it in her short life.

"I'm sorry, princess." He held out his arms. "Your mommy doesn't really love anybody."

"Maddie's mom loves her. She hugs her and reads her stories and makes cookies with her." Avery walked into his embrace.

Mason held his daughter close. "I know."

"Everybody has a mommy 'cept me and Christopher. I've asked Jesus and asked Him. Why doesn't He listen?"

"That's a good question." One Mason had asked many times himself.

"Is it because He's too busy?"

"No, that's not how it works. God is never too busy, even though He's listening to the prayers of many people. He's not like us. We can only think about one thing at a time." Like he'd been thinking of Liz nearly constantly lately. "God isn't a person. He's... He's like a superhero, only even better because He's God."

"God is a superhero?" Avery narrowed her eyes at him as she tilted her head.

"No, not really. But He's not the same as regular people. He's extra special and can do things we can't."

"So He could give me a mommy. If not my regular mom then a new one."

"Well, yes. He could. But He also knows things we don't know. He knows when is the best time to fix something."

Tears pooled in Avery's eyes. "But I need a mom now. When I'm an old lady I won't need one anymore. Or even a teenager."

Mason squeezed his daughter. "I think we always need moms. High-schoolers need them as much as little kids do." He thought for a minute. "I even need mine. She helps take care of you guys when I have to work."

"If we had a mommy, Grandma wouldn't need to."

There was that, of course. "I'm glad you have grandparents who can pitch in. And I know you like going to their house."

Avery nodded. "Grandma always sharpens the coloring pencils so I can draw."

"She likes displaying your pictures." The one on their own fridge bothered Mason every time he looked at it, though. A dad and two kids, with a woman way off on the other edge. A woman with straight blond hair, not curly like Erin's.

"I'll make you a new one next time."

"Sounds good." What would she come up with? "Meanwhile, we need to keep praying for your mom so God will know we haven't forgotten."

"And so He won't forget either?" Avery pushed away enough to look in his eyes.

"God won't forget, but He wants us to tell Him what's important to us."

"Okay." Avery let out a dramatic sigh. "I wish He would hurry up and answer."

Mason squeezed her shoulders. "Me, too, princess." Who would God send to be the twins' mom? Would Erin accept Jesus into her life and return? Would Liz be the one... or someone else? Maybe this was a prayer God would answer with "no" for some reason. He needed to be ready to accept that answer. *God? It doesn't seem fair to punish Avery and Christopher for my sins. The sins of mine You've already forgiven.*

Who was he to tell God how to run the universe? No one. He kissed the top of Avery's head and smoothed her hair. "I need to get a couple of loads of laundry done before we go next door.

Aunt Claire invited us for supper tonight."

Her face brightened. "Yay! I get to play with Maddie!"

And Mason got to say goodbye to Liz.

o0o

"But I thought Keanan and I were on cleanup." Chelsea stood in the kitchen archway holding a stack of plates.

Uhhh. Liz looked from Chelsea to Claire.

"Change of plans," Claire said crisply. "I had to rearrange the schedule a bit. Liz volunteered as she'll be away for a few days."

"Okay. But I don't mind helping." Chelsea smiled at Liz, looking a bit shy. "I haven't gotten to know Liz at all yet."

Claire took the stack of plates from Chelsea and set them on the counter. "Everything's taken care of. Enjoy your evening off. I'm sure you'll have plenty of time to get to know Liz after she returns." She steered the other woman out of the space.

Liz stared after them. She wouldn't have minded the help, truth be told. Of all the women who called Green Acres Farm home, Chelsea was probably closest to her own age.

Mason appeared with several serving bowls balanced on his hands and arms. "Hey, Liz."

"Hi?" Her voice sounded like a squeak.

"Want me to wash pots or load the dishwasher?"

"Um, you're on cleanup?" She glanced at the larder door where the schedule was posted on the dry erase board, but she couldn't read it from across the room.

"Sure am. I try not to freeload too often. I'm not a very good cook, so the least I can do is help with the other chores." He grinned, his blue eyes crinkling. "Like dishes."

"I'll wash pots." She'd already rinsed them to start the soaking. The pan from the scalloped potatoes was going to need the longest.

"Okay, I'll load the dishwasher." He opened the appliance and began angling plates in.

Here was her chance to tell him she was leaving. That would give him the chance to try to stop her. What did she want? After so many long discussions, how could she be so tongue-tied now? She washed out the pot that had held green beans and glanced at him.

Mason leaned over the dishwasher as he worked, his backside turned her way. A distracting sight that turned her mouth dry. "I'm headed to Vegas tomorrow." She got the words out.

He turned and straightened. His eyes searched hers. "You have a job interview?"

Liz nodded. "Three of them."

"Wow. I'm sure they'll be bidding for your services."

Her heart warmed at the thought. "I doubt that."

"Text me and let me know how the interviews go? I'll be praying for you."

"What exactly will you be praying for?" Liz held her breath, unable to break the deadlock with Mason's eyes.

He took a step closer, and his hand swept the side of her face. Just one gentle touch before his hand dropped back to his side. "I pray that God will give you more than you ask for."

Not what she'd expected to hear, but maybe Mason didn't know what, exactly, she would ask for if she thought God was listening. She pushed her chin into the air. "Like what?"

"I pray for you every day, Liz. Many times a day. I pray that God will give you a desire to renew your relationship with Him. I pray that He'll give you healing and wisdom." His gaze dropped to her mouth then back to her eyes with a rueful grin.

"Anything else?"

"Nothing else I ask for is possible until He answers those requests."

What did he me—? Heat flooded her face. It wasn't her

imagination. He did find her as attractive as she found him, but he wasn't planning on acting on it. Not unless she became a Christian again. Or was she still one, even if she never prayed and was rather angry with God? It was so confusing.

Who could answer those questions? Maybe Mason, but that was adding pressure she wasn't sure he could handle. Her parents. Her brother. Anyone here at Green Acres, most likely. It was just deciding whom she could trust.

And she was leaving in the morning.

"One other thing." Mason was so near his whispered words tickled her cheek.

She didn't dare turn her head. "Oh?"

"I ask God to bring you back to Galena Landing."

Liz swallowed hard. "I'll be back." At least long enough to pack up her things. Was she absolutely certain she wanted a position elsewhere? But what were her options, really? Mason needed time. She needed time. And she needed to know if God was really worthy of her trust.

Mason's lips brushed her temple. "You're always on my mind, Liz." Then he turned back to the dishwasher as though he hadn't just rocked her universe.

Chapter 16 --

Snowflakes drifted across the beams of the car's headlights as Liz drove north to the farm. The roads weren't too bad yet, but another storm was in the forecast, the deciding factor in catching a flight back Tuesday evening instead of waiting until Wednesday. That, and she didn't need another night with the expense of a hotel.

At least that's what she told herself. In reality, it was Mason that brought her back as quickly as she could. His texts hadn't been frequent, and they hadn't been passionate. He'd simply touched base with her several times a day with a quick exchange.

Liz navigated the sharp turn on Thompson Road by Elmer's farm, and the car slid a little. She clenched her teeth. Not much farther. A light was on in the living room of her childhood home, even though it was past midnight.

Mason? Was he up? She'd let him know she was on the way.

A shadow crossed the window.

Without conscious decision, she veered left, the plum trees that lined the familiar driveway bare of fruit or leaves but clothed with a layer of fresh snow.

Though your sins be as scarlet, they shall be as white as snow.

That verse again. She might have to look up the context.

This was silly. Why had she pulled into Mason's yard at this time of night? She should've driven next door and texted him that she was safely back. Tomorrow would be soon enough to see him.

But it wasn't soon enough. He'd be at work all day.

Besides, the outside light had come on. He'd seen her.

Mason clomped across the yard without a jacket, his Henley-style shirt untucked and his feet shoved into untied boots. He pulled her car door open before she'd turned off the ignition. "Liz."

How could her name seem like such a caress when he spoke it?

"I made it."

"I'm glad. Come in for a minute and tell me all about it?"

"Don't you have to work tomorrow?"

He scrubbed a hand through his hair. "Yeah, but it won't be the first time I've survived on less than optimal sleep. A cup of tea?"

Liz undid the seatbelt clasp. "Now you're talking." She caught his hand as they walked toward the house, and he looked at her, surprised, before tightening his grip on hers.

So she was being a little forward. Whatever. She knew what she felt, and he seemed to need a little help.

Mason held the door as she stepped into her childhood. The old painted cabinets. The vinyl floor in need of replacement. The Formica table with matching padded chairs in bright yellow. It was clean. Cleaner than she'd expected without a woman in the house, but that was stereotyping.

She'd been the little girl running in the back door clutching a handful of wildflowers. She'd been the one standing on a chair wrapped in an oversize apron helping her mom make supper. She'd been the one tucked up to the table with cookies and milk, chattering to her mom about a day at school or at a friend's house.

Not peering in from outside. Inside. Belonging.

"Liz? You okay?" Mason undid the four big toggles on her coat and slid it from her shoulders. Then his hands cradled her arms.

She blinked. "Long drive, with lots of swirling snow."

He nodded. "Have a seat."

"Let me take my boots off. I don't want to get snow all over the floor."

Mason snagged a chair over to the mat without fully releasing her. "Here."

So considerate. She dropped into it and, before she could reach down, he tugged one tall boot off with an expert twist. Then the other.

He grinned at her. "I'm good at other peoples' boots. Avery is incapable."

"Thanks." Liz smiled back, reaching out to touch the stubble on his face.

Something flickered in his eyes as he straightened out of reach. Without another word, he strode over to the sink and filled the kettle from the faucet.

With his back to her, Liz felt free to let her gaze trail the length of him. His blond hair had been cut while she was away. The muscles in his shoulders and arms rippled even with the simple motion of moving the kettle to the range. His narrow waist and hips flexed, faded jeans not too tight and not too loose. Bare feet poked out beneath the frayed hems.

Mason turned and leaned against the counter with arms crossed against his chest.

Liz's heart sped up. Did he have any idea how crazy attractive he was? If he so much as twitched, she'd be across the room in two seconds flat. All she needed was a welcoming gesture or word. Anything.

That's all it would take for her to decide to stay in Galena Landing.

They stared at each other for a long moment. "What kind of tea would you like? Not much choice, sorry. I have black tea and green. Maybe some chamomile."

So he needed a bit more time. She could allow him a few more days. "Green, of course."

His chest tightened as he breathed in. "You've got it."

A few days would be long enough, right? She'd turn down the job for him, if she were even offered one, of course. He couldn't deny the attraction between them. It went both ways. No way was he this good an actor.

The kettle steamed and he turned to fix two mugs. "Honey? Cream?"

"Both, thanks."

Mason opened the fridge. As the door angled toward her, she saw half a dozen childish drawings. One in particular caught her eye. Three people: a man, a boy, and a girl. And crammed against the far edge, a woman.

Liz surged to her feet and closed the gap as the fridge door closed. She took in all of the artwork, but that one pulled her gaze again. "Avery?"

She caught Mason's nod in her periphery. "She likes to draw. Here's your tea." He walked over to the table, set down both cups, and took a seat on the other side.

But Liz wasn't done. "Is this Erin?" She pointed at the woman half-off the drawing.

Silence.

Liz turned. How hard a question was that? Surely Avery had announced who she'd drawn. "Mason?"

He shook his head. "Nope. Come have your tea before it gets cold."

Okay, so he didn't want to talk about it. But that didn't make any sense. Unless... Liz took a closer look. While a kindergartner's skills were not exactly realistic, she could make some deductions. The woman in the picture had blond hair, straight to the shoulders, a blue top, and gray pants. Hadn't she worn an outfit like that?

"Mason, did Avery draw me?" Her voice cracked as she turned toward the table.

His face was buried in both hands with his elbows planted on the table.

Liz took a step closer. "Did she?" Why wouldn't he look at her? Here was this golden opportunity to move their relationship forward, and he held back. Liz closed the gap and crouched beside his chair, resting her hand on his thigh — his very muscular thigh — as she tried to see his face.

Mason lurched to his feet, nearly knocking her over. He spun the chair between them, gripping the back of it with knuckles white from the pressure. "Liz, don't."

Whoa. Not what she'd expected to hear. She straightened. "Don't what?"

"Don't push. Please."

A chill wormed its way through her body and settled in her heart. "So this is all a game for you."

He took a deep breath and let it out slowly before his eyes met hers again. "No. Not a game."

She steeled herself. "It has to be. You wanted to see if I'd repeat the mistakes of my past and throw myself at you. It's high school all over again. Well, I hope you're satisfied, Mason Waterman." She reached for her cup of tea. Everything in her screamed to throw it in his face. No. She was more mature than that. She had to prove she wasn't a hormone-ridden teenager with a sharp temper.

"Liz." His voice was quiet. Controlled. "Please sit down. Let me explain."

"I don't think there's anything to explain. Once again, you've led me on and dumped me. I guess I can be thankful we didn't have sex. Again."

Pain flashed across his face.

Good. He deserved it after all the anguish he put her through.

"That's not how it is. At all." He turned the chair back to the table and sat on it. He pointed at the one she'd vacated. "Sit. Please."

The overload of the past three days slammed Liz like an avalanche. Three days of travel, interviews, another world. Which world did she belong to anymore? She had no clue. Not Mason's, obviously. Would it hurt to listen to him? Not if she guarded herself. She could get some ammunition for later, maybe. She might need it.

"Fine." She dropped into the chair and picked up the mug. At least she could control the trembling of her hands as she took a sip. No sloshes on the table to give her away.

Liz stole a glance. His gaze was filled with so much compassion — there was no other word for it — it took her breath away.

"Liz." Mason laid his hand palm up on the table.

Now he wanted to touch her? The game was unending. She looked him in the eye, raised her brows, and tucked both hands under her thighs.

He pulled his back and had a sip of tea.

Liz eyed her cup, but she couldn't very well drink it without hands, and they were busy making a statement. She didn't need tea that much.

"To answer your question, yes, Avery said she drew you on that picture. She really wants a mom. Her and Christopher both. They pray about it every single day."

Pray. Right. That's what made Mason different. Just her luck. If only he'd become the decent man in front of her without Jesus. Then he'd be perfect. Probably maddening at times, but perfect.

"Avery prays that Jesus will make you happy."

Liz resisted the urge to roll her eyes. "You are brainwashing your children."

Mason shook his head. "Teaching them. Doing my best to

give them better grounding in life than I had. Yeah, my parents went to church, but they didn't exactly model daily faith. They figured I'd learn what I needed from Sunday school, and you know how that turned out. I want more for Christopher and Avery. My son especially is so much like me it scares me at times."

She couldn't deny it would be a good thing if Christopher had a less self-indulgent swagger as a teenager than his father'd had. Pity the girls at Galena High. A vision of a teen Maddie gazing adoringly at a puffed-up Christopher slid into her mind. *Yeah. Let's prevent that.*

"I'm not sure if stuffing your kids with religion is the answer. My parents did that." She leaned over the table, boring holes in his blue eyes. "And you know how I turned out."

"It was my fault."

That was the easy answer. She could accept it and let him take all the blame. She'd tried that for over a decade, and it hadn't made a difference. "It took two. I threw myself at you." She raised her chin. Let him think what he wanted about tonight.

"Look, I'm not proud of who I was then. I knew what I was doing to you. The guys dared me, and I did it willingly."

She clenched her teeth and stared at him. "I know. I'd like to say that was then, and this is now, but it seems like history is repeating itself. I'm an adult, Mason. I'm no longer that insecure teen. I'm not a victim anymore."

"You're beautiful."

If she hadn't read his lips, she might not have heard the faint words. She blew out a breath. "You are so confusing. What do you want from me?" Could he be coming around after all?

He seemed focused on his hand tracing a design on the table. "Nothing, Liz. Just friendship."

That would be a snowball down her shirt if she believed him. "Nice try."

"You say you're no longer that insecure teen, but you still seem... vulnerable. I care about you too much to take advantage of that."

"So you want more than friendship."

There was silence for a long moment before Mason shook his head. "Not right now. Maybe not ever."

She opened her mouth, but could think of nothing to say. She took a sip of the lukewarm tea and glanced at the clock. One-thirty. She gulped the rest of the tea and stood, planting both hands on the table and leaning toward Mason. "It seems you've graduated from checkers to chess."

He looked up, a frown furrowing his brow. "Meaning?"

"Meaning the game you're playing is more complex than it used to be, but it's still a game."

"I'm not toying with you. Please believe me."

"I don't know what the rules are, but I'll figure them out." She turned and reached for her coat.

"Liz."

She stilled, her back to him. "What?"

"I would like nothing more than to hold you close and kiss you. To have you as a permanent part of my life."

Liz turned slowly, half expecting him to be standing beside her, waiting to get started. He wasn't. "But?"

"But since I became a Christian, it isn't all about me and what I want."

Good reason to steer clear of religion, then. She raised her eyebrows.

"I have the twins to think about. I can't — I won't — jeopardize their future for my own desires."

She poked her chin toward the fridge. "It looks like I'm what your daughter wants."

He scrubbed his hand across his face. "That's what she thinks now. But I'm the adult. I need to make sure for the long haul."

Liz could do long haul, if only he gave her the chance. She really could.

"But that's not the big one."

Oh, brother. She knew where this was going. She pulled her coat on and slid the toggles through the loops.

"Liz, I can't have anything more than friendship with a woman who doesn't love Jesus with all her heart."

She jammed her feet into her boots. "Guess that's a problem, then. Don't get up." Not that he'd made any move to. "I'll see myself out."

Chapter 17 --

*A*n entire night without sleep hadn't done Mason any good. He'd paced the main floor of the old farmhouse for over an hour before getting on his knees. More pacing. More praying. Then he flipped the coffee pot on at five o'clock.

In the few weeks since Liz had re-entered his life, he'd fallen for her, completely and utterly. Those quiet evenings last week after the twins were tucked in bed had been the highlight of his Christmas week.

He'd been filled with hope that she'd walk back into her Christian faith as easily as she'd returned to Galena Landing. He'd pushed to one side how *not* easily that had been. She'd struggled for eleven years before setting foot in Idaho again, and he'd guess she never would have if she'd known he was there.

Her words rang through his mind. *Guess that's a problem, then. Guess that's a problem, then. Guess that's a problem, then.*

She had no intention of letting God work in her life. He'd keep praying for her, but he needed to back off. All the way off. Even more, he needed to protect his children. It might be too late for Avery. She adored Liz. But it was better to cut Liz out now than to wait until the bonding went even deeper.

At least he hadn't kissed her.

He wished he'd kissed her.

It would have sent the wrong message, and it would have been so hard to stop with a kiss. Especially last night in the farmhouse, without Claire and Noel down the hall. No one would have needed to know.

Liz was certainly willing.

But Mason wasn't that guy anymore. He'd dedicated his life to following Jesus. No matter how bleak this day looked — gray skies met gray hills and more snow than any man should have to shovel — he had done the right thing last night.

He dropped the twins and Finnley off at the school as usual then drove down to the tire shop, where Roger used the small Bobcat to clear the lot. Mason waited until staff parking was plowed then pulled into his stall. The shop door was already unlocked and the coffee started. Roger had even turned up the heat, though it wasn't noticeable yet.

Nobody was going to come in today. Those who needed tires the most could never make it through the snow. He checked voice mail. No messages. Flipped through the day planner. One job for this afternoon.

Roger came in the door, stomping the snow off his boots. "Man, what'd we get overnight? Eight inches? You had no trouble getting into town?"

Mason quirked a grin at his boss. "I left early, and I have good tires. Perks of the job."

Roger laughed. He tossed his mitts and cap onto the desk and unzipped his jacket. "Brr." He zipped it back up.

"Yeah. My sentiments exactly."

"Looks like it's going to be a checkers kind of day."

Mason would never look at a game of checkers the same after Liz's accusation last night. Life had become more complex for sure. He tipped his head at his boss. "You sure you want to pay me to play games?"

"Well, you're here, aren't you? If it stays quiet, you can leave when your kids are out of school instead of staying until five."

It wasn't like Mason didn't need his paycheck. "Sounds like a plan."

Roger clomped over to the wall and wiggled the thermostat knob. "Is this thing working? I turned it up an hour ago and it's still freezing in here."

"It's warmer in here than last week."

"Yeah, well, it's also warmer out there. Only twenty degrees instead of sub-zero." Roger touched the baseboard heater. "Great. The thing is dead."

No wonder it was so cold. "Got a portable heater kicking around the back?"

Roger grimaced. "No. Listen, why don't you walk over to the hardware store and grab one? Put it on the tab. We're going to need it today and maybe longer. I'll give the electrician a call and see when he can get someone over here." He gave the baseboard a kick. "Of all the days to be without heat."

"Sure. I'll go." Mason shoved his knit cap over his head and gathered his gloves. "Be back in a few."

"Swing by the bakery and get some doughnuts!" hollered Roger as the door swung shut.

Mason grinned and raised his hand in acknowledgment. He waded three blocks through snow nearly deep enough to swamp his boots just as the hardware store clerk unlocked the door. A few minutes later he'd secured a heater and made his way to the bakery next door where a young woman, all bundled up, struggled with a heavy shovel on the sidewalk.

"Here, let me." Not that there was any place to put the box.

"Thanks, but I'm sure I can manage."

"No, really." He set the box in the snow. Roger would toss the cardboard into recycling anyway. It wasn't like it had to be pristine for that. Mason reached for the shovel and made quick work of the section of sidewalk.

"Thanks, Mason. I appreciate the gallant gesture."

He followed her into the bakery. This was more like it. A place that was actually warm and bright.

"What brings you in so early?"

Just a sec. She knew his name? He took another look at the woman behind the counter.

"Kassidy North. I'm the twins' Sunday school teacher."

"Oh. Uh, hi. My boss asked me to swing by for some doughnuts."

"Roger likes the jelly-filled. Want a dozen?" Kassidy smiled as she crouched to fill a paper bag with confections from the display case.

Mason nodded. So she not only knew his name and his kids' names, but also where he worked. He took a closer look. Her red-gold hair was pulled into a high ponytail, and she was kind of pretty. As if someone could be the total opposite of Liz Nemesek and still be pretty.

Kassidy set the bag on the counter. "Your kids are so sweet, Mason. I was looking forward to seeing them in a different environment when I accepted that invitation to your parents' house last week. I was disappointed when the power outage and nasty weather kept you from joining us."

Wait. This was the woman his mother had been trying to set him up with? Why had he assumed someone over thirty-five with buck teeth instead of a tall woman with a perfect figure? Mason found himself smiling back. "That kept us occupied for several days." He hoisted the boxed heater in his arms. "It's amazing how addicted we all are to electricity and heat."

She laughed. "And water. I heard the pipes in your house were frozen."

Mom had said a lot, apparently. "They were. I had heat tape on them, but when the power went out, it didn't help much."

"Funny how that works."

"It is. How much do I owe you for the doughnuts?" After he'd paid, he juggled the box and bag to open the door. "Nice to meet you, Kassidy. See you around."

"Call me Kass. See you Sunday."

Mason trudged back down the sidewalk. What had all that been about? Was God trying to tell him there were other women out there? Women who loved Jesus and adored his kids? He'd been so sure a week ago that it was only a matter of time before Liz renewed her faith. She'd all but severed that hope last night.

She was actively seeking employment in distant places. One of those interviews was bound to result in a great offer. They'd have to be crazy to pass up on Liz.

He was crazy to.

No. It wasn't the same. He opened the door to the tire shop and plunked both packages on the counter. "Success on both counts."

Was meeting Kass a success as well? Time would tell.

oOo

Liz swiped her phone off and flung it on her bed. That made two jobs Glenda said she hadn't been offered, leaving only the one she'd been least interested in.

Great. What was she supposed to do now? She'd burned her bridges with Mason last night.

Guilt slammed her. She'd pushed him too far, and she'd even done it on purpose, wanting him to commit. Well, he hadn't. She hadn't meant they should go upstairs and have sex right then — though she wouldn't have said no — but to have him shut the door completely? She'd expected the game to continue.

To be fair, he'd left a thread of hope. He wanted her to get back with God, but that wasn't happening. God hadn't taken care of things with Mason in the past, so why would He now? No, she was finished.

She stared out the window at the palette of white and gray. Mounds where she knew there were bushes. Another mound for her car and one for Sierra and Gabe's vehicle next to it.

A distant motor droned closer. She peered at an angle until she got a glimpse of a tractor with a blade clearing snow in the driveway. Was that Dad's old John Deere?

Once upon a time, her daddy had been strong and vibrant. He'd been her hero when she was a little girl. Now he struggled to get around, and she was still avoiding him. Planning to leave again as soon as she could.

If she could get a job. Maybe it didn't matter so much what she did for a living, so long as she got out of Galena Landing. She'd had enough memories to block before yesterday, but she'd added a doozy at one-thirty this morning.

What had she been thinking, pushing herself at Mason in the middle of the night? She'd tossed and turned for hours, replaying the conversation, wishing things had turned out differently. Maybe wishing she'd woken up this morning next to him in her parents' old bedroom.

She grimaced as she turned from the window. That was kind of a disturbing thought.

Okay, she needed a plan. If that third job didn't pan out, she still needed to leave Idaho. Where would she go?

Kara was in a new relationship in California since Liz had been there in December. Liz couldn't crash in on that, but she hadn't kept in touch with anyone else. The thought of her sisters barely brushed the back of her mind. Nope, not happening. Well, she'd gone to Bangkok on her own and survived. She could simply point her car south and drive until she felt like stopping and looking for work. She'd make new friends. She could do this, but maybe she should wait until this storm had passed and the roads were clear again.

Liz heard two voices laughing then someone knocked on her

door. She narrowed her gaze in that direction then shrugged and crossed the space.

"Good morning, Liz! Wow, you must have gotten home late last night!" Chelsea entered, unwinding her scarf, assured of her welcome.

Home. An interesting word that meant nothing.

"It's good you made it." Allison unzipped her coat. "Were the roads awful? They're asking people to stay off the highway today."

"Uh, come on in." Liz backed up. Not that the women had waited for her invitation.

"I brought some granola bars I made yesterday. I hadn't seen you over at the house this morning, so I figured you might not have had breakfast yet." Chelsea bustled over to the table and began emptying her pockets.

"I slept in." True enough. She didn't remember looking at the time from five to eight. She might've slept. Some.

"And I brought loose tea." Allison held up several small jars. "Your preference?"

"Whatever you like." Liz had imbibed enough tea to float a battleship in the past few weeks. It would likely remind her of Mason for the rest of her life.

Allison opened a jar, sniffed it, and passed it to Liz. "This is my new favorite. We added whole cloves, slices of dried ginger, and slivers of cinnamon sticks to dried mint leaves."

"Sure. Sounds good."

"How did your trip go?" Chelsea dropped to one of the chairs at the table as Allison made herself at home in the small kitchenette. "Any promising leads?"

Liz shrugged. "Two of the three have offered the job to someone else already."

"Oh no. That's a bummer."

"Maybe, maybe not," came Allison's voice from the

kitchenette.

Liz's eyebrows went up of their own accord. How nice. Someone else thought they knew what was best for her life.

Chelsea chuckled. "Just wait and hear us out."

So there was something behind this visit. Not so impromptu after all. Liz took a seat at the table and crossed her arms.

"Here, have one." Chelsea nudged the cloth package closer.

Liz examined it. "What is that?"

"Granola bars."

"No, the wrap."

"Oh, we're trying to completely eliminate our use of plastic. That's a piece of cloth that's been soaked in beeswax to make a covering that's sealed and can be wiped clean."

Interesting. Life without plastic wrap?

Allison poked her head around the corner. "Sierra is our beekeeper. I must admit, I find bees completely fascinating." She came out carrying three cups of tea.

"Thanks." Liz might as well make the best of it. She unwrapped the granola bar and had a bite. It was delicious. She'd been hungrier than she thought. When was the last time she'd eaten? The drive-through in Coeur d'Alene before that long drive in the heavy snow?

Allison set the tea on the table and pulled up the last chair. "Those jobs you didn't get. Were they exactly what you wanted? I admit I don't really know what your skill set is."

Liz swallowed the bite of granola bar. "Apparently little that's marketable in the U.S."

The two women exchanged glances. They were fishing for information. Had Mason set this up?

No, he'd only be glad when she left for good so she wouldn't be a bad influence on his children. Bile rose in her throat, and she set down the rest of the bar. Too much. Too sweet. Too something.

Allison cradled her mug. An exquisite set of diamond rings gleamed on her left hand. "You have experience teaching."

"Yes. English to Thai nationals. Not particularly useful on a resume."

"Any credentials?"

Liz glared at a spot on the table. "Just a diploma for that. And a bachelor's degree in education that's almost completed. I've been doing that via Distance Ed."

"Good, good." Allison glanced at Chelsea. "We're looking to expand our farm school."

"That's nice."

"Interested in working with us?"

Liz surged to her feet. "Not really. I mean, no offense, but I don't really fit in."

Chelsea leaned back in her chair, eyeing Liz through her pink glasses. "How's that?"

"I'm not really into this whole farming thing. The food here has been amazing, but I'm fine with the easy life. You know, supermarkets and restaurants." She held up both hands. "You've got the wrong person."

"We do work pretty hard." Chelsea sighed.

Both women's nails were short but done up. Chelsea's rings looked artisan-made. That was another thing. This place was full of married couples. Families. Oh, and Mason. No thanks.

"I suspect you know more about farming and gardening and food preservation than you think you do," Allison went on. "We have a full syllabus of the class work."

Liz's head was already shaking. "No. I appreciate the thought, but no. Whether I get that last job I applied for or not, I'm leaving the panhandle as soon as the weather clears."

Allison's perfectly plucked eyebrows rose. "You'd leave without a job to go to, when we're offering you a term position here? We haven't even discussed salary or expectations."

"Not interested." She'd almost kept her voice steady. If only she hadn't all but propositioned Mason last night. There was no way she was sticking around now. Not that she wanted to teach farming, anyway.

"Okay. Well, we'll put the word out then. I'm sure we'll get some qualified applicants."

And here she'd wondered if they'd invented a job for her. For Zach's sister. Of course they hadn't. What a ridiculous idea.

Allison stood and crossed to the doorway where she put on her coat and boots. "Coming, Chelsea?"

Chelsea glanced between them. "Go ahead. I'll catch up."

Allison nodded and left.

Liz stared at Chelsea. Now what?

"Anything you want to talk about? I'm a good listener."

"Not really." Like she was going to spill her guts to someone she'd met last week? Not a chance.

"I didn't think I fit in here when I came a year and a half ago. It turned out I needed to work through some things in my faith."

Liz's eyes narrowed.

"I grew up in a Christian home, like you did. What I somehow missed was how much God loved me, Chelsea Riehl." She grimaced and shook her head. "Sorry, I keep forgetting I'm Chelsea Welsh now. Or Chelsea Welsea as Maddie likes to say. But back to the point. I knew God loved everyone. I mean we were taught that in Sunday school when we were little kids, right?"

That required an answer? Liz gave a terse nod.

"It didn't seem personal. But Keanan helped me a lot. He gave me these." Chelsea fished in her pocket and came out with a small stack of note cards. "I'd like to give them to you."

Was this where Liz told Chelsea to take her gift and leave? She couldn't find the gumption to be that rude.

Chelsea stood, compassion radiating from her, so welcoming

that Liz took an involuntary step closer before catching herself.

"I'll leave them on the table. Have a look. You might find them interesting." Chelsea reached for her coat. When she was bundled up for the wintry day, she turned back to Liz. "I think I understand a lot of what you're feeling. I'm praying for you."

With a blast of cold air, the door opened and shut behind Chelsea.

Liz eyed the note cards on the table. Did she dare?

Chapter 18 --

*H*is father looked up from reading his newspaper when Mason entered the house. The twins had spread toys from one end to the other and were running around like banshees.

"Daddy!" yelled Christopher.

Autopilot kicked in. "Inside voice, please."

The decibel dropped and Avery smashed into him, sending him reeling. "Avery. Slow down."

How could Dad even pretend to read with all this going on? This was an awful lot of mess for two hours after school. Guilt poked at Mason. He put his parents out enough on days Mom was home, but this was the result when she was at work.

"Put the toys away, kids. You have ten minutes before we need to be on the road home." He removed Avery's arms from around his hips. "Hurry it up."

"Aw, Dad..."

"Don't even start, Christopher. Did Grandpa make this mess? I doubt it. You know where the toys go."

"I'm hungry, Daddy." Avery tugged at his arm.

"Please clean up. Then we'll head home for supper."

Dad got to his feet. "Your mother will be home from work soon."

Like she needed to cook for three extra people. They weren't her responsibility. Mason twitched his head toward the kitchen. "Can we talk for a minute, Dad?"

A guarded look crossed his father's face. "Uh, sure."

Mason made eye contact with each twin in turn and pointed at the mess. "Get a move on."

Drooping like two flat tires, they each reached for a toy.

"Dad, I'm sorry I asked you to do after-school care today."

His dad straightened. "I know things got a bit out of hand—"

"You don't have to let them walk all over you, you know." Mason shook his head. "But it's not just that. I need to think of a better solution."

"They're my flesh and blood."

"Well, yes, but that doesn't make them your responsibility. They're mine." And that was the problem. His alone. "I'll apply for subsidized spots at the county-run after-school program."

His dad's eyes narrowed. "We Watermans don't take charity."

"You know what, Dad? This one does. This one needs help, and he's willing to ask for it."

Dad shot a glance over his shoulder toward where the kids were elbowing each other as they reached for the same toy. "I thought they went to Green Acres after school on the other days."

"They had been. But everyone's busy there, too." To say nothing of Avery getting too attached to Liz. "Allison and Brent and Finnley are leaving Monday for two weeks away. And it's just not fair to keep taking advantage of them. Or you."

"You need a wife, son."

And he figured Mason didn't know that? "Yeah, well, God hasn't seen fit to send someone. I can't wait around on my knees forever." *Liz. Oh, Liz. Why so stubborn?*

"Pickings are slim in a small town like this, but your mother has some ideas."

"I'm sure she does." Mason glanced into the living room. The twins were making reasonable progress. "But I'm a grown man, Dad. Would you have let Grandma pick a wife for you?"

A ghost of a smile poked at the other man's cheeks. "She did point Emma out to me. I hadn't really noticed her before. Mama was right. We suited well."

So much for that argument.

Dad thumbed over his shoulder. "Those two need a mother. Seems you need help finding someone. They're not gonna be young forever."

It sure seemed like it some days. But hey, he'd made it through diapers and bottles and tantrums. He could make it through after-school care and last-minute suppers, too. Somehow.

Tires crunched in the snow outside. A car door slammed. The back door opened and closed, and Mom appeared, stripping gloves off her hands.

Mason closed his eyes. He'd really hoped to pass his mother's car on the road. Wave at her as they went opposite directions.

"You're home!" called Avery. She ran into the kitchen and hugged her grandmother.

Mom patted Avery's shoulders. "Good to see you, sweetie. What are you and your brother up to?"

Avery shot Mason a look of disgust, complete with curled lip. "Daddy's making us clean up the toys."

Mom looked at Mason. "You're not staying for supper?"

He shook his head. "Not tonight, Mom. Thanks."

She pursed her lips. "It has to be better than the diner."

Touché. "No diner tonight. I picked up a meat pie at the bakery."

"They have such good food." Mom nudged him. "Kassidy works there."

Avery looked from one grown-up to the other.

"Off you go, princess. Put everything away, please."

Her lip protruded, but she turned and flounced back into the living room.

"Have you met her?" Mom removed her coat. "She's a lovely woman in her mid-twenties. Single. A Christian."

Dad hooked his thumbs through belt loops and grinned at Mason.

Mason took a deep breath. "I've met her."

Mom beamed at him. "Of course you have. She's the twins' Sunday school teacher. She finds them charming."

"I'm glad. They enjoy Sunday school."

Dad cleared his throat. "What your mother means—"

"I have a pretty good idea what she means." Was this what it felt like to ride an avalanche? A man couldn't stop the snow and rocks and trees from sliding. He could only hope to keep his head above the turmoil and not break every bone in his body before it all ended.

His heart was already broken, but that didn't stop the avalanche. It may have muffled his own need, but he had to think of the kids. His parents might not have the best marriage in the world, but they did okay by the looks of it.

He wanted more than okay. He wanted mutual love and passion. He wanted the sun to rise and set upon his beloved, and for her to feel the same about him. He wanted Liz. She wanted him, but she didn't want God.

Was the situation really non-negotiable? Maybe she'd come around after a while when she saw Jesus in his life.

A slippery slope, indeed.

Wait. Mom was talking, and he'd checked out. "Pardon me?"

"I said, Kass is off on Tuesday. I'd like to invite her for supper, but I don't want you to bail on me like last time."

"The power was out and the roads were closed."

"We had power on this side of the valley." Mom leaned closer. "You need to put some effort into this, son. Erin's not coming back."

Mason choked down a laugh that may — or may not — have come out sounding like hysteria. If Mom only knew Erin was planning a visit, but he sure wasn't saying so when the kids could hear. Mom was right about one thing, though. Erin might return, but it would always be temporary. The chance of him marrying and sharing responsibility with the twins' other parent was less than zero. Less than Liz and, after the other night, that was saying something. His prospects weren't looking very good.

He spread his hands. "Fine. Tuesday. The kids are coming on the bus after school, right? That still work?"

"Monday and Tuesday are good." Mom eyed Dad. "How did it go with the children today, Gary?"

Dad's gaze shifted from Mom to Mason. "Uh. Okay."

If that's how Dad wanted to spin it. Hadn't looked that way to Mason.

oOo

"It's always good to spend time with you, Lizzie Rose." Mom smiled brightly at her across the table in the bakery. "How have you been keeping?"

That smile was going to disappear in a minute. It was like Liz couldn't help being a disappointment to her parents, but she had her own life to live, separate from theirs. Separate from Mason's.

"Pretty good." Liz dredged up some enthusiasm. "I found a job!"

Mom beamed. "Jo said they were going to offer you a teaching position. I'm so happy."

"No, not that. I'm leaving for Des Moines on Sunday."

"But..." Mom's smile faltered.

"I'm really looking forward to it." She'd spent the last decade and more perfecting her lying technique. She could do this.

"I didn't know you applied for a job in Des Moines."

Liz pushed out a carefree laugh. "I didn't, exactly. But the business I applied to in Las Vegas has a satellite in Des Moines. They've already filled the position in Vegas."

"So you'll be teaching English?"

This was where it got dicey. Keep it upbeat. "Part time teaching and part time office." The offered pay was definitely lower. "It sounds like a full-time position might open up in the next few months and, if I'm right there, it's sure to be mine."

Mom's eyes searched hers. "Is this what you really want to do?"

No. Absolutely not. But she couldn't tell her God-fearing mother about the mess with Mason. Either the one from high school or the one from this week. She couldn't stay in Idaho, even if she wanted to.

She'd spent two days trying to decide if it was worth pretending to be a Christian for Mason, but she was pretty sure he wouldn't be that easy to fool. She knew the language, but she no longer spoke it like a native. No matter how she tried to spin it in her mind, it wasn't going to work. The only solution was to get away from Galena Landing and forget he ever existed.

Because that had worked so well for her in Thailand.

She shoved the thought aside with a well-practiced mental motion. What had her mother's question been, again? Right. "I think it will work out fine. I've never been to Iowa, and I'm ready to explore someplace new."

Mom pursed her lips. "You're flying?"

Liz shook her head. "Driving. I thought I'd head out Sunday morning."

"Lizzie, it's the dead of winter. There's more snow coming. You shouldn't drive by yourself."

"I'll be fine, Mom. I'll take it easy. They'll keep the interstate in good shape. From Billings it's southeast to Des Moines. All major routes. Don't worry about me."

Mom stretched her hand across the small table and squeezed Liz's. "I'll always worry. You're my baby. Did Cindy call you about that possibility in Denver?"

Like she was going anywhere near a city where her perfect sister and brother-in-law worked at a church. "My mind's made up, Mom. You'll be proud of me. You'll see."

"It's not about that, Lizzie Rose. I'll always love you and be proud of you. You're a beautiful woman and smart as a whip. I only want to know you. You've been here for what, three weeks? And I've only seen you a handful of times. I'm not ready to let you go again."

Liz forced herself to lean back in the chair. Too bad they hadn't done more than taste their sandwiches before getting into it. Her gut was churning too hard now to eat. "I don't know what to say."

"Say you'll wait until spring. Teach with Allison one term. See how things look when the snow's gone."

Liz's head was shaking long before her mother's words were finished. "I can't. There's more to it, but we don't need to go into all that."

"Why not? Give me a try."

Liz picked at the crust of her sandwich. Right. Mom might think she wanted to know, but she didn't. There were things mothers and daughters simply weren't meant to discuss.

Mom's voice lowered. "Does it have something to do with Mason Waterman?"

Tears prickled Liz's eyes. She peered at her mom through lowered lashes. Mom only looked concerned, no more. Whew. She didn't know.

"He's a good man, Lizzie Rose. He sowed his wild oats, but he's stable now. A good Christian man and father." Mom paused. "Single."

Liz tried to blink the tears away, but she could barely make out the napkin in her clenched hands through the blur. How could she ever respond without giving everything away? Her voice would break, for sure.

Mom chuckled. "Why, there he is now."

Not falling for that one. No looking up. It could be true, of course. The bakery was right downtown, not far from where Mason worked. But he should be busy swapping out tires on some old lady's car right now, not on break.

"Hi, Mason!" called Mom.

Liz stared at the wall beyond her mother and counted to ten. No patter of footsteps. She picked up the napkin and dabbed her eyes, hoping Mom was too preoccupied to notice.

The urge to see him for herself became more than she could deny. Liz angled her head slightly and peeked over her shoulder.

There he stood at the counter with his hand on a cardboard container. The pretty clerk smiled, her eyes twinkling, and laid her hand on top of Mason's as he leaned closer to her.

Liz scrunched her eyes back shut. He might have said he loved her, but words were cheap with Mason. They always had been. He'd obviously be fine when Liz disappeared again.

She only wished she would be.

Chapter 19 --

Now that had been some bad timing. Mason hesitated, but there was nothing more to be said to Liz. They'd said it all the other night. He couldn't force her into a relationship with Jesus. That step had to be all hers. Neither could he and the twins wait for years hoping she'd come around.

The bakery door whisked shut behind him and the swirling wind encompassed him, tightening around his heart. He tromped back to the tire shop and stowed the empanadas in the car. Kass had assured him they would reheat nicely at 350 for half an hour. Picking up supper at the bakery on his coffee break was an improvement over swinging past the diner on his way home. Better food for less money. Win-win.

Or win-lose. Liz hadn't turned to see him, but Rosemary had said hi. Would she have told Liz she'd seen Kass squeeze his hand? Kass had only told him what Christopher had said in Sunday school.

His phone buzzed with an incoming message as he reached for the tire shop door. He glanced at it. Claire. He took a deep breath. What now?

Did you know Liz got a job in Des Moines?

No giving up for Claire. Mason swallowed hard. *No, but I'm not surprised.*

She's leaving Sunday already.

159

She'd take Mason's heart with her. How could he live without a heart?

He stared at the phone and tapped a reply. *That's really soon.*

And yet, with her gone, he could try to pick up the pieces of his life. He had to do a better job of making a real home for the twins, with or without a wife. These healthier suppers were a good start. Maybe, in time, Kass might find a place in his life. Or someone else. Hard to imagine. *God, help me here, please. I don't know if I can do this.*

The phone buzzed. *Come for supper Saturday?*

If only that would make a difference. If only. But it wouldn't. It would only make it worse for all of them. For him. For Liz. For the twins. *I think it's better if I don't.*

Don't give up so easily.

I can't do it, Claire. I just can't.

It took longer for a reply to come this time. Maybe she'd shown her phone to Noel. *We won't stop praying.*

At least she was taking it to the only authority who could make a difference. *Thanks.*

His coffee break over, Mason pocketed his phone and pulled the door to the tire shop open.

oOo

Liz white-knuckled her way up Lookout Pass out of Coeur d'Alene. The only good thing about this slippery interstate was that it took all her attention, leaving little to spare for the last two days she'd spent at Green Acres. Glimpses persisted.

Allison, asking her to reconsider the job.

Chelsea, pressing a Bible into her hands, telling her it was a fresh new translation she might not have read. Liz hadn't had the heart to shove it back. Instead, she'd buried it in her suitcase with the note cards she hadn't looked at yet, and never planned to.

Zach. Her big brother saying he'd failed her. Asking her to stay.

Her little niece, prancing around rhyming "Liz" with everything she could think of. "Liz fizz. Liz whiz." Then hugging her and kissing her goodbye.

But no Mason. No Avery and no Christopher. She'd overheard Allison asking Claire if they hadn't been invited, but Liz hadn't caught the answer. It didn't matter, anyway. It was better this way.

The car slid toward the rail and Liz's heart stopped. She pushed on the accelerator and turned the wheel. *Please God please God please God.*

The tires caught traction again and straightened. She dared to breathe.

Huh. She'd actually prayed. But she'd also remembered what to do in a spin, and it had worked. Was going her own way going to be the death of her? Wasn't there a Bible verse about that? Probably. There had to be one for everything. She'd memorized hundreds of them as a child.

Romans six twenty-three. In her mind, she could hear her little girl sing-song voice. *For the wages of sin is death, but the gift of God is eternal life in Christ Jesus our Lord.*

Who taught little kids about sin and death, anyway? And why on earth did she remember those words? Others crowded into her head. She tightened her hands on the wheel.

For all have sinned and fall short of the glory of God.

That was all too true. She'd sure fallen short. Mason had fallen even farther and yet seemed to think God had forgiven him. If those old memory verses were to be taken at face value, he had grounds.

Why couldn't it be that simple?

The car skidded again.

Enough of those thoughts. She had to focus on driving. She wasn't ready to die today.

oOo

"Daddy, did you know God smacked Paul and made him blind?" Christopher rammed one fist into the other, eyes lit up. "Kerpow. Knocked him to the ground."

Avery slid her hand into Mason's. "That's what Miss North told us."

Miss North. Mason looked across the crowded church foyer to see Kass chatting with Allison, both women laughing. No wonder he hadn't put two and two together and realized Miss North wasn't some middle-aged spinster.

"Do you like your Sunday school teacher?" he found himself asking the children. No more dreaming about Liz. She didn't love him, didn't love God, and was so desperate to leave Galena Landing that she'd driven out of here in iffy road conditions early this morning. At least she had good tires.

Christopher shrugged. "There's Finnley!" He darted off between Zach and Ed Graysen, nearly causing the old man to slosh his coffee.

Mason started over to apologize for his son when Avery's hand tugged him back. "She's nice and she's pretty." Avery grimaced. "But she likes mushrooms."

Mason chuckled. "I didn't see you picking them out of your meat pie the other day."

Avery tilted her head at him. "What does Miss North have to do with my meat pie?"

"She works at the bakery. You have to admit those suppers the past few days have been better than burgers and fries every night."

Kass's chuckle reached his ears, and there she stood beside

162

Avery, who stretched her other hand to her teacher. Kass grinned down at her. "I want to hear your answer, Avery. Do you like my cooking?"

Mason shifted from one foot to the other. Why did that feel like such a loaded question? But it wasn't disloyalty to Liz to appreciate Kass. Not her cooking, for sure, since it had been purely an exchange of cash for supper from a business with an established service.

"It was yummy." Avery looked up with adoring eyes. "Thank you."

It wasn't all about him. His little girl became fixated on any woman, young or old, who gave her the slightest encouragement. She needed a mom in her life.

And Kass was pretty. Reddish hair curling past her shoulders. Green eyes and a freckled nose. She glanced at him and her mouth curved into a smile. Plus, she already knew and liked the twins, she loved the Lord... and she was here. Obviously interested.

Wasn't this where his heart was supposed to melt a little? Where he was supposed to make a flirty remark back? He'd used them all up the past few weeks on Liz. Maybe he just needed a bit more time to get over her. Maybe a lot more time. But for his kids' sake, he'd try.

Allison came up beside him. "You're coming for lunch, right, Mason? The boys are planning to build a snowman army with all that fresh snow."

"I, uh. I wasn't planning on it."

She tapped two fingers on his arm. "He's a stubborn one, Kass."

Mason's ears heated. "Now what's that supposed to mean?" Allison had better not have been talking about him to Kass. He'd handle his own love life, thank you very much. Or lack of one, as the case may be.

Allison leaned closer. "So what do you have planned for today that is more important than relaxing with friends?"

Someone from Green Acres invited him and the kids nearly every Sunday, like they were a charity case. "I was thinking of cracking open one of the recipe books my mom gave me for Christmas, if you must know. Try to actually plan a week of meals rather than let every day catch me by surprise."

"Oh, I have some terrific recipes you could try, Mason." Kass slid her arm across Avery's shoulder. "Some of them don't even have mushrooms in them. I used to teach some classes on once-a-month cooking."

Allison tilted her head to the side. "Do tell."

Kass looked from Allison to Mason. "That's when you plan ahead for a month of meals, and buy all the stuff you need — well, except for fresh produce like lettuce, of course — and then have one marathon prep day to get all the supper starters into the freezer so they only take a few minutes when you want to use them."

A month of meals mostly ready to go? Sounded like the next best thing to heaven. "What kinds of food?"

Kass caressed Avery's shoulder, and Avery leaned against her.

Mason would hazard a guess Kass wasn't even aware of the gesture. She didn't seem the kind to manipulate his kids to get close to him. Not that many women would. Most wanted guys without baggage.

"It depends on your family's needs and budget. I mean, there are lots of options. If you want gluten-free, for instance, or someone has allergies." She wrinkled her nose at Avery. "Mushrooms don't count. They're always delish."

Mason chuckled. Kass sure had Avery's number on that one. "Sounds interesting. I could definitely use some help in that department." He rubbed the back of his neck. "Well, you know."

"I'm fascinated, too." Allison pursed her lips. "My brain is whirling with possibilities. Mason, I've already invited Kass out to the farm for lunch. I think you and the twins should come, too, and we can talk about this some more. Maybe set up a plan to do some batch cooking for you."

"Allison, you don't have to—"

"I know. But you and the kids are part of our Green Acres family. We *like* having you around. Besides, you could be our guinea pig."

That sounded ominous. He raised his eyebrows at her. He knew all about the matchmaking that went on at Green Acres. They'd even tried it on him and Liz.

Liz. Oh, Lord, take care of Liz. Let her know You love her.

But Allison had turned to Kass. "That sounds like a terrific course or workshop we could offer through the school."

And Mason had thought she meant him and Kass. Yeah, it wasn't always all about him.

"Batch cooking for busy people," Allison went on. "Whether they've got families, or even for older folks who find it hard to trim back to cooking for one or two. Using good, local ingredients. I really love this idea."

Kass beamed at Allison. "It's definitely one of my passions."

Allison elbowed Mason. "You're coming. You need in on this."

"What, and deprive my kids of burgers and fries five nights a week?" He chuckled to cover his discomfort. Hopefully they'd understand.

Allison shook her head. "And with what for veggies?"

He wasn't that bad. "Baby carrots?"

"I'd like to think I've already helped start him on the road to better eating," Kass said, a twinkle in her eyes. "He's picked up dinner from the bakery a few times now."

Thanks, Kass. By the way Allison's plucked brows rose, Mason was pretty sure she was adding things up. Maybe even adding in the fact that Avery nestled against Kass's side.

"Well, the budget would probably look a lot better if I got this under control so, yes, I'll be your guinea pig." He raised his own eyebrows and stared hard at Allison, hoping she'd get the message exactly what he was volunteering for.

She grinned back at him. "I'm glad that's settled. It's only fair to warn you both that Brent and Gabe are on lunch today, but you're not allowed to back out on account of it. They're perfectly capable. Well, mostly."

Mason chuckled and poked Avery. "Go find your brother. Let's get going here."

Someone opened the door from the church foyer to the parking lot. A wall of swirling white was all he saw.

Liz was out driving in that, and she had so little experience with winter road conditions. *Lord, please...*

Please what? Mason didn't even know how to pray for Liz anymore. *Please take care of her.*

Chapter 20 --

*I*t was a miracle she was still in one piece.

Liz tried to peel her fingers off the steering wheel, one at a time, to keep them from cramping. She peered into the unrelenting white. She'd seen red taillights a minute ago, but they'd disappeared again. How close was she to the vehicle in front of her? She was barely crawling as it was. If there was an impact, it could hardly do any damage. Unless someone rammed her from behind.

She glanced in the rearview mirror, not that she could see anything but white. Then forward again. Red circles! She tapped the brakes. The car slid a little then held.

Liz inhaled sharply and tried to restart her heart as the back of a semi loomed. If she could just keep it in view, she'd be okay. It was the not knowing that was the problem.

That and the fact she hadn't seen a plow since coming down the pass. Soft snow pulled at her tires. Maybe she could keep the car in the semi's tracks, now that she could see them.

Breathe. In and out. Keep watch. One foot poised to tap the brakes. Slamming them would send her into a skid she couldn't recover from.

Was she like Jonah, running from God? Only he was the lucky guy who got swallowed by a whale, not a blizzard.

She was dumb, dumb, dumb. How bad could it have been,

staying at the farm for another day or two, at least until the storm passed? Maybe forever?

But Mason. She couldn't be the woman he needed. To be the mother Avery and Christopher longed for. The daughter her parents craved. The respectable aunt Maddie and John had a right to. Never mind. She wasn't kidding even herself. It was all about Mason.

And God. The two were intertwined. She couldn't do Mason without God. Truth? She didn't want to. She'd known the pre-God Mason, and he'd been a dangerous bad boy. The with-God Mason was mature, thoughtful, and easy to talk to.

She'd been infatuated by the teen version. The man? She was in love with the man, but she wasn't in love with his God.

oOo

"We have an announcement to make." Gabe looked around the farmhouse table then grinned at Sierra, who nestled against his side. The adults lingered over dessert and coffee after the kids dashed off to play.

Everyone perked up, including Mason. He knew they badly wanted a baby, and this had all the trappings of that type of announcement.

"Well, spit it out already," said Jo as she offered John a heel of bread to gnaw on.

Mason remembered the endless teething. Times two.

"We've started filling out paperwork for adoption." Sierra's nose wrinkled. "There's a lot of it."

Claire leaned onto the table. "Babies are hard to come by." Her face reddened. "I mean in the adoption system."

Jo raised an eyebrow at Claire. "Are you trying to tell us something?"

Mason looked from Claire to Noel, whose eyes twinkled before he gestured back to Gabe. "Claiming innocence until proven guilty. Back at you, man. Don't let this gang distract you. How can we help? I imagine a home study will be part of the process?"

Sierra nodded. "Do you think Green Acres will be a pro or a con to the officials?"

"A pro, definitely," Allison said firmly. "Being part of this community made my bid to keep Finnley more attractive to the state. When I started the paperwork, Brent wasn't really in the picture, so I figured on parenting alone. Having the support of all of you made the difference to the officials."

"And Maddie was the only kiddo on the farm, then. Now there are six." Jo angled a significant glance at Claire. "And possibly more on the way."

Claire spread her hands out with a wide innocent expression.

Wait. Jo had said six kids? Mason leaned over the table. "You can't count the twins. We don't actually live here. But still, four kids in three homes proves this is a family-centered place."

Zach set his mug down on the table forcefully. "Waterman."

Mason raised his eyebrows. "Nemesek?"

"Green Acres Farm owns the house you live in. You help with chores, and we help watching the twins. Plus I keep seeing you at this table."

A slow burn crept up Mason's ears. "That's only because I keep getting invited. I try not to take advantage of it."

"Oh, Zach, stop it." Claire shook her head and turned to Mason. "You're taking him wrong. He didn't mean that as a negative. You are most definitely not freeloading. Ever. Get that right out of your head."

"But—"

"Agreed. We'll return to this discussion another time. Soon." Allison turned to Sierra. "Meanwhile, back to you."

What did Allison mean? It sounded like a veiled threat. Mason forced his gaze not to linger when it passed Kass. What must she think of him and this whole situation? Yeah, he needed help. That had to be plenty obvious, even to a visitor. But he was trying. Doing his best. Parenting solo was the hardest thing he'd ever done in his life. When the twins were teens, he'd probably look back on the terrible twos as the good old days.

"We've talked on and off about building you guys a house," Brent said to Gabe. "Do you think living in the duplex might be a negative?"

"It does have two bedrooms," said Sierra. "It would still do us for a while."

"If you're sure." Brent shook his head and looked at Mason. "The old farmhouse is desperate for remodeling, and that's my top priority starting as soon as we can in the spring. I'll bring in my Timber Framing Plus crew. Maybe Keanan can help when he's not needed on farm work?"

The big redheaded man nodded. "Definitely."

"But it sounds like it may be more important to get Sierra and Gabe into their own place." A sudden thought choked Mason. "Maybe they'll want to move into the farmhouse when it's renovated."

The couple in question didn't even glance at each other. "Not at all." Gabe shook his head. "That discussion came up when we all made the decision to buy out Zach's parents. It doesn't suit what we want, long term."

"Plus we're not desperate." Sierra toyed with her coffee mug. "No, Brent should definitely keep to the current schedule."

"Well, that includes a new house across the valley that will take the better part of the year to complete. That's the one that will bring the cash influx for the farm for the year."

"No problem." Gabe spread his hands. "Really. Maybe pencil us in for starting a year from now. We'll discuss final plans while we wield paint brushes over at Mason's."

Sierra raised a disbelieving eyebrow at Gabe. "So now you're an expert painter?"

He slid his arm across the back of her chair and caressed her shoulder. "I know my way around a roller."

"I wouldn't trust him," she said to Mason.

It wasn't his decision. Man, this was a lot to take in. Didn't they usually discuss this kind of thing in closed meetings? Today, not only was he present, so was Kass, who sat between Chelsea and Sierra across the table taking it all in.

"So. Adoption." Jo tapped a fork against the table. "Any idea of a timeline? Like Claire said, babies are in high demand."

Sierra and Gabe exchanged a look. "We're open to kids a bit older. Maybe a set of siblings. We've also decided ethnicity doesn't matter to us."

"That should up your chances. Please do keep us in the loop. We'll help in any way we can." Jo's gaze softened as she looked at her friend. "I'm happy for you guys. I hope it all works out."

Noel cleared his throat. "I think we should pray about it. Starting here and now." He closed his eyes and launched into a heartfelt plea. Several others followed suit.

Mason should've asked Noel to pray for Liz. He shook his head slightly. No doubt the man — the entire group — already did. She was Zach's sister.

There was quiet after the last "amen" sounded then Allison cleared her throat. "You've all met our guest, Kass North. While I've known her for a few months as Finnley's Sunday school teacher, I also know her as a wonderful person who has a passion for real food. You may know she works at the bakery. Anyway, she said something after church about batch cooking that sparked my interest. Care to share, Kass?"

Kass's gaze flitted between Allison and Mason. "It's not that remarkable, really, and I'm not sure how it applies to most of you here, cooking for so many. But I was involved with a group of girls in Spokane who got together once a month and did all the prep and assembly for meals. We had a lot of fun and each took home twenty-five packages ready for the freezer. We took turns planning the menus and buying the ingredients. I mean, everyone paid their share every month, but there didn't seem to be any point in all six of us spending a couple of hours at the supermarket when one person could easily pick up everything and often a bit cheaper with the bulk."

"So a cooking cooperative," mused Claire, looking around. "Add that to homegrown ingredients..."

"Don't we kind of do that already?" asked Chelsea. "I mean, we batch cook soups and stews for the freezer, and make a year's worth of pasta sauce in October. That kind of thing."

"We do," Allison agreed. "We could possibly do a bit more, but I wasn't thinking so much of implementing it for the farm as seeing if we could adapt Kass's idea in some way for the farm school. Offer it to folks in Galena Landing. They could buy in on a monthly basis for a set amount of money, and someone would source the ingredients and get everything together. Then all the participants could get together in the school kitchen and do the prep and take their meals home. We have a commercial kitchen, after all. I'm seeing this as an ongoing program."

"You'll always have some who can't make it on the scheduled day." Claire pursed her lips. "Like someone who always works Saturdays, or is on shift."

"That's true." Allison drummed the table thoughtfully. "First we need to determine if there's need for the service before crossing that one. We could potentially offer it twice a month on different days of the week. Or we could do the cooking ourselves and sell a week's worth of meals at a time to subscribers."

"Kind of like Meals on Wheels?" Chelsea leaned over the table and looked toward Allison. "I'm in, either way. At least if Claire is. She's the chef, but I'm absolutely willing to organize this and help cook."

172

"Me, too." Keanan nodded. "Unless we're in the middle of haying or something else that can't be scheduled."

"We definitely need to look at all the angles before jumping in," said Claire. "It sounds like a full-fledged business of its own. Not a full-time one, perhaps, but we still need to do our homework to make sure it's worth our time."

Jo shrugged. "It sounds like it fits our mandate of teaching people to eat more healthily. We can include education on the benefits of local. Mind you, they'll taste the difference."

"Kass and I decided to use Mason as our guinea pig," said Allison. "He needs healthy, quick-prep meals, especially for work days."

Mason's head swam. Did he want all these people who lived to poke their noses in each other's business to take over his meal planning? They did seem to get along, even with all the intrusiveness, but — whom was he trying to kid? — he needed help. No two ways about that.

He cleared his throat and leaned forward. "I gratefully accept the challenge, just so long as you remember that two thirds of us have a thing against mushrooms."

Chapter 21 --

She'd hoped to do the twenty-five hour trip — according to her car's GPS — in two extended days. Instead, that's how long it had taken to get across Montana, crawling eastward in the blowing snow. Meals consisted of sandwich after sandwich made from the deli meat and sourdough rolls she'd picked up in Missoula, topped off with cookies, chips, and so much coffee she'd had to pull off at every rest area. Sometimes she caught a nap beside the idling rigs while she was there anyway.

Liz tapped a phone number on her dashboard display. The phone rang seven times then went to voice mail. Seriously, what was up with that? They couldn't be closed every time she called. Maybe her job would be to answer phones. Someone certainly needed to.

The beep sounded. "Hi, this is Liz Nemesek, and it's four o'clock on Tuesday afternoon. I'll be at the office tomorrow at eight, ready to work." She bit off the need to explain to the answering machine why she was late. She'd done that twice already.

Now to find a truck stop where she could pull off for longer than a couple of hours. Preferably a place with coin-operated showers. Yeah, she had some savings, but she needed to make sure they stretched until her first payday, at least. Who knew how much an apartment might cost?

She bit her lip and glanced at the phone display again. Before she lost her nerve, she tapped another number.

Her mom answered on the second ring. "Lizzie Rose? How are you? Where are you? Is everything all right?"

"I'm okay, Mom. That storm lasted all the way through Montana, but it's been better since then. I'll be getting into Des Moines soon."

"She made it, Steve." Mom's voice was a bit muffled, as though she covered the microphone with her hand.

"Thank the Lord." In the background, Dad sounded relieved. "She wasn't anywhere near that fatal pile-up near Billings, was she?"

The *what?* Liz hadn't listened to the radio, just an unending stream of pounding rock to keep her awake and focused. "I hadn't heard about an accident. When was that?"

Mom gave her the information.

"Sounds like it happened not long after I went through there. The highway was pretty ugly."

"Your dad and I have been praying for you nearly constantly." Mom's voice broke. "I'm so glad God sent His guardian angels to keep you safe."

The flippant answer would be that she didn't need God's help. He was too sporadic about when He decided she was worthy of it. If a person couldn't depend on God, what good was He?

Yet she sure couldn't claim her own driving skill to have been the deciding factor. Not after all those harrowing hours. A lifetime of them. Who knew? The angels might've made the difference. "Thanks, Mom."

"Do you have a place to stay tonight?"

"I'm still a couple of hours out of Des Moines. I'll start watching for a spot when I'm closer." Her parents didn't need to know she meant a truck stop or rest area.

"And you're starting your new job tomorrow? Give us a call when you get off work, and tell us all about it. Please?"

The wistful final request nearly broke Liz then and there. She'd done such a good job of keeping her parents at bay, even through three weeks in Galena Landing. She knew they loved her. She knew it. Why couldn't she let them into her life?

Why couldn't she let God back into her life?

She shoved the thought aside. "Will do, Mom. Thanks."

"I hope this job is everything you want it to be."

Liz hadn't told anyone she'd been downgraded to a different position. She didn't even know what exactly she'd be doing. "I hope so, too." But she had a sneaking suspicion it would prove to be a disappointment.

oOo

Mason's phone beeped with an incoming text as he locked up the tire shop.

Rosemary heard from Liz. She made it okay.

It seemed he hadn't taken a deep breath since she left on Sunday. *Thank God*, he tapped back to Claire. The storm had hit Galena Landing hard, too, but the direct path had been further south. He could only imagine how it howled across the plains.

He headed toward his parents' farm west of town. Mondays and Tuesdays were his mom's days off work, and the twins caught the school bus there after kindergarten. Mom had invited Kass today. Not that she'd consulted Mason. Kass had told him on Sunday.

Now that he knew Liz was safe, could he set her out of his mind? She'd made a choice to walk away from both him and God. Pursuing her wasn't an option. He would've done something like that before the twins. Before Jesus had claimed him. Now, even in his piercing pain, he knew he couldn't do it. He could pray for her, but he had to let her find her own way.

Liz wasn't coming back.

Kass was here. Pretty, bright, and a believer who liked his kids. Interested in him, too, unless he missed his guess. For everyone's sake, he should focus on Kass. Maybe God, not Mom, had sent her into his life.

He drove into his parents' yard and parked beside Kass's white Rav4. He closed his eyes and rested his forehead on the steering wheel. *God? Please help me be open to Your leading. Help me to think of the kids' needs before my own, and Your will above all else.* He took a deep breath. *And please be with Liz and love her back to a relationship with You.*

Mason pushed open the car door to see Dad striding across the yard from the barn. "Hey, Dad."

"Hello, son. Good day at work?"

"Nothing out of the ordinary."

"Good, good." Dad pointed a thumb at the house and lowered his voice. "Your mother is up to something, you know."

A small smile poked the edges of Mason's mouth as he shut the car door and fell in step beside his father. "Yeah, I figured that out."

"She's just trying to help."

"I know."

Dad angled a look at him. "You okay with that?"

Mason shrugged. "So long as she doesn't push too hard. I know she's thinking of the kids."

"Don't sell yourself short." Dad punched him lightly on the arm. "Your mother wants what's best for you. A good, stable woman. She was worried when you paid so much attention to that Nemesek girl. She's a flighty one."

Mason blocked the farmhouse steps as he turned to face his father. "Dad, I know you two mean well, but whom I see is my decision, not yours."

"Your mother—"

"Both of you. That Nemesek girl is a woman, and her name is Liz. I've known her since we were kids, and it was good catching up with her over Christmas. We're friends, Dad. Nothing more." Not that he didn't want more, but no need to explain that to his parents at this stage of the game.

Liz was gone.

Kass was here.

Mason took a deep breath. Man, he hated being pushed. Always had. If he didn't already like Kass simply as a nice person, he'd grab those kids of his and be off the farm in two minutes flat. Even if it meant the diner instead of his mother's home-cooked meal. For today, he'd play along, and after that it would be his decision — his and Kass's and the twins' — if anything more would come of it. Not his parents.

"Supper's likely getting cold," Dad said mildly.

Mason gave him a sharp nod and mounted the steps. A moment later he entered the kitchen to the aroma of sweet-and-sour ribs and the sound of Christopher's laughter.

Huh. Usually his son was pretty glum here.

Kass and both kids sat on the floor around the coffee table, playing cards in hand.

"Go fish!" yelled Christopher.

"Hi, Daddy!" Avery jumped up and ran to Mason.

He scooped her up and nuzzled his cheek against hers.

"That tickles." She giggled. "Look, we're playing a game."

"So I see." He set Avery down, and Kass glanced over and smiled at him.

"It's time for supper now," Mom called. "Come to the table."

"But Grandma, I was winning." Christopher flopped dramatically to the floor and groaned.

"You can finish after you've eaten. Come now."

Avery tugged a laughing Kass to her feet and dragged her over to Mason. "I helped Miss Kass and Grandma make cookies.

Grandma said we can take some home."

"Are they good?" He rested his hand on his daughter's shoulder.

"They are scrumptious."

"I can hardly wait to try one."

Avery shook her head. "Grandma won't let you have one unless you eat all your supper."

He glanced at Kass to see her wide grin then looked back at Avery. "Supper smells so good I don't think it will be a problem. Did you help make that, too?"

"No. Grandma said to go play."

Mom pulled out a chair. "Kass, have a seat beside Christopher. Mason, you're on the end, and Avery, come sit by me."

Subtle, Mom. She'd get after him if he didn't seat Kass, so he did then took his chair around the corner. And yes, of course, they held hands for grace.

Kass's hand was soft. Her long tapered fingers were tipped with pale pink nails. But the touch didn't stir anything inside Mason. Too soon after Liz? Hard to know. He'd give it a try to please his mother and for the sake of the twins.

The chatter was light around the supper table. Mom had cooked corn to go with the rice and ribs bathed in a delectable sauce. There wasn't a mushroom in sight, and Mason didn't need to argue with Christopher over corn. Win-win.

It didn't escape Mason's notice that his daughter stared at Kass across the table with rapt attention as the visitor explained the monthly eating plan to his mom.

"So you're going to be cooking together?" Mom asked him, practically beaming.

"Sunday afternoon," he affirmed.

Mom's smile widened.

"We need to get together to finalize the menu before that."

Kass glanced up from her plate. "Are you free any evening this week? I'm afraid I work Wednesday through Saturday."

Yeah, Mason knew what days she was at the bakery. He shrugged. "Any evening is fine. I don't live a very fast-paced life."

His parents exchanged significant looks at the other end of the table. So not subtle. If either were closer, he'd give a poke with his toe.

"Thursday then? Let me bring supper. You're off at five, right? Same as me."

"Sounds good."

Christopher angled a sideways look at Kass. "What are you bringing?"

"Hmm." She narrowed her eyes at the five-year-old, a grin twitching her lips. "I was thinking of mushroom soup and maybe mushroom sauce over rice. I see you like rice."

"But I don't li—"

"Miss Kass is just teasing you, Christopher. Right, Miss Kass?"

Kass giggled as she nudged the boy. "Avery's right. I'm teasing."

Christopher scowled and crossed his arms.

"What do you like best, Christopher?"

She was a sly one, this Kass. Mason could do worse. Much worse. Maybe in time he'd find an attraction to her.

"I like meat and potatoes. And rice. I don't like vegetables." The boy glanced at his grandmother. "Broccoli is 'specially yucky."

"I see." Kass nodded thoughtfully. "How about you, Avery?"

"Hmm. I like macaroni and cheese. And I don't like broccoli very much, either."

She was winning over the twins. Maybe for most guys the old adage was true. *The way to a man's heart is through his stomach.*

For a single dad, the way to his heart lay through his kids.

They both liked Liz, too. He pushed the thought out. Liz wasn't here. She'd left them all, and he couldn't hold onto hope she'd return when every day Avery and Christopher were a little bit older. They needed a mom sooner rather than later.

"How about your dad, kids?" Kass's voice lowered into a conspiratorial tone. "What is his favorite food?"

Uh oh. Kass was smarter than he'd given credit for.

Chapter 22 --

*T*here's no point, you know." Vonnie's dull eyes focused on Liz. "It ain't gonna stay nice."

Liz scrubbed years' worth of smudges off the conference room window with a wad of paper towel. "Sure it will."

"No. Nobody cares."

Speak for yourself. Liz bit the words back before they came out. "I can't work in the midst of dirt and grime."

Vonnie shrugged. "It don't much matter."

Liz turned and looked at the girl. Really looked. Vonnie couldn't be more than twenty, if that. Way too young to be so jaded. "What's your position around here?" The girl seemed to have nothing better to do than watch Liz clean.

Vonnie's eyebrows rose. "You don't know?"

"I'm here to teach the employees English. You obviously don't need my help, but Larry hasn't given me a lot of details about who my students will be." It smelled like an entire nest of rats, though. And looking at Vonnie didn't alleviate Liz's worry.

"Yeah, the girls he brings in from the Philippines and Mexico."

"The girls..." Liz's words trailed off as her brain leaped to its obvious conclusion.

Vonnie smirked. "Yep. But don't think you're beyond being put to work. He don't need a full-time teacher, fer sure. Just enough so's the girls know what's expected of them."

Put to work? Expected of them?

Liz dumped the paper towels in the trash and reached for her coat. "Come with me, Vonnie."

The girl stayed in the chair. "Where you going?"

"Away. Not coming back."

"Larry ain't gonna like that."

"I don't care what Larry thinks." Liz did up the toggles and grabbed her purse. "Are you coming?"

Vonnie shook her head slowly. "Can't. Nowhere to go, anyhow."

"I'll help you." How? No clue. Liz had no idea how she'd help herself, let alone Vonnie.

"No, thanks. Have a nice life, though."

Liz wrenched the door open and bowled straight into a solid body. Larry's hands reached to grasp her arms. She kneed him then shoved as hard as she could. He staggered backward a step, eyes narrowing. She took the purse by its sturdy strap, prepared to swing it at his head. "Don't touch me."

Still bent over, he held up both hands. "You just surprised me is all. Where you going? You don't get off until five."

"I quit."

"Aw, you can't do that, baby." He looked past her into the conference room. "What, Vonnie telling tales out of turn?"

"Don't blame Vonnie for you being a sleaze bucket." Liz eyed the path to the door. "Told you, I quit. I'm gone." The quicker the better. She dashed past him.

Low laughter came from behind her. "Don't think the cops are interested, baby. They're not."

A moment later she blinked in the bright sunlight, the cold wind blasting against her. She ran down the block to her car, thankful she could beep the doors open. No need to fumble with keys.

The brick building was behind her. The job she'd come halfway across the country to accept. Tears burned Liz's eyes. She'd been so stupid. So desperate to get away from Galena Landing she hadn't done due diligence.

But now what? She was in a city far from anyone she knew with no resources. Just like when she'd deplaned in Bangkok. She'd landed on her feet then, though. Right? She could do it again.

The fuel light came on in her dashboard. This wasn't the same as Thailand at all. There she'd had a job. Here she could freeze to death without shelter. She couldn't keep sleeping in the car indefinitely.

Liz pulled in at the first gas station and fueled up the car. Then she went inside for a cup of coffee and a cheap meal. If they had wi-fi, she could log into the local job website and see what else was available.

At the counter, she opened her purse to pay for the coffee. She stared into the open wallet, her gut plummeting. Only one twenty? She'd had a couple of hundred in there. Must've been Vonnie. She closed her eyes a second and blinked back tears.

At least she hadn't been stupid enough to have all her cash in her purse. At least Vonnie had left her charge card in place. Live and learn... but man, she'd better learn quickly if she expected to live.

oOo

"This is yummy chili, Miss Kass." Avery smiled at Kass.

Christopher stared into his bowl, his nose curled. "Is it hot? I don't like spicy food."

Mason choked back a chuckle and caught Kass's grin.

"It's not very spicy." Kass pushed Christopher's food closer to him. "Have you even tried a bite?"

Christopher scowled. "This isn't meat and potatoes."

"That's enough, buddy," Mason said firmly. "There's meat and beans and corn and tomatoes. And Miss Kass made cornbread, too."

His son picked up his spoon and captured one kidney bean then glared at Mason for a second before putting it in his mouth.

"There, that wasn't so bad, was it?" Mason leveled his son a no-nonsense look.

"It's okay. I guess."

"High praise from a five-year old." Kass grinned at Mason.

"We're almost six," announced Avery. "In February."

"Really? What are you going to do on your birthday?"

Avery glanced at Mason. "I don't know. Daddy said he has secret plans."

Yeah, Erin. She was either going to be a terrific surprise or a nightmare. He should never have suggested she come for the twins' birthday. It would have been better on some random day that wouldn't taint their memories as badly. Too late now. Erin had texted him her arrival time at the Spokane airport a few days before the birthday. At least the twins would be in school, and they could have their first meeting in private.

Bad idea, Mason. Such a bad idea.

His gut clenched. He had too many women in his life. His mother, pushing him at Kass. Claire and Allison, holding out for Liz. Nobody rooting for Erin — not that he'd told anyone she was coming. Kass herself, making inroads with his kids.

And Avery, smiling at Kass between every bite.

It was almost enough to quit his job, pack up the twins, and move somewhere else where he could start over. Alone. But he had a safety net here. He couldn't yank the kids away, no matter how tempting.

Mason took a bite of the cornbread. A minute ago it had been sweet and warm and melting in his mouth. Now it tasted like cardboard. He forced another spoonful of chili to his mouth.

"I don't like surprises," mumbled Christopher.

Something snapped inside Mason. "Quit whining and eat your supper."

Christopher glanced at him and seemed to see he meant it. The boy straightened slightly and took a bite.

"I'm sure your daddy only has good surprises for you," Kass said brightly into the silence.

Right. She was such an optimist. Obviously believing she could have a future with him and the kids. Tonight he couldn't imagine it. Not even with the four of them sitting around a home-cooked meal in the farmhouse kitchen. If she was meant for him, shouldn't this feel right, somehow?

If only he'd met Kass before Liz returned. He might have fallen in love with her. Maybe he still could, but it would take time. He'd have to forget Liz first, setting aside the anguish that scraped his soul. She'd demanded what he could not give while refusing to take the step that would make it all possible. If only she'd turn back to God.

Mason cast a sidelong glance at Kass as she chatted with Avery. Kass was at least as pretty as Liz, long reddish curls instead of Liz's shoulder-length blond hair. A longer straighter nose than Liz's upturned button. Lips curved into a smile, but not lips that cried out to be kissed.

He closed his eyes for a second. *Lord, help me here. I don't know what to do.* Kass? Liz? Erin? Someone he hadn't met yet? Or maybe he needed to set aside his desire for a wife, a companion, a mother for his kids, and simply learn to be a better parent by himself.

That was likely his life lesson.

Until he looked again and saw the adoration in Avery's eyes as she replied to something Kass had said to her. Even Christopher had joined the conversation while his dad had completely checked out.

Being a better parent required paying attention. With an effort, Mason tracked the discussion and jumped in when he knew where it was going.

oOo

Mason jogged down the stairs and into the kitchen, where Kass stood at the sink, drying the last bowl.

She turned and smiled at him. "They're asleep?"

"Probably not, but they will be soon. Thanks for reading to them." This was the type of pictures he needed to fill his mind with: Kass with a twin snuggled on either side, reading them a chapter from their Bible storybook.

"No problem. They're great kids." She set the bowl in the cupboard, shut the door, and hung up the tea towel before turning back to him. "Shall we sit down and look over my menu ideas?" She glanced into the living room.

Another picture took shape in his mind, of him and Kass sitting close together on the sofa. He pointed at the table. "Let's do it in the kitchen. You'll have plenty of room to spread everything out here."

She glanced at the table then back at him, expression unreadable. "Oh, wait. I brought a special dessert for you and me." She went over to her bag by the door and retrieved two containers and a folder. "A little bird told me you love strawberry cheesecake, and we happened to have a couple of pieces left at the end of the day."

Mason stood in the middle of the floor. "That little bird must have been my mother."

Kass smiled as she slid each piece onto a plate then added a dollop of whipped cream to each. After perching half a berry on top of each, she handed one to him. "Yes, it was. Do you mind?"

Mason snagged two forks from the drawer and held out a chair for Kass before seating himself around the corner. Did they have to have this conversation tonight, when he was so muddled inside?

"You know my mother is trying to set us up."

Kass focused on slicing a sliver of cheesecake off with her fork. "I kind of figured."

"She thinks the kids need a mother. That I need a wife. She thinks it is her duty to make sure it all happens."

Kass pushed the bit of cheesecake around on the plate. "I see. What do *you* think?"

"About what? About you?"

She nodded slightly and darted him a glance.

"Kass, I-I don't know. I'm not sure I'm in a good space to commit to a relationship right now."

"Your mom said it was a long time since you'd heard from the twins' mother. That it wasn't likely she'd ever return."

Mason released a long breath. "There are a lot of things my mother doesn't know. I heard from Erin over Christmas."

"Do you still have feelings for her?"

"What? No. It's not that. It's just... she's the surprise. She's coming for the twins' birthday. I think it's a really bad idea, but I don't know how to say no. I mean, she's their mother."

"Oh." Kass cut another bite of cheesecake.

Mason noticed she hadn't eaten the first one yet. "I don't know if she'll want a bigger part of their life. I don't think so, but I can't know for sure. Legally she has no recourse."

"So it's complicated, but not insurmountable."

He stared at her. She was willing to work within those confines? Why again didn't he love this woman? He should. She was a gem.

"Mason, I..." Kass took a deep breath and met his gaze. "I like you a lot. I like Avery and Christopher."

His brain told him to run with it, but his heart and his body told him to run away, instead.

Her eyes fell as she caught his reaction, that slight pulling back he'd tried to curtail. "But I see it's not mutual."

"Kass." He waited until she looked up again then he pushed out what he could only hope was a warm smile. "I do like you, and I'm thankful to have you in my life. But I've made snap decisions before about women. Li—" He bit off Liz's name. "Like Erin. And others. I once had a reputation, but Jesus has saved me from my past. And with the twins — regardless of my mother's opinion — I can't afford to act quickly. There's too much at stake, and I need to know for sure I'm moving forward with God's blessing."

She nodded. "I want God's best, too."

Words he'd give anything to hear from Liz's lips. Almost anything. He pushed her back out of his mind. "Then can we just be friends for now? Maybe it will grow into more, given time." He doubted it. There wasn't any spark, but maybe a lasting love could grow without that initial attraction. How could he know for sure?

Kass slipped her hand over his. "Thanks. I'd like that."

Mason turned his palm to meet hers and gave it a squeeze before pulling away. He poked his chin toward the closed folder on the table as he picked up his fork. "Now, tell me about this menu plan."

Chapter 23 --

No, I'm sorry, but we're not hiring right now."

"Do you have experience in this field? We need someone who can hit the ground running."

"Try again in spring."

"Didn't the ad clearly say applicants needed the requisite degree?"

Back on the street for the umpteenth time in a week, Liz huffed a breath. It turned to fog in front of her before dissipating. Just like everything else.

Surely someone in a city the size of Des Moines was hiring. Surely there was a position she was suited to. She stepped around a woman slumped in a doorway.

Liz wasn't too many weeks from being that woman unless she found a job. The wad of cash in the trunk of her car was shrinking steadily. She needed fuel for the car so she could run it a bit at night to keep from freezing. She needed warm food here and there, to say nothing of coffee.

A sign on the snowy sidewalk offered a free meal. She angled a glance at the closed door. No windows afforded the opportunity to see the setup. What would she be expected to give in exchange? There'd be a catch somewhere. She thought of Larry, and her gut soured. There was always a catch.

Two hours later and chilled to the bone, she retraced her steps.

The sign still stood on the sidewalk, which had been recently shoveled. Liz's stomach growled.

She'd take a chance. She pulled the door open and stepped inside, all senses on alert.

A few people sat at one of several long tables. At the back of the space, a middle-aged man glanced up and smiled at her from behind a restaurant-style warming table. "Here for a meal? There's a bit left. Help yourself."

Savory aromas wafted toward her and tugged her forward. "What's the catch?"

The man chuckled. "No catch. I'm Warren, and I'm glad to meet you. There's bowls over on the end. Help yourself to some stew and a roll."

Liz eyed him, and he backed away from the table. She filled a bowl, grabbed a roll, and found a spot with her back to the wall where she could keep an eye on him and the others. Not that anyone looked like a threat, but she didn't want to find out the hard way. Not after Larry.

A woman about her mom's age came from a door at the back, carrying two cups. She scooted one across to Liz. "Want a coffee?"

Did she ever. "Thanks."

The woman settled into a chair across from Liz. "I don't believe we've met. My name's Linda Thompson. Warren's my husband."

"I'm Liz." She took a big bite of the stew, laden with savory root vegetables. It was hot, filling, and reasonably tasty.

"We're open every day for those who need a warm meal and a place out of that nasty winter wind."

Liz eyed the woman. "Why?"

Linda's face wrinkled when she smiled. "Why not? The good Lord has given us so much, we want to give in return."

The food soured. The good Lord. Liz should've known. "So is

this the Salvation Army, or what?"

"Something similar, but not run by them." Linda sipped her coffee. "How are you doing, Liz? Is there anything you need help with?"

She probably looked the homeless part pretty well. No matter how hard she tried to keep clean at the truck stop showers, she couldn't pamper herself the way she'd always done.

"I'm doing okay. I just need a job. Do you know anyone who's hiring?"

Linda's lips pursed together as she shook her head slowly. "I don't know of anything right now. Have you checked the paper?"

Liz nodded and dipped her roll into the stew before eating a bite.

"They've got a website for employment opportunities, too. There's wi-fi here if that helps."

"That does help. I've had trouble finding consistent Internet." The jerk at the truck stop had changed the password on the weekend. Probably only to keep her from using it. She hadn't dared ask for the new one.

"Other than that, it's a matter of avoiding scams while going from business to business." Linda eyed her.

Liz sighed. "Yes, the job I came here for proved to be a front for something else. I didn't stick around long enough to figure out exactly what."

Linda's hand, callused yet warm, covered hers. "I'm sorry, dearie."

"Yeah." What was keeping Liz in Des Moines? She should head south where it was warmer. Or back to Idaho. Where her parents and Mason could feel sorry for her and say *I told you so*.

Surely she could find an acceptable job while she weighed her options. Mason wasn't one of those options. She needed to get him right out of her head, but the memory of his smoldering gaze helped keep her warm. Made her feel like a valuable person.

He cared about her. Maybe even loved her, but he loved God more.

"Take your time." Linda levered out of the chair. "Feel free to drop back tomorrow, too, if you're in this part of downtown."

"Thanks." Liz lifted her spoon. "This is really good, and very welcome."

Linda smiled. "Enjoy." She wandered to the next table and engaged an older man in conversation.

Liz watched a minute, though she couldn't overhear. Soon she shrugged and pulled her phone out of her coat's inside pocket. She logged in through the password-free wi-fi.

One text from Mason. Surprise. An email from Mom and another from Zach, plus one from Allison. Liz clicked away without reading any of them and switched to the Internet browser button to check employment listings.

Maybe today there'd be something just right for her.

o0o

Over the past week, Mason had seen Kass a few times. He'd popped by the bakery for lunch twice, but of course she'd been busy. He'd stopped short of inviting her out to the farm for a meal. Asking her for a date had crossed his mind, but he hadn't acted on it. *Just friends* didn't date. People without chemistry shouldn't date.

He and the kids were eating better, though. They'd all spent Sunday afternoon in the Green Acres kitchen assembling meals he could finish off quickly after work, with nary a mushroom in sight.

Want to come for dinner tonight?

Claire again. Mason, just home from work, stared at his phone.

We've got something to discuss with you.

193

Sounded ominous. *Will Kass be there?*

Do you want her to be?

Not really. Just wondering.

Not this time. This isn't about her unless you want it to be.

Such a helpful reply. *I do have supper planned.* Thanks to Kass. All he needed to do was pop it in the oven before walking over to collect the twins.

LOL. Stick it in the fridge for tomorrow. Pls say you'll come.

Fine. I'll be there.

He walked over on the packed trail between the two farms. Christopher and Finnley whooshed down the drive on their sleds. Zach and Brent had given up keeping the upper drive cleared with so much snow. Everyone walked in from the main parking area this winter.

"Supper's ready," Mason told the boys.

"One more run!" yelled Christopher, cheeks pink from the cold.

"Only one more. Then come in."

"Okay." Both boys grabbed the ropes from their sleds and trudged up the path again.

Mason went into the house and removed his boots and jacket.

"Hey, Waterman!" greeted Zach.

"Oh, man. Your night in the kitchen? Claire didn't warn me."

Avery ran over from the great room for a quick hug then dashed back to where she and Maddie were playing with dolls.

"My good wife is keeping me on track here. Meatloaf and baked potatoes will be out of the oven in a few minutes." Zach held up a bowl. "I'm on coleslaw."

Mason slid onto a tall stool at the peninsula.

"Girls!" called Jo. "Want to ring the gong?"

"Yay!" yelled Avery. Both girls scrambled into boots and raced outside. A minute later the dinner gong echoed across the farm.

Mason heard it nearly every night from next door. Usually it wasn't for him.

"Heard from Liz lately?" Zach asked.

Mason shook his head. "Not since she left. You?"

Zach frowned as he stirred the cabbage and carrot mix. "No. I've emailed her a couple of times, but she hasn't answered. Nor does she pick up when Mom calls her."

"I've texted a time or two," Mason admitted. "She hasn't replied."

"I hope she's okay." Zach gave a wry grin as he shook his head. "She's a stubborn one."

"All we can do is pray for her."

"There should be more."

"Yeah, but doesn't she have to welcome it? Or at least allow it?"

Zach let out a long breath. "I have to go out to Des Moines for a veterinarian conference next week. It will kill me if she keeps avoiding all contact. She's my kid sister, and I'm worried about her, you know?"

"It's probably my fault."

The other man stopped mixing the dressing. "How so?"

The clomp of boots on the deck saved Mason from needing to respond. He just shrugged and turned to greet the other Green Acres team members as they came in, shedding outerwear and making room for the next wave. Noel and Claire entered from the other wing of the straw bale house. Claire shot him a quick grin before tucking her son into his high chair, while Noel snagged John off the floor and did the same.

Soon everyone gathered around the long table, and Zach asked the blessing over the food, the conversation, and his sister.

Whatever the big discussion was about, Mason needed to be patient until the children had gone off to play again after the meal. He eyed the meatloaf. That would be something he could prepare in advance, right? Maybe not baked potatoes, though. He was still trying to figure out what froze well and what didn't.

Finally the meal was cleared away and the kids had scooted off to the great room.

Noel leaned toward Mason. "We've been talking." He circled the table with his finger, indicating each gathered adult. "We'd like to invite you to be part of the Green Acres team on a permanent basis."

If a kick to the gut could feel welcome, this was it. What he'd been braced for, he couldn't have said. "Really? But I have a job, and no skills you guys need."

"Everyone brings something different to the group. Some are good cooks." Sierra grinned at Zach. "And this was a pretty decent dinner, buddy."

"Some are teachers," Chelsea put in. "Some are organizers."

"Some of us are simply good at doing what we're told." Keanan spread his hands on the table as everyone chuckled.

"All of us work hard to make it happen," added Jo. "No slackers allowed."

"Zach and I both work off the farm." Brent caressed Allison's shoulder. "When there's lots going on, it makes for long days, but I wouldn't trade it for anything."

"I appreciate the offer, but I still don't really know why you'd want me."

"You and the twins have become part of our family," said Jo simply. "When the topic came up, we were all immediately agreed."

If only it were really true that he and Jo belonged to the same family. She was happily married to Liz's brother. A knife went through his heart again. How could he ever get over Liz when her family surrounded him?

But leaving Galena Landing again with the twins was out of the question. He was done running. This was where God wanted him. Did that include Green Acres itself?

From meeting Allison and Finnley at the lake soon after his return, he'd been inextricably drawn into the group here. But it was too big a decision to make hastily. "Please lay out everything you're thinking of," he said at last. "Then give me a few days to pray about it. But either way, know I'm really honored."

"One more thing," said Gabe. "You need to know that we won't evict you from the farmhouse if you decide against it. No strings, Waterman."

"Thanks." Mason's throat choked up. "I can't tell you all how much this means to me."

"We'll get more work out of you," Zach said with a chuckle. "But here. Let's go over everything. Rubachuk, you have the documents?"

Gabe nodded and spread a folder open on the table. "All here."

To think these wonderful men and women wanted to call him brother. Wanted to be a permanent part of Christopher and Avery's life. Mason shook his head as he focused on Gabe's words.

Chapter 24 ---

*W*aterman, spill." Zach stripped off gloves and knit cap in the farmhouse kitchen.

"Spill what? And shush, man. The twins just went to bed."

"Sorry." Zach shed his coat. "I'm so worried about my sister I'm not thinking straight."

"Did you hear from her?"

"No." Zach's eyes bored into his. "Have you?"

Mason shook his head. "But then, there'd be no reason for her to contact me." He indicated the kitchen table. "Have a seat. Want coffee?"

Zach scrubbed his hand through his hair. "Better not. I'm already so wired sleep is unlikely, but there's no point in making sure."

"Tea then? Claire gave me some chamomile."

"Yeah, sure. Sounds good."

Mason turned to put on tea. "When's the last anyone heard from Liz?"

"Two weeks. We know she got to Des Moines safely, and that's about it. She was going to call Mom after her first day at work, but she didn't."

Not good. "Maybe she lost her phone?"

"And her laptop with its email program? Not likely. The

veterinary clinic is dead easy to find online, at the very least."

Mason nodded slowly.

"Besides, her phone is charged. It rings three times before going to voice mail. So it seems unlikely it's not on her."

"Makes sense."

"What I want to know is why, Waterman? Why would she leave in the dead of winter and not stay in touch? What caused her to run?"

Zach's gaze bored into Mason's. "And one more thing. Is it related to why she ran eleven years ago? I can't help wondering if there's a common denominator."

The look in Zach's eyes was not just that of a concerned brother. He was on Mason's doorstep for a reason. He knew. Not the details, most likely, but that Mason was linked in some way.

The only question was, did he owe it to Liz to keep quiet? Or was it his story to tell? If she were in some kind of danger, wasn't it Mason's duty to provide all the clues he had?

Not that he had any, really. He could certainly explain why she'd fled — both times — but not why she'd disappeared from contact, unless it was to punish him.

Mason spooned honey into two cups of tea, set them on the table, and sat across from his friend. He stared into his tea for a long moment. *God? I could use some help here. But I think Liz needs You even more than I do. Please give me words, and please help Zach find Liz.*

He raised his eyes to meet Zach's. "It's a long story, and I'm not sure it's of any help."

Zach's gaze didn't flicker. "I've got time."

"I've kept quiet because it didn't feel like my story to tell. I'd like to ask you to keep it under your hat, but maybe we're beyond that point by now."

"Spit it out, Waterman."

"Liz and I were in the same class all through school. She was such a good little girl I had no time for her." Mason shrugged. "For some reason I cannot explain, I was popular. Everyone wanted to be my friend. Play with me at recess. Sit with me in the lunchroom. And then we hit high school."

"Go on," Zach said into the lingering silence.

"Every girl I asked out was happy to date me. I, uh, had sex with many of them. You have to understand I didn't know Jesus then."

Zach's jaw twitched. "And then..."

"Some of the guys asked Liz out, but she refused. We all figured she was just playing holier-than-thou." Mason rubbed his day-old scruff and shook his head. "She *was* better than us."

Zach said nothing, but neither did his piercing gaze leave Mason's face.

"So, uh, the guys started betting on whether or not she'd go out with me. Have sex. Seemed obvious to everyone that she liked me, and if anyone was going to get anywhere with her, it would be me."

"Uh huh."

Man, that wasn't an encouraging sound. "So, I, uh, asked her to our senior party."

"And she said yes." Zach's voice was flat and hard.

Mason nodded. "She said yes."

He'd accepted high-fives right in front of her. And afterward... Mason chewed his lip and glanced at Zach. "Afterward, we went out along the river and had sex. She'd been a virgin, but she gave herself to me willingly."

No response.

"I told my friends I'd won the bet. By noon the next day the news had swept the school, and Liz was the laughing stock."

"Do you have any idea how much I'd like to deck you right now?"

"Bring it. I deserve that and more."

Zach shook his head, but his knuckles remained white as he clenched the mug of tea.

"She left town a few days later, right after graduation. I didn't see her again until that day in your parents' kitchen."

"You've told me what the intervening years were like for you. How Jesus met you and saved you from the life you'd been leading." Zach ran a shaking hand through his hair. "But Liz. I didn't know. What kind of brother was I? Why didn't I even know something was wrong?"

Zach had been at Washington State, studying hard to get one of the coveted spots into veterinary college.

"Look, if you guys want to retract the invitation to join Green Acres, I understand. I can find another house to rent. Or I can leave town. Whatever you want."

"No, Waterman. That's not a solution." Zach closed his eyes for a moment. When he opened them again, he looked straight at Mason. "Do you know anything about her years in Thailand?"

"Not more than she told everyone when she showed her photos that day."

"Rumor has it that you two spent a lot of time together when the water was froze up here."

Mason nodded slowly. "We talked late into the night several times. I asked Liz to forgive me."

Zach's eyebrows rose. "Did she?"

"She said so. It's God she can't forgive."

"Okaaay. Allison offered her a temp job here, but she left anyway. Any idea why?"

Mason chewed on his lip. "Yeah?"

"Waterman, don't make me beat it out of you. I don't think there's much you can add to what you've already said. What you've already done to my sister."

"She was looking for an excuse to stay."

"Yet she left."

Did Mason have to spell everything out for Zach? Apparently. "She wanted to, uh, come upstairs with me, and I said no."

Zach's fist hit the table.

oOo

Maybe today would be the day Liz would find a job. A woman needed to stay positive.

She peered into the mirror of the truck stop washroom and carefully applied her makeup, trying to hide the dark circles under her eyes and the way her cheeks had hollowed out. The new coral sweater she'd received for Christmas — had that been only a month ago? — no longer molded to her curves but hung on her thinning frame. She'd already picked up a package of safety pins to tuck in the waistband of her dress pants.

Gel in her hair helped a little. Liz eyed herself in the mirror speculatively. If she owned a business, would she hire the person staring back? Sure she would. Someone had to.

She gathered the few items she'd brought into the building with her and wove her way through aisles of junk food toward the exit. The paunchy man behind the till smirked at her.

"Have a nice day, Maurice." She'd be pleasant to the man if it killed her. When she'd asked him for a job, he'd offered her *more* and seemed offended when she'd turned him down. This truck stop had the best facilities closest to the downtown core. She couldn't afford to annoy him further.

No reply from Maurice, but that wasn't a huge shock. Liz pushed open the door to the swirling white in the parking lot. Man, if she didn't get a job today, she was heading south. Winter was terrific if you weren't living in your car. Winter was terrific in Galena Landing, she amended mentally, remembering the startling beauty of the hoar frost and the glee on the kids' faces as they chased each other in the deep snow. Winter in the city was something else again.

She trudged around the corner of the building just in time to see a tow truck at the far exit pulling a white car. Her gaze shot to where she'd left her vehicle.

Gone.

No way. Liz swallowed her fury and ran toward the tow truck, but it already signaled a right turn onto the highway. She slipped on the ice, falling hard onto both hands in the middle of the parking lot. The truck disappeared.

This absolutely could not be happening. Could there be a more final last straw than this? Hot tears poured down her face.

Oh, God.

Though your sins be as scarlet, they will be as white as snow.

She didn't want to see anything as white as snow ever again. But how could she leave Des Moines without her car? Wait! It was even worse. The remains of her stash was in that trunk. She didn't keep much in her wallet.

Liz slammed her fist against the icy pavement, welcoming the fierce pain.

Honnnnnnnnnnnk.

A semi-truck loomed in front of her, and Liz scrambled out of its way. The contents of her gear bag lay scattered where she'd fallen, but the truck rolled right over the spot before stopping. The driver's window slid down and a burly older man peered out at her. "You okay, sweetheart?"

"I just slipped on the ice is all." Liar.

"It's sure slick, all right. Hope your day gets better." The window rose between them as he put the truck into gear and eased forward.

Yeah, she hoped so, too. Because there weren't all that many ways it could get worse.

When all eighteen wheels had passed over the spot where she'd fallen, she retrieved the contents of her bag. The driver had somehow missed most of the items, but her foundation and bottle of gel had both been crushed.

Liz scooped the remains and tossed them in the trash, catching sight of her scraped, bleeding hand. She leaned against the side of the building, hopefully out of Maurice's sight, closed her eyes, and tried to regain control of her breathing.

What had she done to deserve all this? Really?

I'm waiting for you, my child.

Her eyes sprang open, but no one stood before her.

Stop trying to do it all on your own, and come home. Accept your Father's love for you.

The voice was not Dad's. Not Steve Nemesek. It was the other father speaking. God.

"I don't really want to talk to You," she whispered. "You abandoned me when I needed You most."

No, my child. It is you who turned your back. I am right here, waiting.

Liz pushed off the side of the building. "It's not that easy."

It is that easy.

Liz summoned back her anger and strode around the corner and into the truck stop. She marched right up to the till and stared at Maurice. "What are you trying to prove? Call that driver and have my car returned this minute."

His smirk widened. "What driver?"

"You had my car towed."

"It was in a no-parking zone."

"I didn't see any signs."

"It's marked on the pavement. You know, them yellow stripes?"

She narrowed her gaze. "The ones covered with snow and ice?"

"It's possible."

"Why didn't you just ask me to move the car?"

Maurice leaned closer, his acrid breath wafting in her face.

"You can't live at a truck stop, cupcake."

"Hello? I was right here. You could've used words. You know, spoken verbal sentences to tell me to move my car." She should've known. Should've seen the signs she'd overstayed her welcome. She'd never dreamed he'd have her car towed without so much as a threat, though.

He slid a business card across the counter at her. "Give 'em a call yourself. They'll let you have it back. For a fee."

Liz's gut clenched. "How much?"

"How should I know? I'm a law-abiding citizen. Never had my car impounded."

Law-abiding? As if.

Maurice laid his hand on top of hers when she reached for the card. "I'm sure we can work something out, cupcake."

Liz yanked the card away and shoved it in her pocket. "I don't think so."

Maurice's eyes hardened. "Have it your way. Don't come back here again."

"No worries. I won't. Ever." She gathered what was left of her dignity and her belongings and strode out the door into the sub-zero wind. Walking the five miles to Linda and Warren's would keep her warm. Or was the impound lot closer?

One thing was certain. She'd wistfully imagined God's voice back there. It was plenty obvious He didn't care a fig for what happened to her.

Chapter 25 --

*F*ury kept Liz going for the first frozen mile. Then she stepped into a doorway alcove and pulled out her phone and the business card.

The phone that was on 4% battery. It was too cold to keep a charge, much like her. She'd planned to spend long enough at the soup kitchen today to get it charged.

The cord was in the car.

Liz sagged against the brick wall and closed her eyes. She could spend that 4% on calling her parents, or she could spend it trying to get her car back. And exactly what could her parents do to help her? Nothing. They were thousands of miles away.

She wasn't ready to let them see how far she'd fallen. No. She'd call the towing company. Her fingers trembled as she pushed the buttons. *Don't die now...*

"Hi, my name is Elizabeth Nemesek, and I think you might have my car." She rattled off the license plate number, make, and model.

"Let me take a look." The guy sounded bored.

Silence for a long moment. Silence that meant her battery was disappearing without anything to show for it.

"Nope, don't got a record of that."

"But I saw your business name on the door of the tow truck."

"George might not be back with it yet. Sometimes it takes a

bit of time to get them all entered in the computer. Give a call back in a couple of hours."

Two percent battery remaining. Great. Liz thumbed off the phone, put her head into the wind, and began her trek once again. Fifteen blocks later, her phone rang. She looked at the display and saw her brother's name. Should she answer?

While she hesitated, the screen went black.

oOo

The mood at Green Acres was somber at their emergency noon-hour meeting. Mason wasn't the only one watching Zach pace the great room.

"This is crazy." Zach slammed a hand against the wall. "How can she have just disappeared?"

"Two possibilities. She *can't* answer, or she *won't* answer." Jo gave Mason a pointed glare.

"If she's choosing not to, there isn't much we can do about it," Claire put in reasonably.

Chelsea dabbed her eyes with a tissue. "But what if something happened to her?"

This was where Mason's mind had been going more and more. What if it wasn't Liz's choice?

"There are ways to search." Allison flipped open her laptop. "We can call the police in Des Moines. We can try the hospitals."

Chelsea pulled out her phone. "Give me a number."

Allison read off the police department number. Then she assigned hospital numbers to several others.

Mason sank deep into the leather chair and closed his eyes. All he could do was pray. Pray one of these calls had results they could act on.

None of them did.

"She might not have stayed in Des Moines," said Sierra. "She could be anywhere, really."

"But this is crazy! I'm going to be in the city for three days. Yeah, I'm supposed to be in meetings, but I'd skip them all to find her." Zach grimaced.

A slow thought niggled at the back of Mason's mind and then erupted. "If I can leave the kids with Allison or someone, I'll go with you. I'll pound the pavement while you're in meetings."

"You *what*, Waterman?"

"I'm the reason she's gone." He choked out the words. How much had Zach told the others? By the way Jo treated him, she knew. But the others?

"How's that, Mason?" Claire's voice was gentle.

"Zach didn't tell everyone about our talk last night?"

Heads around the room shook as his friends glanced between them. Would they still be his friends? Not only that, but Rosemary and Steve were here as well. Liz's parents.

Mason focused on Steve as he recited the short version of his relationship with Liz. "I wronged your daughter," he said at last. "Can you ever forgive me?"

Steve's fingers tightened around Rosemary's. The couple exchanged a look then Steve turned back to Mason. "We forgive you, son, as God has forgiven us. All of us have sinned, and God doesn't categorize those sins into hierarchy. You have asked His forgiveness and received it. I cannot withhold mine."

Mason stared at his feet. "I don't deserve it."

"None of us do," put in Rosemary mildly. "But this explains a lot."

"Steve's right," said Noel. "Each of us here has had a struggle. We've all fallen short of God's standards. I forgive you, brother."

"I do, too," said Claire softly. Others murmured similar words.

Tears blurred Mason's vision. The next thing he knew, a gentle hand rested on his shoulder. Steve's. Then more hands touched him.

"Father, I escort Your child to Your throne." Steve's deep voice spoke into the hushed room. "I thank You for bringing Mason into relationship with You. I thank You for saving him and making him a new creature through Jesus' blood."

The anguish in Mason's soul eased with every word from Steve's lips.

"Lord, you know where my little girl is." Steve's voice broke. "You know what she's going through. Please forgive me for failing her."

"Yes, Lord, me, too," whispered Zach.

Tears dribbled down Mason's cheeks. He'd failed her the worst.

"God, I believe You are working in Lizzie's life," Steve went on. "If she did not feel the prodding of the Holy Spirit, she wouldn't need to run away. I claim Your victory over her soul. Please work in her life and turn her eyes back to You. Please put God-fearing people in her path. We rest her in Your hands, Lord. You love her more than we do."

Hands still touched Mason's head, arms, and legs as several other team members prayed for him. Prayed for Liz. His body warmed, and a level of peace he hadn't felt in days settled on him.

One by one, the hands were removed, but the peace remained. And with it, an even more certain sense he needed to go to Des Moines. Zach had his meetings. Besides, the man had never lived in any city's seamier side. Mason had. Not in Des Moines, but he'd find his way around. If things had gone really wrong for Liz, he'd find her.

"What airline are you flying?" he asked Zach.

"You're serious."

"Totally."

"Of course the twins can stay with us." Allison glanced at Brent, who nodded. "They can catch the school bus just as easily from here as from next door."

"What company did she accept that job from?" asked Claire. "Anyone get a name?"

Mason wracked his brain. "Pretty sure she never told me. But they have a head office in Vegas."

Sierra shook her head. "That's not enough to go on."

"And all the information would be on her laptop and her phone. Neither of which we have access to." Jo tapped her fingers, deep in thought.

"What recruiting company was it?" asked Noel.

Mason looked around the group, where heads shook in unison. He didn't know, either.

"How many can there be?" asked Chelsea. "It can't take that long to call each one and see if she was registered with them."

"Good point." Jo nodded. "I'll help work our way through them."

"They probably won't release that information," said Sierra. "Confidentiality and all that."

Chelsea glanced at her sister. "It's worth a shot, especially if we say she accepted a position and then went missing."

"Yeah, maybe."

"Delta." Zach's voice came from close beside him.

Mason blinked. "Huh?"

"You asked about my flight."

"Oh. Right. Sorry."

"Leaves at one-thirty-six. One hour stop in Minneapolis. I don't have the flight number on me."

Mason pulled out his phone and toggled the browser on. "I can find it."

"Can we pay for your flight, son?" asked Steve.

"No, it's okay. I've got it." His charge card had space, and he'd pay it off, even if it took a few months. Anything for Liz.

Rosemary's dry voice interrupted. "We insist. She's our daughter. If Steve was in any position to go, he'd be there in a heartbeat."

They should hate him. God's grace was bigger. "Thank you. That would be a huge help." His fingers danced on the phone's screen as he found Zach's flight and tapped to purchase a ticket. A seat was available! *Thank You, God*. He handed the phone to Rosemary to complete the payment section.

Uh. He'd better get back to work so he could ask Roger for the rest of the week off. The flight's confirmation number flashed on his screen as Rosemary passed it back.

More like *tell* Roger. How would that go over?

oOo

Liz staggered in the soup kitchen door, as frozen as juice concentrate. Her cheeks were numb, and she'd lost feeling in her toes a while back.

"Liz! Linda and I hoped you wouldn't be in today. That you'd find a warm place to hole up. We must be pushing minus twenty out there." Warren steered her to a table near a heat register. "Are you okay?"

Liz stared at him, trying to make sense of the question. What did okay even mean? She shook her head slowly, sluggishly. "So cold," she murmured.

"Have you eaten anything today?" Linda hovered in front of her.

Had she? "Dunno."

"Go heat up a cup of broth," Linda said to Warren. "Now, dearie, we need to get your boots off and have a look at your feet. How are your fingers?"

Liz pulled trembling hands from the depths of her pockets and held them out for inspection.

"Child, where are your gloves? I know you have some." Linda clasped one of Liz's hands between both of hers.

"In my c-car."

"And where's that?"

"I don't know. Th-they towed it."

"Oh, dearie." Compassion flowed from Linda's voice. "There you are, Warren. Can you get Liz's boots off? Here, child, have a sip. Warren heated it, but not too much. We want to warm you, not scald you."

Warren knelt in front of Liz and unzipped one boot before tipping it and pulling it off her foot. Then the other. How could the room feel even colder without them?

"You sit with her for a minute, Warren. I'm going to get some warm blankets. Don't worry, dearie. We'll get you warmed up. I don't think you've done any permanent damage."

Did that mean none of her toes had frozen off? They were going to hurt like crazy as they thawed. "I'm s-sorry." Great, now her teeth were chattering.

"For what?" Warren asked as Linda bustled away.

For everything? For being such a nuisance? For living? "For imposing on you."

"You're not an imposition, Liz. Never. You and others like you are the very reason Linda and I are here. To make a difference. To be God's hands and feet to those in need."

Well, Liz was in need. Pretty hard to deny.

"Here, have a sip of the broth. We need to start getting some heat inside of you. Finish this, and I'll get you a coffee."

Liz forced a smile. After even this short time, Warren knew it was coffee she really craved. If she had to get through a mug of beef broth to get there, she'd do it. She swished the warm liquid in her mouth for a few seconds before swallowing.

"You said your car was towed? What happened?"

"I was in the truck stop having a shower when the owner decided I'd been there too much, I guess. I tried to stop the tow truck as he drove away. When I called, the guy said they had no record of my car." Liz closed her eyes. "And then my phone died."

"I see." Warren sounded thoughtful. "Which impound company?"

Liz pried unwilling fingers from around the warm mug and dug into her coat pocket. She laid the business card on the table as another shuddering spasm wracked her.

"Here, dearie." Linda wrapped a large blanket around Liz's shoulders then tucked another around her feet.

"How did you get them so warm?"

"Just tossed them in the dryer for a few minutes. I can do that as many times as needed."

The fuzzy warmth cradled Liz. Maybe, just maybe, sometime in the vague and distant future, she wouldn't be frozen straight through. She had a gulp of the warm broth then buried her hands in the depths of the blanket.

Warren chuckled. "Here, girl. I'll get you a coffee. The car can wait another half hour or so. It's not going anywhere."

Chapter 26 --

*M*ason stomped the snow off his boots at the back door to the tire shop after his extended lunch break.

Roger glanced at the clock. "You're late."

"Yeah, I know. I'm sorry."

"What happened that was so important? One of the kids sick?"

"No." Mason shook his head and took a deep breath. Here went nothing. "I don't suppose you know the Nemesek family?"

"The vet?"

"Yes, them. They've lived in the Galena Valley for decades. Anyway, their youngest daughter — Zach's sister — has gone missing."

Roger frowned, clearly puzzled.

"So..." Mason shot up a prayer. "I need the rest of the week off work. Zach and I are flying out to Des Moines tomorrow to try to find her."

"To Des Moines."

"That's where she was last known to be, about ten days ago."

Roger tipped his head, still frowning. "I'm sorry for the family, but what's that got to do with you? You don't have any vacation time accumulated, Waterman. And even if you did, we need to plan stuff like that in advance."

"Is the shop busy right now?"

"That's beside the point."

"Look, I know there's not much scheduled. If I take a few days off without pay, it will save you money. And I really need to go."

"Didn't know you were independently wealthy, man. Thought you needed this job."

"I do need it." Mason forced himself to meet Roger's eyes. He didn't want to lose his job over this. How could he have felt so strongly that he needed to go find Liz if it wasn't meant to be?

Trust Me.

"This isn't the way a man who needs a job acts, Waterman. He doesn't come in and demand time off with no notice."

"I understand, but emergencies don't come on a schedule."

"So this is an emergency."

"Yes."

"To go chase a woman who obviously doesn't want to be found. Is she cute, Waterman?"

"That is completely not part of the equation, Rog."

Roger's eyebrows rose as he leaned back in his desk chair. "So this is a romantic endeavor."

"Probably not. She just needs help."

"Why you?"

An interesting question, and one with no easy answer. Mason took a deep breath. "I need to do this, Roger. Are you going to fire me for it?"

"Would you go anyway?"

Mason's head swam. How had they gotten to this point?

Trust Me.

"I'm sorry, but yes. Though I'd prefer my record of employment said I quit instead."

Roger swore. "You're dead serious."

"Yes. I am." How he was going to pay rent and feed his kids without this job, he didn't know. Maybe he could work full time at the farm. Some of them did.

"Waterman, you're back on the clock next Monday at nine. If you're not here, you are definitely fired. I can't run a business with workers who show up only when they feel like it."

His lungs found air. "Thanks, Roger. I'll be here."

"I'm no bleeding heart, man. Next time the answer is no. The only emergencies from here out are deaths in the family."

"I understand."

Hopefully an emergency like that would be a very long time coming.

oOo

"Now let's see if we can find a cord for your phone." Warren dumped out a bag of cords. "People forget them here all the time, so we have quite a selection."

Liz's fingers still throbbed from the ebbing chill as she dug her phone out of her coat pocket.

He took it and turned it to the business end. "Hmm. This one's state-of-the-art. Not too many folks who wander in here can afford a phone like this."

Did that require a reply? Liz knew how far she'd fallen when her only friends ran a soup kitchen for street people. Oh. Realization shot through her. Without her car, where would she sleep? No. She'd get it back today and be more careful where she parked in the future. Definitely not at that truck stop.

Warren whistled tunelessly as he searched for a match. He shook his head. "Doesn't look like we've got the right one."

The door opened and two elderly men entered, the wind swirling in around them. The temperature in the room dropped ten degrees instantly.

Liz shivered. "Where's the nearest store I can get a replacement?" And how much might one cost? She was almost out of cash. Even with access to her car, her stash had been dwindling rapidly. Without it? Dire.

"This brand? West Des Moines, unless there's a kiosk in a downtown mall. Too far to walk, at least in this weather, but you might be able to catch the bus."

How much farther than she'd already walked today? Not that she wanted a repeat.

"Well, here. You can use my phone to call about your car. Then we'll go from there." Warren slid his across the table.

Tears prickled Liz's eyes. "Thanks." She keyed in the number again. The same bored man answered.

"Yep, we got that car," he said to her repeated inquiry.

"How can I get it released?"

"No sweat. Show up before five o'clock with one hundred eighty-five in cash. Oh, plus twenty-five. You'll also need your registration and driver's license."

"Two ten? Cash?" She hated how her voice squeaked. Was he just making up numbers now?

"Yep. Good math skills." He chuckled.

Liz swallowed hard. Two ten. "My registration and driver's license are in the car, so I'll need access to that first."

"Not the way it works, lady. You'll need proof of ownership and some ID before we go out back."

"I have the keys."

He chuckled again. "Sorry, lady. I don't make the rules. You don't have access to the car until you prove you own it."

Her patience was wearing thin. "Who carries their registration around in their pocket?"

"Most folks have other paperwork at home. Or get a copy from their insurance company." She could almost hear him shrug. "Doesn't much matter to me how you get it."

Most people actually had a home. She didn't. Not anymore. She thought with longing of the cozy duplex on her brother's farm. Where they'd offered her a job. But no, she had to do her own thing. She shoved the memory away. "So you're saying I can't get anything out of my car before I've proved to your satisfaction that I'm the owner."

"Yep. And paid up, of course."

"Of course." She sure didn't have two hundred bucks in her pocket. After Vonnie, she'd kept it down to a couple of twenties. Where was she going to get the funds? In cash, no less. If she could borrow it from someone — Warren, maybe? — she could repay him from the trunk.

"Oh, I should tell you. We add twenty-five bucks a day for storage."

Of course it would be a moving target. Was this even legal?

"Anything else, lady? Other line's ringing."

"Uh, no. Thanks."

He laughed and the line went dead.

Had she seriously just thanked a highway robber who'd explained his ransom demands? Liz slowly set the phone down on the table.

Warren met her gaze. "What's the damages?"

"Two ten. Today before five. Tomorrow it will be two thirty-five instead." It was already well past noon. She cringed. Better count on the extra.

"Anything else?"

Liz's shoulder's sagged. "Registration. Driver's license or other identification. All of which is in the car. I'd gone into the truck stop to have a shower, for goodness sake. I didn't take all my belongings."

"Okay, first things first. Where is your car registered?"

"California."

Warren shook his head with a tiny smile. "Shoulda stayed there until spring, hey? If you know the name of the company there, get them to fax it over."

Somebody still had a fax machine? Liz hadn't seen one in years. But wait. She needed Kara. All she knew was that the

DMV was within walking distance of Kara's apartment in Fresno. Not enough info. Plus Kara's cell number was locked in her dead phone.

The phone was her first priority. She'd barely thawed out. How could she get back out in this weather and get all the way out to West Des Moines?

Liz put her head down in the crook of her arm on the table and let the tears flow. Why didn't life come with a rewind button? She'd rewind it by a few weeks for sure. She'd stay in Galena Landing. Maybe she'd rewind it further. How about all the way back to her seventeen-year-old self before she decided it was a good idea to give her virginity to the high school bad boy?

So many regrets. Sobs wracked her body. There was no stopping them now. *Oh, God...*

I'm here.

She hadn't meant it as a prayer. But what if she had? What if she forgave God for something she'd done out of her own willful disobedience? She'd blamed it all on Him, but she was the one who'd barricaded her conscience into a back corner. She'd been the one who wanted Mason's attention, whatever the cost. It had cost her, all right. It had cost her an entire decade of her life. It had been a bad trade-off from day one, and it hadn't gotten any better.

Oh, God...

Though your sins be as scarlet, they shall be as white as snow.

Scarlet sins. She'd never figured out what that meant, but she sure knew how white snow in the mountains could be. How clear and pure and bright.

"Want to talk?" Linda's hand rubbed circles on Liz's shoulder.

"I give up," Liz mumbled.

"Don't give up, dearie. Warren and me, we'll help you all we can. The good Lord has plenty more for you."

The good Lord. Liz shook her head. *I give up, God. I've had enough of Liz's way. Here You go. Have at it.*

"He loves you, Liz. He has a plan for your life. He wants to give you a hope and a future. That's in the Bible."

"Jeremiah twenty-nine eleven."

Linda's hand stilled. "You know the good Lord?"

Liz dabbed her tear-streaked face with the blanket. "I did, as a child. I know more memory verses than I could tell you."

"He wants you back."

"I know. I just told Him He can have the whole mess. I'm done doing things Liz's way." She gave a wry smile. "It hasn't worked out so well for me."

"Well, hallelujah! The angels in heaven are rejoicing. Warren, did you hear? The lost sheep has come back to the fold."

Liz laughed between her tears and accepted Linda's hug. The decision didn't change anything. Not really. She still had a huge mess with very few options, but somehow she felt lighter inside.

"What now, dearie?"

What now indeed. "I need a phone cord. All my contacts are in here. I can't even phone my mom or my brother. They have cell phones, and I never memorized the numbers."

Linda chuckled. "Your head was too full of Bible verses."

"I guess." It was kind of funny. Or it would be, if she ever got out of this mess. No. *When* she got out.

"Hmm. No one has a publicly listed number?"

A light bulb came on. "Wait. My brother is a veterinarian. I can call his clinic." She glanced at the clock. Mid-afternoon in Idaho.

"Sure, use Warren's again."

"Is it a smart phone? I mean, can it go online?"

"I think so. Right, Warren?"

He nodded from the table over where he talked to the two old men and gave her a thumbs-up.

It took a few minutes to navigate his browser to find the phone number. She tapped it. On the third ring, voicemail kicked in.

"You've reached Landing Veterinary Clinic. We're closed until Monday as Dr. Nemesek is out of town. In case of emergency, call Dr. Taubin at home. Have a safe and healthy weekend!"

Zach's clinic was closed? In the middle of the week? What on earth was going on?

Liz slowly lowered the phone and pressed the 'end' button. This worry would have to get behind others that were more pressing. It wasn't like Zach could have done much for her anyway, so far away. He could have sent her money for her car's release via PayPal, but how would she turn that into cash?

Either way, she needed to charge her cell. *God? If we're on speaking terms now, I could really use a cord for this stupid phone. I know You're not in the business of waving Your wand and making things magically appear, but I wouldn't say no if it happened.* She opened one eye and peered at the table. Nope, still no cord.

Chapter 27 --

A whisper in the stillness caught Mason's attention as he unlocked his car after shift. He whirled to find Kass standing there with a box.

"Hey, long time no see." She shifted from one foot to the other.

"Yeah. Sorry. I've been busy."

"Twins okay?"

He nodded. "Avery has a bit of a cold, but nothing too serious."

Kass held up the box. "I was wondering if I could invite myself out for supper? I've got pizza."

Mason's brain had been so full of worry for Liz in the past few days he hadn't given any thought to Kass. "I have chicken pot pie out to be reheated." He grinned. "Thanks to you."

She tilted her head at him. "It can wait for tomorrow?"

Tomorrow he'd be in Des Moines. Looking for Liz. But that wasn't Kass's fault. "Maybe I can toss it back in the freezer for next week."

Kass shook her head. "You're not supposed to thaw and refreeze food. The quality breaks down."

Pizza from the bakery, though. And time with Kass. The twins would like to see her. "I'll worry about the chicken pot pie later.

Come on out."

"You're sure? I don't want to intrude."

"You're not." It wouldn't take long to explain to the kids that he'd be away for a few days. It also wouldn't take long to toss a change of clothes or two into a carry-on. A toothbrush and a couple of pairs of underwear, and he was good to go. "We'd love to have you."

"Okay. I'll follow you out."

True to his guess, the twins were excited to see Kass. They were happy with the pizza as well. Kass had remembered the one kind all three of them liked, no mean feat in itself. The four of them indulged in a few rounds of Go Fish before Kass read the kids their Bible story.

"I'll be back down in five minutes." Mason herded the twins toward the stairs. "I hope you can stay a bit longer?"

She nodded with a smile.

At the head of the stairs, Mason set his hand on his son's shoulder and guided him into Avery's room. "I need to talk to you both for a minute."

Avery's eyes shone. "Is it about Miss Kass? I like her."

"No, it's not."

Both children sat on the edge of the bed, watching him.

He squatted in front of them. "Tomorrow after school, you two will go to Finnley's house."

Christopher nodded. "That's what we usually do on Wednesday, Dad."

"Right, but I'm not coming after work. I'm going away for a few days with Uncle Zach. You two will stay at Finnley's house while I'm gone. I'll be back by Sunday night for sure, okay? Do you think you can manage that long without me?"

Avery flung her arms around his neck. "I'll miss you, Daddy."

Christopher crossed his arms. "Where are you going?"

"I'm going to a city called Des Moines in an airplane."

"I want to come!" Avery tightened her grip. "I've never been in a plane."

"I'm sorry, princess. You two can't come this time." Mason disengaged Avery's arms. "You remember Miss Liz? Des Moines is where she went a few weeks ago, but she's not answering her phone or her emails. Uncle Zach is worried about her, so we're going to try to find her."

"Like in a TV show where the bad guys got her?"

Mason forced a grin. "Oh, I doubt that happened to her. I'm sure she's fine. Maybe she just lost her phone or something." No need to saddle two kids, not quite six, with the worry he felt.

"Did you pray for her, Daddy? God can take care of her."

"I sure did, princess. But sometimes God wants us to do something more as well. Both Uncle Zach and I believe God wants us to go find her. That doesn't mean we aren't praying, because we are. You can pray for her, too. Both of you."

The kids exchanged a look.

"Okay," said Christopher. "We can right now, if you wanna."

Mason reached for the twins' hands and bowed his head as he listened to their simple prayers.

"And please bless my mommy and keep her safe," Avery finished.

One of these days Mason was going to have to tell the kids Erin was coming, but not before he got back from the Midwest. "It's time to tuck you both in bed. I'll see you on the bus in the morning before I leave, okay? And then you guys need to listen really good to Aunt Allison and Uncle Brent."

Christopher nodded. "We will."

"Can't I stay with Maddie instead?"

Mason chucked his daughter under her chin. "Not this time, princess, but you'll see her lots. Sweet dreams."

After kissing them both, he made his way back downstairs to where Kass waited on the sofa. She glanced up at him, her smile warm and inviting.

She was so pretty. So sweet. He really ought to fall in love with her. Maybe once he'd seen that Liz was safe, he could do that. Oh, and survived Erin's visit.

Mason scrubbed a hand over the stubble on his face. Life was so complicated.

A shadow crossed Kass's face. "Everything okay?"

He settled onto the end of the sofa, turning to face her. "Kinda."

"Tell me? Or maybe I shouldn't be here." She started to rise.

Mason reached over and caught her hand, tugging her back down before letting go. That probably did little to relieve her worries.

"I'm going out of town for a few days. I just told the kids they'll be staying next door at Brent and Allison's."

"Oh? Where are you off to?"

"Des Moines."

Kass's eyebrows rose. "What's there?"

"Zach's sister Liz. At least, she was there last we heard. She's gone missing. Zach's really worried about her."

Kass's look was direct. "And you are going because?"

Mason swallowed hard. "Because I'm worried about her, too. And because I believe God wants me to go."

"I see."

This time when she stood, Mason rose, too. He caught both Kass's hands. "I have a lot going on right now. Please don't write me off just yet."

Kass pulled one hand free and rested it on his chest. "I don't want to be just friends, Mason," she said softly. "I really like you. A lot. But I can't keep showing up if you don't feel the same. It's too hard."

"I understand." Mason leaned closer and brushed his lips across hers. He meant for it to be a reassuring gesture and nothing more, but Kass wrapped both arms around his neck and kissed him with surprising passion.

Pushing her away now would push her away for good, and he wasn't ready for that decision. Too much in his head was muddled. So he kissed her back.

Danger, danger!

He rested his forehead against hers and held her for another minute before releasing her.

Kass's eyes shone. "Wow."

It had been more *wow* for him than he'd expected it to be. Maybe this was a good direction for him, but he had to find closure with Liz before he could pursue Kass. He slid an arm around Kass and walked her to the door. "I'll be back in a few days. Take care."

He helped her into her coat and watched as she pulled on her boots. "I'll be praying for you, Mason." She stretched to give him another kiss.

He managed to keep this one short, sweet, and to the point. "Thanks. I'm going to need it." He needed it in more ways than Kass could possibly know.

oOo

"I don't know what to say besides thank you." Liz followed Linda up the back stairs.

"Being thankful is enough, dearie. It's not the Hilton, but it's better than outside."

"I didn't even know you let people sleep here."

"Just when someone seems to need the extra." Linda's jaw clenched as she pulled open a door at the landing. "I only wish we could take in everyone who comes through our door."

A stack of mats sat under a shelf with white sheets and blankets. Two women looked up from making a bed on the floor.

Liz stifled something between a gasp and a laugh. She really was homeless, just like the gaunt people she'd seen in the soup kitchen downstairs, like she'd seen on the street. Lord willing, it was temporary for her. What must it be like to have no hope of anything changing soon?

Lord willing. How long had it been since she'd thought in those terms?

"Girls, this is Liz. Liz, meet Anne and Martha."

Liz smiled and nodded. "Hello." No response.

"Let's just pull out a mattress for you and get a bed made up. A few more women will come in before we lock up at ten. There's a washroom right through here. Warren and I will be upstairs if you need anything." Linda expertly tucked a thread worn sheet around the mattress then flipped a blanket over it. "Pick a pillow if you like."

They sure weren't down. Liz reached for what looked like the fluffiest one then glanced at Martha and Anne. Both women had paused to watch her. She selected a lumpy pillow and slid it into a white case. This was no time to assume she deserved the best. She didn't.

Who knew what circumstances had caused these women to be here in a shelter in Des Moines? Were they local people down on their luck, downsized from promising jobs and evicted when they couldn't pay rent? Surely there weren't too many who were here out of the same kind of stubbornness she possessed.

In the morning she'd get a phone cord, charge her phone, and call Zach. Surely he'd send money to rescue her. By the end of the day, she'd have her car out of impound and be pointed west to Idaho.

Home.

Mason. She pushed the thought of him from her mind. No assuming he'd want her back after all this. Not with the way that woman from the bakery had looked at him.

No. Tonight she'd think about her parents. They would, once again, treat her like the prodigal daughter. They'd welcome her back and roll out the party. Sure, they'd be shocked at the depths to which she'd fallen, but that wouldn't matter in the long run. They loved her.

"See you in the morning, dearie." Linda turned and crouched beside Anne then slid an arm around the thin shoulders. "How was your day?"

The woman murmured something Liz couldn't hear.

"The good Lord knows all about it, dearie. Warren and I will keep asking with you."

Anne nodded slightly.

"Martha, it's your turn to help make soup in the morning. You okay with that?"

Martha glanced at Liz and shrugged. "Sure."

"I can help," said Liz. It must take a lot of work to keep this place humming.

"Not tomorrow. It's Martha's job. You have a busy day ahead and need an early start."

"True, but if there's anything I can do, point me at it."

"Thank you. Now, don't you girls talk all night and keep Warren and me awake, you hear?" Linda chuckled as she walked to the door.

Liz grinned, but the other women didn't. The room had been dead quiet since they walked in, and Liz was pretty sure it had been no noisier beforehand.

A stack of Gideon Bibles sat on the shelf beside the bedding. Liz plucked one off the top and sat cross-legged on her mattress. Opening it made her think with longing of Chelsea's gifts locked in her trunk. A Bible and a ring of note cards. Tomorrow she'd have a look at those.

What would she read tonight? Liz cracked open the slim hardback close to the middle. Psalms. She'd memorized tons of those as a child. She didn't remember the thirteenth, though.

O Lord, how long will you forget me? Forever? How long will you look the other way?

Man, she could identify with those words.

How long must I struggle with anguish in my soul, with sorrow in my heart every day? How long will my enemy have the upper hand?

No more. Her prayer today in the soup kitchen had broken that pattern.

Turn and answer me, O Lord my God! Restore the sparkle to my eyes, or I will die.

That's what it was about Martha and Anne. No sparkle. Just a flat gaze that spoke of no hope. Could she help?

Don't let my enemies gloat, saying, "We have defeated him!" Don't let them rejoice at my downfall. But I trust in your unfailing love. I will rejoice because you have rescued me.

Oh, sweet rescue. Inside, she was rescued already, and she'd be bodily rescued soon.

I will sing to the Lord because he is good to me.

Liz's heart nearly exploded from the songs that wanted to well out.

Chapter 28 ---

Is it my imagination, or is that wind colder out here on the flat lands?" Mason hunched his shoulders against the flurry as he followed Zach to the rented car.

Zach chuckled. "No mountains to slow it down." He pointed the key fob at the car and beeped it. "Toss your stuff in the trunk, and let's get to the hotel."

Mason did as he was told then rounded the car. "Heated seats, I hope." The car purred to life at the press of a button. "This vehicle is a grade or two above mine."

"Me, too. I'd have probably just taken city transit downtown if I didn't think you'd need a car to look for Liz."

"Well, thanks. I refuse to feel guilty for the expenditure."

Zach glanced at him as he backed out of the parking stall. "I just wish I knew where to start. Maybe I should skip the conference. Two can cover more territory."

"I have three days. I've been praying like a mad man that God would direct me to her." Three days. If he weren't back in Galena Landing Monday morning, would Roger really fire him?

"Yeah, me, too." Zach sighed heavily as he merged with traffic. "She's my little sister. I feel like I should be the one searching."

"I can't very well pretend to be you at the conference."

At least that got a grin out of Zach. "True enough. But I'm not sure the conference will change my life as much as finding Liz."

"I get it." They'd had this discussion a dozen times if they'd had it once. "Give me a day to do some scouting and we can re-evaluate in the evening."

Zach sighed. "Right. That's probably best."

The car's GPS guided them northeast into the city. Mason stared out the passenger window, trying to get a feel for the layout.

Lord, where is Liz?

He couldn't shake the feeling she might be long gone. Florida might've sounded good to escape from this bitter winter. But no. He had to assume she was here somewhere. That was the only way to keep utter hopelessness at bay.

"Hey, this thing has Bluetooth."

Zach's voice pulled Mason from his circular thoughts. "What?"

"Here." Zach flipped his phone at Mason. "Go to settings and try to connect. I should give Jo a call and let her know we've landed."

Mason did as he was told. It was easier than dwelling on the fact he had no one to call. Kass would be happy to hear from him, but that was more message than he wanted to send.

The dashboard display showed the connection complete. "Tap Jo's number," directed Zach.

A few seconds later, Jo's voice sounded through the car. "Zach? Everything okay?"

"Yep, we're good. We're on our way to the hotel."

"Well, I hope Mason is driving if you're on the phone."

The guys exchanged a grin.

"The car has Bluetooth."

The GPS announced an immediate left turn.

"Then you should be paying attention to it and not on the phone. I could've waited half an hour to hear your voice."

"I missed you, too, Jo." Zach chuckled. "Everything okay there?"

"Yeah. I went into town to pick up some items at Nature's Pantry. Your receptionist was in there shopping."

"Nadine seemed glad for a few days off." Zach turned left.

"Your destination is on the left."

The car slowed as Zach signaled.

"She said she popped by the clinic to check something and glanced at the phone. An out-of-town number registered on the call display."

Mason held his breath as Zach veered into the hotel parking lot.

"Oh?" Zach asked.

"Area code five-one-five."

The guys glanced at each other then Zach pulled to the side. "That's significant how?"

"That's Des Moines, Zach. Nadine looked it up. She thought it might be about your conference or something, but it was too late as you'd already left."

Mason turned in his seat to watch Zach's face. He couldn't help the hope burbling inside him.

"So was it the conference?"

"Nadine couldn't find out who the number is registered to, so she took note of it and left it with me."

Mason whipped his phone out and poised his thumbs over the notes app. "What was the number, Jo?"

"Oh, hey, Mason." She rattled off the number as he entered it in his phone. "Avery's here playing with Maddie. She'll go over to Allison and Brent's at bedtime."

"Good enough. Give her a kiss for me."

"Will do."

Zach cleared his throat. "We're at the hotel now. We'll get checked in and give this number a call. I'll talk to you again in a bit, okay?"

"Okay. Love you."

"Love you back." Zach tapped the dashboard to end the call.

Mason tried not to think about the relationship he was missing as he followed Zach into the hotel, his carry-on rattling behind him. A few minutes later they opened a door on the eighteenth floor to reveal a room with two queen beds.

"Home sweet home." Zach swung his bag onto the first bed.

"You going to call this number or am I?" Mason held his phone out to his friend.

Zach raised his eyebrows as he took the device. "I am. Whoever it was contacted the vet clinic."

"So call it." Mason leaned against the wall.

Zach tapped the number. "This is Dr. Nemesek calling ... Someone from this number phoned my veterinary clinic in Galena Landing, Idaho ... My first name is Zach ... Yes, I have a sister named Liz." He clenched the phone and met Mason's gaze. "She's not there?"

Mason's legs couldn't hold him up. He slid to the floor, holding his breath, never taking his eyes off his friend.

"Do you have a way to contact her? ... I see ... I'm here in Des Moines for a few days, and I'd really like to see her. Make sure she's okay ... So I should be able to call her later or tomorrow? ... Please call me back if needed. Thanks."

He thumbed the phone off and dropped to the end of the bed. "Well, that was sort of helpful. Guy's cautious about giving me any real information, but he says she's safe. He'll let her know to call me."

A guy? Liz was with a guy? Mason rubbed both hands over his face. She wouldn't want to see him. Not if she had someone else already. He'd told Kass he and Liz were just friends. He needed to remember. Somehow his imagination had zipped off to envision a moment where he swept a repentant Liz into his arms and kissed away all her fears and doubts.

She'd left because she didn't want that. He had no reason to believe anything had changed. Liz was the one who'd broken contact with her family and friends back home. She wouldn't welcome him as a saving angel. He'd be lucky if she spoke to him at all. If he even had the chance.

"She lost her phone's charge cord. The guy said she'd gone out to get a new one. He's expecting her back within the next hour or so."

"So her phone's dead."

"For now. You look a wreck, Waterman. Coming down with something?"

Mason shook his head. "I'm okay. Really."

"Could have fooled me."

"It's not that hard."

Zach chuckled. "Let's go downstairs and get something to eat. We can't plan much until we see if she'll call me back."

Mason grimaced. "Why would she? She hasn't called in weeks. Has her cord been missing that long?"

"Waterman."

Mason stood and looked at Zach. "Yeah?"

"I think you're not over caring about my sister. I think have reasons of your own for being here." He held up a hand. "I'm cool with that. What I don't get is why when we got our first solid lead it drags you down instead of making you bounce off the walls. Care to explain?"

"Nothing has changed." Mason pushed past Zach to the door. "Dinner sounds good." In theory, anyway. He wasn't sure he'd be able to do it justice.

oOo

"...and then there was an accident in front of the bus. A semi flipped on the ice and blocked the entire street. We had to wait half an hour for the wrecker to clear a lane."

"Why didn't the bus take another route?" asked Linda, serving up a bowl of soup.

"It happened seconds before we got there. There was no time for the driver to react before we were packed in like sardines on the parkway."

"You must be starving." Linda set the bowl in front of her.

"I am. Who knew a quick trip to the other end of the city would turn into an all-day event?" Liz dug in her pocket and held up a package. "But look! I got what I needed."

Linda beamed. "That's wonderful. Plug your phone in and get the thing charging while you eat. How long does it take?"

"From flat dead? I don't know." Liz pried the cord and USB port out of the package. How long would it take to get her car released? Could she sleep upstairs that long?

She started the charging process, but the screen stayed black. No surprise. Liz turned to the soup. "Thank you! This smells wonderful." Man, nothing could keep her down for long now. All day, even amidst the struggles of taking transit in an unfamiliar city, she'd felt like singing. She'd actually done a twirl in the mall food court, even without enough money in her pocket to buy lunch. People had looked at her strangely, so she'd stopped.

The street door opened and Warren entered, carrying a large, heavy-looking sack and stomping fresh snow off his boots. His eyes brightened when he saw her. "You made it back."

She grinned. "Sure did." She pointed at the phone lying beside her bowl. "And I got the cord, too."

"Excellent."

"Did you get the parsnips, love?" Linda rushed over to give Warren a hug.

"I did, but it will be a few days before we can replenish the carrots. The contents of one of the storage rooms froze."

"Oh, no. But the good Lord will provide, and the parsnips are a big help."

Curiosity poked at Liz. "Where do you get all the food you serve here, anyway?"

The couple glanced at each other. "Local farmers provide some of it. Some restaurants donate at times. Other times the good Lord provides cash and we can go on a shopping spree."

When she had a job again, she'd send money. Hands down. These people had saved her life. Okay, maybe God had done that, but He'd certainly used Linda and Warren in the process.

Warren carried the sack into the kitchen then returned with a bowl of soup in hand. He settled into a chair across from Liz. "Had an interesting phone call while I was out."

She paused with the spoon halfway to her mouth. "Oh?"

"A man named Zach is looking for you. He's here in Des Moines."

Liz shot to her feet. "My brother?" She threw her hands in the air, and the spoon flew across the room. "Thank You, God!"

Warren grinned as he picked up her spoon and snagged her a clean one.

"Where is he? Is he coming here?"

"We never give out any personal information, Liz. It's not our place. It's up to you to make contact."

Liz jiggled from one foot to the other then reached over and tapped her phone. Still dead.

Chapter 29 --

*Z*ach was in the shower when the cell on the nightstand began to ring.

Mason rolled over and looked at the lit display. "It's Liz!" he yelled.

"Answer it!" called Zach, turning off the water.

Mason hesitated an instant then slid the phone on. "Hello?"

"Zach?"

Oh, her sweet voice. Mason leaned back against his pillow. "No, it's Mason. Zach will be here in a sec."

"Mason?" she squeaked. "But Warren said Zach..."

He clenched his jaw. "Warren?"

Silence. Not a good sign.

"Look, Liz, we've all been really worried about you. You just dropped off the map. All I want to know is if you are okay. If you don't want to talk to me, I get it. Really."

"Who said I didn't want to talk to you? I just thought I was phoning my brother is all. This *is* his number, isn't it?"

"It is."

"Warren said Zach was in Des Moines."

That name again. "He is."

"And you're with him?"

"Yes."

"That's great, but why?"

"Because we were worried about you."

"We?" Her voice softened. "Or you..."

Mason clenched the phone. "All of us. Your family. Everyone at Green Acres."

"I see. What about Mason Waterman?"

"Liz. I've been sick with worry." He groaned. "But it sounds like you've landed on your feet after all."

"Mason? I have no idea what you're talking about. Although that first bit sounded somewhat promising."

How could she toy with him now, when he'd come so far?

Zach came out of the bathroom in boxers, toweling his hair. He raised his eyebrows and Mason stretched toward him with the phone, shaking his head. Who knew what was going on in Liz's head?

"Lizzie Rose?"

Mason fell back against his pillow. He felt like pulling it over his face. Why couldn't he get his mind off her? It was justice, probably. He'd ruined a decade of her life with one selfish action as a teen. She'd forgiven him, so why couldn't he let her go? She didn't need him. Never had.

"Wow." Zach dropped into the chair beside the desk. "What a scum."

Mason focused on Zach's face. Scum? Who? That Warren guy? He'd pound him if he abused Liz.

"Oh, man. No way. Liz, you should have phoned me before it got that bad."

Mason's stomach soured.

Zach shook his head. "Yes, I can definitely help with that. How much cash do you need? ... Totally doable. Where? What time?"

She was being blackmailed?

"Listen, we can come get you right now. I can get a room for you here ... You're sure? ... Okay, if you're in a safe place ... Sounds like a long story. I can't wait to hear it all ... I'll send Mason for you in the morning then. Just give me the address."

Zach mimed writing at Mason, who stretched for the hotel writing pad and a pen then recorded the address as Zach repeated it.

"Yes, I'll find a bank machine and withdraw the cash beforehand ... I'm so relieved you're okay. Call me again if you need to ... Okay, see you tomorrow. I have a long break at lunch. Love you, sis."

Mason raised his eyes at his friend as Zach tossed the phone at the other bed. His gut churned with inexplicable emotions. Relief, yes, but so much more. "Spit it out already."

"She thinks the original guy who hired her was a john, that the ESL thing was a front. She didn't stick around long enough to make sure."

"No way." Mason dug his thumbs into his temples, trying to dislodge the sharp pain the words caused.

"She's been unable to find another job and was living in her car. Until it got impounded a few days ago."

Mason surged to his feet. "Why didn't she call?" He could see why she didn't call *him*, but her family? Zach, at least?

"Pride, I guess. And then when her car got towed, her phone battery was almost drained from the cold, and the cord was in the car."

"Why'd she call the vet clinic and not you? Or your parents?" Or him...

"She didn't have any numbers memorized, and we all run on cells, so the numbers aren't readily available. She found the clinic online. Nadine would have passed my number to her, but she caught voice mail."

It sounded too easy. Too explainable. "Who's this Warren guy?"

A slow smile curved Zach's lips. "Now that's an interesting question."

Mason hardened his eyes. "What do you mean?"

"Out of that entire story, all you heard was a man's name? Waterman, stop trying to tell me you're here because of guilt from hurting Liz a bazillion years ago."

Mason raised his eyebrows. "I'm not sure what you're getting at. Why not answer the question? Why is he blackmailing her?"

"Bla—? You've lost me completely."

"The money."

Zach laughed. "That has nothing to do with Warren. The impound company requires cash, and Liz doesn't have that much on her. The rest is in her trunk, but she can't get to it until the car's released. Catch twenty-two."

"Oh, I see." And he kind of did, about the money part anyway.

"Want to explain to me how you have feelings for my sister? I mean, other than guilt."

"You know I do," Mason growled, turning from the window. "So stuff it already."

Grinning, Zach cupped his hand behind his ear. "What was that? Didn't quite catch your words."

"I love Liz!" snarled Mason. "Are you happy?"

"Fairly happy at the moment, yes. Are you?"

"No. Nothing's changed. She's the one who ran away, Nemesek. She's hooked up with a guy here already and only tried to call you because she was in trouble. Why didn't *Warren*—" he all but spat the name "— get her car out of impound for her? She's not in that much trouble if she wanted to stay with him tonight rather than with you. Probably because I'm here."

"Waterman. You are jumping to a whole raft of conclusions."

"Am I? Then why don't you explain it already?"

"I don't have all the information." Zach shrugged. "But I'm willing to wait until tomorrow before I assume the worst. Didn't you hear her voice? She sounded so happy. Whoever Warren is, he's not a predator. More like a rescuer."

Zach didn't know the inner city like Mason did. Truly good

guys were few and far between. Des Moines couldn't be that different from cities he'd known in his own seedy past.

"If you're going to treat her with suspicion, maybe I should skip my lecture and take her to the impound yard tomorrow myself. She's been hurt enough. You've got a chance to find out the real truth behind it all and state your case with her, but if you're going to treat her like a pariah, I'd rather take you back to the airport right now. You're no good to me here. No good for Liz."

Mason dropped into the chair at the desk and covered his face. "Sorry, man. She's got me in such a turmoil, I hardly know which way's up."

"Then I think we need to do some praying."

Yeah. That'd probably help.

oOo

Liz flung open the soup kitchen door at the knock. "Mason!" Her first instinct was to jump into his arms, but his hands were firmly in his pockets, and he had a wary look on his face.

Better go with her second instinct. She smiled up at him. "Good to see you."

"Likewise." Something flickered in his eyes, but it wasn't exactly welcoming. "You ready to go?"

"If you've got the money?"

He nodded.

Liz turned and waved. "Thanks for everything, Linda!" Would she ever see her friend again? She ran across the room and squeezed the woman. "I appreciate you so much. I'll keep in touch."

"Your young man doesn't look very happy," Linda whispered, glancing past her. "You gonna be okay?"

Liz let out a breath. "He'll come around. I'm sure of it."

"All right then." Linda patted Liz's back and gave her a nudge. "Off you go before it costs another twenty-five."

Liz grimaced. "Need you remind me?" She hurried back across the space and opened the door.

Mason followed her out. "I'm parked around the corner."

"Thanks so much. I can't even tell you how excited I am to see you."

He raised his eyebrows but said nothing.

What was wrong with him, anyway? Why had he come all this way if he was just going to be surly? She slipped a quick prayer heavenward as Mason opened the car door for her.

A moment later he coded the impound yard's address into the GPS then, with a shoulder-check, pulled into traffic.

Liz tapped the switch for the heated seat and the blessed warmth began to seep into her body. It didn't do anything to lessen the chill between her and Mason, though. If she didn't get some words out of him soon, he'd drop her off at the depot and she'd be on her own again. "Mason? What's wrong?"

His jaw twitched, and both hands tightened on the steering wheel. "What do you mean?"

"You're treating me like a leper."

"Am not. I'm helping you get your car."

She sighed. "Because Zach sent you. Why did you come to Des Moines?"

"It seemed like I might be able to do some good. I didn't realize you'd already rescued yourself."

"Hello?" Liz swiveled in her seat to face him. "Where on earth did you get that idea?"

"So why didn't *Warren* get your car out of impound?"

He said the name like a dirty word. Liz's gut clenched. "Warren?"

"That's what I said, Liz. Warren."

"He doesn't have money just lying around. If he could've

done it, I'm sure he'd have offered, but I didn't want to make any demands."

Mason's eyebrows shot up, but his gaze remained on the road. "It seems like the least he could do."

"You aren't making any sense. It wasn't his fault, and he's not a bank machine. He has to be careful to treat everyone the same."

He groaned. "What have you gotten into? Treat yourself with some respect."

Liz stared at him. Her brain clicked through the things Mason had said. The things he hadn't said. "Just one little minute, Mason Waterman. Do you think I'm working for Warren? That he's a pimp?"

His hands flexed on the wheel.

Her fury soared. "You make me want to hurl, you know that? You lived in the inner city too long if you think that is everyone's lifestyle. Not only that, but you obviously don't know me at all if you think I'd go along with it. I'd rather freeze to death under a bridge."

"What am I supposed to think?" He ground the words out through gritted teeth.

"How about not jumping to conclusions? Instead, how about saying, *Liz, tell me what Warren means to you.*"

"Fine. What does Warren mean to you?"

"Warren is married to Linda. They run a soup kitchen for those who need it. Not only that, but he's a Christian who has given up everything to help people living on the streets. He's ten times the man you are. He doesn't play games with women's emotions." Liz rammed her arms across her chest and sank her teeth into her lower lip before she told Mason exactly what she thought of him.

"Oh."

Mason might've flicked a glance her way, but she wasn't looking. Not a chance.

"I'm sorry. You're right."

Ya think?

"It's just... I was worried sick. I've thought about you every minute since you left."

"And here I thought I wasn't that important to you."

"I never said you weren't important. I said I had to follow God."

"Oh, yeah? What if I told you I found my way back to God? What then?" She couldn't help that her voice sounded demanding. He'd started with the accusations first. He was going to have to grovel for forgiveness. Big time.

"I'd be really glad for you. If it were true."

She twisted on the seat to see his face. "You have got to be kidding me."

"What?"

"Do you not believe anything I say? The bit about God is true. Two days ago I gave up fighting Him. I don't know why I wasted any thoughts on you in my entire life. You've always assumed what you wanted and didn't credit me with any worthwhile motivation. Forget it. I'm so done with you. Completely."

"Did you really pray?"

"Yes, I did. Is that so hard to believe? I've even been reading the Bible some. The Gideons left a stack at the shelter. Linda and I've talked and prayed together." She glared at his profile. "Don't fool yourself into thinking I did that for you. You're so full of yourself. Get over it."

His jaw clenched, but he said nothing.

Chapter 30 --

*L*iz swerved into a strip mall parking lot heading back into the city from the impound lot. Anything to get the back bumper of Mason's rental car from filling her windshield. She was never following him anywhere, ever again, even if their destination was the same hotel. She had her own GPS, thank-you-very-much.

Her dashboard Bluetooth lit up with an incoming call. Mason's number. She glared at the display before jabbing to accept.

"You took a wrong turn."

Liz glanced around the plaza and spotted a small pharmacy. "I need to pick something up. I'll be at the hotel in time for lunch."

"I'll turn around."

"Don't bother." Slamming old-style telephone handsets was so much more satisfying than tapping an end button. She jumped out of the car, hit the lock, and ran for the little store.

Ten minutes in there and all she could think to buy was a tube of lip gloss. Through the store window she could see Mason's car parked beside hers. He was so stubborn. If she spent two hours in here, he'd probably still be there and she'd miss lunch with her brother.

She was going to have to face him.

Again.

Liz pushed the store door open and strode across the parking lot in the icy wind. She spared no glance for Mason but slid into her driver's seat and started the engine.

This time he followed her, never allowing enough space for another car to come between them. When she flicked a glance in the rearview mirror, all she saw was his grim face and two hands on the wheel.

Lord, why did he even come?

For some reason she'd at first thought he'd come because he cared, but his surly attitude didn't align with that. She'd lost her chance with him in Galena Landing. The chance she'd never wanted anyway.

She signaled and eased into the right lane at the GPS's direction. Maybe Zach could give her some guidance. She couldn't wait to see her brother again.

oOo

Why had he picked the chair across from Liz at the lunch table? Oh yeah. To be as far from her as he could. Too bad that put her straight ahead.

Mason fidgeted with the cloth napkin in his lap. This place was more upscale than he'd expected, and that set him on edge, too. In the bit of traveling he'd done, he'd been more a Motel 6 kind of guy.

Him being here was costing the Nemeseks a pretty penny, and he'd done nothing useful yet. Taking Liz to the impound yard didn't count. Zach would only have had to skip one session of his conference to do the same.

Mason had stitched his heart to his sleeve for everyone to see, had insisted it was his God-given right — or something like that — to accompany Zach, and he should never have done it.

Liz didn't need him. She never had. He'd blown everything out of proportion. Her disappearance. His panic to find her.

Warren.

"...and then Maddie said, if I was a cat, I'd be afraid of broccoli," Zach said.

Liz laughed, as she was no doubt supposed to. "She's so funny. I miss her."

Zach leaned closer to his sister. "Liz, will you come home?"

Mason didn't miss the flick of her eyes toward him then away even as he studied the dreary view out the nearby window.

"I've been thinking about that," she said softly. "I have no place else to go."

Did he want her to come back? Of course he did. He'd been such an idiot. Still was, but it was hard to reverse direction when she made a wreck of him and his conflicting emotions.

Mason caught his name and pulled his attention back to his tablemates. "Pardon me?" he asked Zach.

"You don't mind, do you?"

"Mind what?"

Zach shook his head, a glimmer of a grin poking up his cheeks. "Driving Liz's car to Idaho."

"Driving L—" His mind blanked as he met her eyes across the table. Then the cogs caught again. What was this, Friday? Two and a half days should be enough time to get back before Roger fired him Monday morning. "I, uh, I could do that. She going to fly with you then?"

"That's what we were talking about, Waterman. I'll cover your expenses, of course."

Mason hated that he needed the help. "I have friends in Billings. I can probably make it to their place tonight if I leave soon."

"Right, I guess that's right on the route, isn't it?" Zach opened a map app on his phone.

"Erin still in Billings?" Liz's voice was flat.

"That's not who I meant. I meant the pastor of my church there."

She raised her eyebrows at him.

Why was she pushing his buttons? "As far as I know, yes, Erin lives in Billings. It's not like we keep in close touch, so that could have changed."

"I see." She poked her fork into her food.

Her plate looked like a war zone, and his had fared little better. Seemed only Zach had a significant appetite.

Zach pushed back his chair. "I need to run for my next lecture." He opened his wallet and thumbed through a wad of bills then handed them to Mason. "This should see you through, Waterman. Call or text if you need anything. Can you haul Liz's stuff up to my room? I'll make an arrangement for her at the front desk on my next break."

Mason stuffed the cash in his pocket without counting it. "Sure. Don't worry about a thing. I've got it." Finally something he could do.

Zach clouted him on the shoulder. "Thanks, man. Drive safe." He turned to Liz. "I'll be up in the room in a couple of hours. Make yourself at home."

She hopped up and gave him a hug. "Thanks for being the big brother I need."

"Aw, no problem." He patted her back. "I haven't always, so I'm glad to be here for you now. I'll pay for lunch then I have to run." Zach gave Mason a significant look. A *don't mess this up* look.

Mason nodded slightly.

Liz slid back into her chair and picked up her fork. Stabbed a French fry and stared at it.

"Not hungry?" Mason tried to gentle his voice.

She grimaced slightly. "I thought I was."

"Yeah, me, too." He took a deep breath. "Look, Liz, I'm sorry."

"For?"

"I've been an idiot. I was so worried about you."

"Thanks. I appreciate that you bailed me out this morning."

With Zach's money. He was making ends meet on his tire shop paychecks, but not getting ahead. Nothing for emergencies. Not enough to stay in hotels like this and order meals like the one he'd plundered and left for dead on his plate. He had nothing to offer Liz.

She hadn't said she'd forgiven him. And why should she? He bungled everything.

The chair grated as he pushed back. "I guess if we're done here, I should get your things from the car. Whatever you'll need for a couple of days, anyway."

Liz nodded and stood. "I need to sort through the trunk. I can meet you back in the lobby."

Or we could drive west together.

The words were on the tip of his tongue, but that was a bad idea on so many levels. Surely they'd push through this impasse with two long days in the car. They'd have to talk, wouldn't they? But they weren't married, and it would look bad. He didn't want to have to explain Liz to his pastor in Billings.

Zip your mouth, Waterman. Don't even suggest it.

"I'll come out with you." He reached for her coat and held it for her. Her fragrance teased at his senses, and he barely resisted the temptation to slide his arms around her along with the coat.

No. He didn't have the right.

oOo

He was such a puzzle. One minute attentive and winsome. The next surly and guarded. It was a good thing he'd be out of her hair for a couple of days so she could try to figure out how to treat him back in Galena Landing.

The wind had died down leaving sub-zero temperatures that seeped into Liz as she stood at her open trunk. She'd tried to keep everything as organized as her home. That's what the car had been for her the past few weeks. A mobile bedroom.

She layered a few changes of clothing and underwear into her carry-on while Mason trucked across the parking lot with her small bag of trash. Her personal supplies and makeup. A pair of shoes. She zipped the case and set it on the pavement while she closed the pieces remaining in the trunk.

Mason reached for the handle. "Is this everything?"

Liz swung her laptop strap over her shoulder. "Yes, this should do me." She walked beside him into the lobby and across to the elevators. They exited on the eighteenth floor and, a moment later, he slipped a key card into a slot. He pushed the door open, and she entered ahead of him.

She surveyed the thick moss-green carpet and the rusty-red bedspreads embossed with gold threads. Through the door on her left she spotted a jetted tub. That would be where she'd spend the afternoon. She could feel the soothing heat already. "Pretty posh."

"Yeah. Not my usual." Mason swung her carry-on to the desk by the window.

She crossed the room and looked down into the parking lot and the gray city beyond. Saying goodbye to Des Moines would not be at all difficult. It was probably a very nice place full of good people. Too bad she'd met the other kind first.

The sound of a zip behind her caused her to turn.

Mason set a battered carry-on beside the door. His gaze met hers across the room. "I guess this is it." He tossed a set of keys on the nearest bed. "We took my car to Spokane, so Zach will need these when you guys get there."

Keys. Liz tugged hers from her purse then crossed the space.

"My registration is in the glove box." She met his gaze as she handed the keys to him. "Thanks, Mason."

His fingers closed around hers, and his clear blue eyes searched hers. Something flickered in their depths.

What was he thinking?

Mason's eyes hardened as she stepped back, too simultaneously to be a reaction. He pocketed the keys and extended the handle on his case. "Take care, Liz. See you in a few days." The door clicked shut behind him.

Liz sucked in a long breath and let it out slowly. She crossed to the window and stared out, blinking back the burn in her eyes. A few minutes later, Mason strode across to her car. The lights flashed and he tossed his bag into the backseat. He sat in the driver's seat for a long moment before starting the car and driving away.

Gone. Just like that.

She bit down on her lip. Had she really expected to simply walk back into his life? That her surrender to God was all that stood in their way? What else was she supposed to make of the fight they'd had in the farmhouse before she left? She'd expected him to be happy for her.

Instead it was like he didn't even believe her. Was he so full of himself that he thought she'd pretend to reignite her faith just for him? He should have known better. She'd have done it in Galena Landing if it were only a sham.

My ways are not your ways, neither are your thoughts my thoughts.

Why was that old memory verse entering her mind now? God wanted her to push thoughts of Mason aside and move on with her life? Fine. She'd do that.

First she'd have a good cry in the bathtub.

Chapter 31 --

*L*iz had never been hugged by so many people in her life. It was worse than the Humbert family reunion when she was twelve. Worse... or maybe better.

She swung Maddie into her arms at the first break in the welcoming committee.

"I missed you, Auntie Liz."

"I missed you, too, sweetness." She nuzzled the soft neck.

"Did you come for my birthday?"

Liz's mind scrambled. What day was it?

"Ours too!" Avery tugged at her arm.

Liz crouched, still holding her niece, and looked into the eyes of Mason's daughter. "You have a birthday soon, too? Wow, so many birthdays."

Avery nodded. "We'll be six. Miss Kass is making us each a birthday cake. Christopher wants a boy cake and I want a girl cake."

"Miss Kass?"

"She helps Daddy cook our food."

Kass. From the bakery. Whoa. There was a woman who'd wasted no time.

Reality rocked Liz to her heels. No wonder Mason seemed so distant. Liz had only been gone a few weeks, but he'd already moved on. He'd been moving on before she left.

"Two cakes sounds really nice."

"Miss Kass promised me real strawberries on top."

"Not that they're in season," Jo said tartly.

"Sometimes it's worth it to please a child."

Who was that? The beloved Kass? Liz set Maddie down and rose. Why hadn't she noticed the woman with the red-gold curls and pretty nose in the welcoming committee?

The smile on Kass's face didn't reach her eyes. "Pleased to meet you, Liz. I've heard so much about you."

Yeah, I just bet you have.

In the next heartbeat, Liz pulled the cloak of God's forgiveness around her. She wouldn't be sarcastic. She hadn't turned to Jesus to win Mason back, but because she'd been at the end of her own rope and heard Him calling.

Though your sins be as scarlet, they shall be as white as snow.

"Nice to meet you, Kass." She'd sing at their wedding if that's what it came to. *God's got it. God's got it.*

Allison reached between them and put her hand on Liz's arm. "I was so glad to get your email yesterday. I had a few students on hold I wasn't sure we could fit in without a bit more help. We'll have a greenhouse 101 class as well as business management and animal husbandry. With twenty sheep due to lamb soon and half a dozen cows, there will be lots to keep everyone's hands busy."

"I often helped Dad with lambing when I was in high school. After Zach left for college." Good memories, working with her father in the dim, pungent barn, watching new lives emerge.

"Terrific." Allison nodded. "Keanan has been doing a lot of that the past couple of winters. We only call Zach when there's a problem. But when he is up to his shoulder assisting a birth isn't a time when he can answer questions and teach. On Monday I'll give you the class syllabus to go through. Students start arriving next weekend."

Liz nodded. Room, board, and a small stipend. This would

give her time to figure out where her life was going. Where *God* wanted it to go. She was done running it herself.

"Mom and Dad are expecting me for dinner, but I'll be back later." She fingered Mason's car keys in her pocket. He'd be here tomorrow, and they'd trade back. Meanwhile, she wasn't going to flaunt them in Kass's face. Wonder what Kass thought when Mason caught a flight to look for Liz? Bet that had burned.

No. She was done with manipulating. Kass was probably very nice. Right now she bent to hear something Avery whispered to her. She was likely much better suited to Mason and the twins than Liz was.

God knows.

Liz whirled for the door and collided with Chelsea. "I'm sorry!"

"It's okay. I wasn't trying to sneak up on you. I heard you were back and wanted to say hi."

Liz reached to hug her. "I can't thank you enough for sending me your Bible and those note cards."

Chelsea smiled. "Did you read them?"

"A lot, in the past few days." Liz forced a chuckle. "Before that I wasn't much interested."

"I get it." Chelsea squeezed her back. "A person has to be ready. I can't wait to curl up with a hot chocolate and hear all about it. Save me a few hours before things get busy, okay?"

"Really?" How long had it been since Liz had a girlfriend who wanted to hang out? Even better, one who could walk beside her as they both followed Jesus? She couldn't remember. "I'd love to. Sometime tomorrow?"

"You're coming to church?"

"I wouldn't miss it for anything."

Chelsea jiggled. "I'm so excited I can hardly stand it. We'll find a time tomorrow afternoon or evening. Now go! I'm sure your parents are waiting for you."

No doubt they were. And for the first time since she'd been a young teen, Liz was ready to open her heart to them. Would they welcome her like the prodigal daughter she was?

They would. She knew it.

oOo

Almost home.

Mason stopped at the one and only traffic light in Galena Landing on Sunday afternoon. He saluted the tire shop two blocks down on his left. "Made it, Roger," he announced as the light turned green.

The ringtone he dreaded most broke through the rock music. He reached to accept the call on the car's Bluetooth. With any luck, Erin was calling to say she wasn't coming after all.

"Hello, Mason here."

"Mase? It's Erin."

"Hey. How are things?" *Please say you're not coming, at least for their birthday.*

"I'm such a mess, Mason."

He took a deep breath. What kind of a selfish, horrid guy was he, anyway? "I'm sorry. What happened?"

"My boyfriend. H-he... I left him. Can I come tomorrow? I can't stay here anymore."

"I... Uh..."

"Please, Mason. I've nowhere else to turn."

"Try Jesus?" Even as the words left his mouth, Mason knew it wasn't that simple. How did that saying go? *You are the only Bible some people will ever read.* He was it. Front line.

He imagined Erin in the same room as Liz and Kass, and his whole body trembled. Wasn't following Jesus supposed to make his life easier? How could he tout that at Erin when his own was still such a disaster?

Not easier. More fulfilling. More complete. Jesus had never promised easy.

"Mason? You there?"

He clenched the steering wheel as he drove across the bridge. "I'm here. Sure. Come."

"Oh, thank you. You have no idea how much this means to me."

"You're taking the bus?"

"I guess so."

He wanted to ask if she had enough for the round trip but didn't dare. "My friends have a spare room you can use for a week or so."

"But..."

"You're not staying with me, Erin."

"But the kids."

"You'll see plenty of them. They have school every day and go to my parents on Monday and Tuesday on the bus. I'm not changing that. I'm not rearranging everything for you."

"I don't want to stay with people I don't know."

Mason turned the car onto Thompson Road. "It's them or my parents."

She sniffled. "Not happening."

He shrugged, not that she could see it. "Those are the options."

"Fine." She sighed deeply into the phone. "I thought maybe... maybe you still loved me."

Why hadn't he whisked Kass off to Vegas for a whirlwind wedding last weekend? That would have solved everything. If only he loved her. He pinched the bridge of his nose. "Erin, please don't start. We don't have a future together. I'm only allowing this visit for the twins' sake." He should never have said *yes* at all.

"Wouldn't it be best for them if we were a fam—?"

"No. I'm pretty sure it wouldn't."

"But I gave birth to them."

"You did." He hadn't been there. He'd been out getting smashed. "Those papers you signed? They gave me full custody of Christopher and Avery. You have no jurisdiction except what I grant you. None."

He drove past Elmer's and into his own driveway. No way was he pulling in at Green Acres with Erin still on the line, no matter how much his heart ached to clutch his kids close after four days apart.

Not Liz. He wasn't thinking about her.

"I see you're as stubborn as you ever were."

"Yep. Pretty much. Look, Erin. I have to go now. Your bus gets in about four o'clock tomorrow. Walk down to—" Oh, man. After ditching Roger for two days this week, Mason couldn't leave early, nor could he have Erin pacing the tire shop for an hour. "Walk down to the bakery on Main. Anyone can give you directions. I'll meet you there when I get off work at five, okay?"

She sighed. "I guess."

"Okay. See you tomorrow." He tapped the dashboard icon to end the call then cradled his face in both hands.

Could God possibly want him to marry Erin? He wanted Liz, but had bungled everything again. And then there was Kass. *God? I'm going to need a boatload of help here. Oh, and patience. I don't even know where to start. Point me in the right direction?*

When wisdom from heaven didn't instantaneously flood his heart, he put the car into gear and headed next door. At least he knew where he stood with his kids. Whatever else happened, they were his primary responsibility, and right now, he couldn't wait to wrap his arms tight around them.

oOo

Liz paced the small duplex. Funny how it seemed like home, though she'd been away again as long as she'd been on Green Acres over Christmas. She straightened the two Bibles on the table: the one Chelsea had given her and the old leather-bound she'd dug out of storage last night at her parents' new house. Their tears had mingled with hers as they'd held each other, another piece of her reconciliation.

She had so much to be thankful for. So much. God's love and forgiveness. Her parents. Her brother and his friends, who'd taken her in and given her a home and a job. What more could she want?

A knock at the door hip-checked her brain from the direction it was headed. Chelsea? She was early.

Liz hurried to the door and swung it wide.

Mason. Her breath caught. Blond hair disheveled, a few days' worth of growth on his face and the wary blue eyes she was all too familiar with.

"You made it!" Why hadn't she heard her car? Oh, his was in the way. He'd parked over by the straw bale house.

"Yep." He reached out, dangling her fob.

"Come in for a minute?" She accepted her keys and fumbled in her purse for his.

"No. I can't, really. I need to pick up the kids from Brent and Allison's and spend some time with them."

"Claire said she'd invited you for dinner."

He shook his head, not meeting her gaze. "Not tonight. I've got meals in the freezer I can quickly thaw and heat."

Realization sank in. "Kass."

"Uh. Yeah." He scratched the back of his neck. "Not that she's coming for supper. She helped me get a bunch of starters in the freezer."

Good? Bad? How could Liz possibly know? But there was time to figure it out. She'd promised Allison to stay at least a couple of months.

He stretched out his hand and she dropped the keys into it, as careful as he'd been not to touch.

"Mason!" Chelsea squealed. She grabbed him and gave him a fierce hug from behind.

He snagged her and returned her hug.

Liz stepped back into the room.

Chelsea's gaze swung from Mason to Liz then back again. "Am I interrupting something?"

"Not at all." Mason held up his keys. "Just doing the car swap." He nodded at Liz. "I'm going to pick up the kids. See you around."

"See you."

He strode up the path toward the houses above, where Allison and Brent lived next door to Zach and Jo.

Liz realized a hand waved in front of her face.

"Liz? I'm sensing quite the story here. I brought cookies." Chelsea shut the door, blocking off the view before Mason disappeared between the trees.

"I don't think there's a story."

"Ha." Chelsea shrugged out of her jacket and peeled off her boots. "That's what you think now, but I'm an expert in these things. I can tell you all about Sierra and Gabe and Allison and Brent."

She probably could, too. Tales that might be fun to hear one day, but not now. Not when her own heart felt fractured. "Where does Kass fit into things?"

Oh man. Had she really asked that out loud?

Chelsea chuckled and pried the lid off the round tin. "Pumpkin raisin?" Her eyes danced.

"They look good."

Chelsea swung the tin behind her back. "I'll let you have one if you tell me why you asked about Kass."

"Maybe I'm not that fond of cookies."

"I'm a good listener, and I don't blab." Chelsea set the tin on the table. "But I'm thinking there aren't that many secrets here. Just dots that need connected. Help yourself to a cookie while I fix some hot chocolate."

No secrets? Chelsea might be correct. From what Zach and her parents said, Mason had already told his version of what had happened their senior year. Her darkest secret had been exposed, and everyone still loved her. "I have a question."

"Oh?" Halfway to the kitchenette, Chelsea turned. "What's that?"

"There's this verse I keep thinking about. *Though your sins be as scarlet, they shall be as white as snow.* What does it mean?"

"Oh, that's Isaiah 1:18. I looked it up not long ago. It goes on to say, *though they be red like crimson, they shall be as wool.*"

"I never really thought about red sins before. What does it mean?"

"Commentators don't agree completely. The obvious answer seems to be that red dye was the worst color to try to bleach out."

"And the other?"

Chelsea looked pensive. "A few believe red represents sexual sin. Like when Rahab the harlot dangled a red thread from her window when the Israelites marched around Jericho."

Sexual sin? Yes, God could remove its stains, too.

Chapter 32 --

The closed sign had been flipped in the bakery window and the main lights dimmed. Two figures stood looking out the window.

Panic clawed at Mason's throat. Nothing would ever be the same after this ugly week, and it was starting right now. He should have known better than to send Erin to the bakery. He should have warned Kass. And said what?

Kass swung the door open and stretched up to kiss him on the cheek. "Hi, Mason. I've got some company here for you."

He should respond in some way. Maybe kiss Kass back, but that would send the wrong signal to both of them. He smiled at her. "Thanks for waiting for me to get here."

Her eyebrows rose. "It's rather cold to make someone wait outside."

"It is."

Erin bumped into Kass as she approached. That could have been more subtle. "Hi, Mason." She'd poured all the sultry she owned into those words.

"Hi, Erin. Ready to go?"

"I sure am." She turned to Kass. "It's been nice chatting."

Mason breathed a prayer. This was worse than he'd expected. He'd been doing nothing but bumbling from one mess to the next lately. Ever since Liz returned in December. At least she wasn't here as well. "Let me carry your bag. I'm parked just down the street."

"Yes, I'm dying to see *our* children." Erin cast a triumphant glance at Kass as she pushed the handle of her gigantic suitcase at Mason. "The little dears need their mama back in their lives."

Mason hesitated. Kass didn't deserve this. He'd tried to tell her nothing could work out between them, but she still didn't deserve Erin. "Thanks, Kass. I'll talk to you soon."

She crossed her arms and shrugged, her eyebrows raised.

Yeah, that'd have to be some apology, yet one that ended short of declaring love he didn't feel. For a guy who once thought he'd been suave with the female gender, he was a dolt. He was in way over his head.

He followed Erin out of the bakery, listening to the lock turn behind them. Erin tucked her hand behind his elbow. "Such a quaint little town. What do you do for fun around here?"

Mason shifted the suitcase to the other side, dislodging Erin's grasp.

She pouted at him, and he pretended not to notice. "Have a good trip?"

"I hate buses."

Not much he could add to that. He swung her suitcase into the trunk. Sure was heavy, like she'd brought everything she owned. He paused, one hand on the trunk lid. She wouldn't have done that. Would she?

"So tell me about your house."

He glanced at her as he started the car. "I'm renting an old drafty farmhouse that needs serious renovations."

"Oh. But it has lots of space?"

"Erin."

He could just make out the batting of her eyelashes in the glow of the streetlights. "What?"

"You're not staying."

"Why don't you want me?"

Where to start? "You're here for a week. I get that. But then I'm taking you back to town and putting you back on the bus. I don't know where you're going, but you're not staying here."

"But the children..."

"Don't start. You haven't thought about them for five minutes in their entire lives. There's no court of law that would give you custody. This is a visit. Nothing more." He glanced at her hand resting on his sleeve. "And don't touch me."

"Are you afraid it will awaken your old feelings for me?"

"Not really."

He must have sounded casual enough she believed him. She stared out the side window for a few minutes at the swirling snow. They'd had so many storms this winter. He was lucky his drive from Des Moines had been relatively uneventful.

"You live a long way from town."

"We're on our way to my parents' house."

"No way. Mason, you can't—"

His patience was about gone, and it hadn't even been half an hour. "I told you on the phone the kids go there on the bus Monday and Tuesday. Mom invited us for supper." He waited a beat. "I said no."

Erin swore.

"Another thing. None of that language around my kids."

"They're mine, too."

"Which you've conveniently forgotten. Make no mistake, Erin. You're in my territory. Play by my rules. The bus goes south every day." He signaled and turned into the driveway. "Want to come up to the house or stay in the car?"

She huffed. "I'll wait here, thanks."

"Suit yourself." He turned off the ignition and pocketed the keys.

"I'll freeze."

Like he was going to leave her with a running car. He wasn't born yesterday. "Not in five minutes if you don't get out. It's the wind chill that will kill you." He strode up the walk and into the house.

Avery bounced over to the door. "Is my mommy here?"

"She's in the car. Hurry up, and get your coat on." Mason met his mom's gaze over Avery's head and shook his head.

Mom pursed her lips but, for once, said nothing.

"Come on, Christopher."

His son tromped over to the entry and shoved his feet into boots. A minute later Mason herded both kids down the steps. They climbed into the backseat and reached for their seatbelts.

"Are you my mom?" Avery asked.

"Yes, I am!" Erin turned slightly as Mason slid into his and started the engine.

"Can you tell good bedtime stories? And make cookies? And give hugs?"

Erin cast him a helpless look.

Good luck pleasing Avery.

o0o

It ought to be beneath her, but Liz couldn't help it. She, Chelsea, and Keanan lingered over cleanup in the straw bale house kitchen.

"I wonder what she's like," Chelsea whispered for the fifteenth time as she scrubbed the butcher-block island.

Keanan shook his head, but a small smile poked at his cheeks. "She isn't any of our business, sweetheart."

Speak for yourself. Erin was plenty of Liz's business. One glimpse of how Mason treated her would tell Liz everything she needed to know.

Nearly everything.

Boots scuffling across the deck accompanied by low voices caused Liz to freeze. She hadn't been to the washroom in ten minutes. What if her hair wasn't in place? What if she'd smudged her mascara somehow? Couldn't be helped. She wiped clammy hands on a kitchen towel and shot a glance at Chelsea as the outside door opened.

Chelsea grinned and gave her a thumbs-up.

Avery and Christopher kicked off their boots and shed their coats on the floor. "Miss Liz!" Avery ran into the kitchen. "Will you read me a story?"

Take that, Erin.

"I'd love to in just a minute, if you're staying long enough." Liz's eyes were trained across the peninsula to where a slight woman in a tweed coat stood beside Mason.

Mason's gaze snapped to hers and he swallowed hard. "Hi everyone. I'd like you to meet the children's mother, Erin. Erin, this is Liz and K—"

"Nice to meet you all." Erin shrugged out of her coat. "I'm sure I won't remember everyone's names."

Liz became aware of Claire, who must've come in from the back hallway that led to their bedroom. "Hi, Erin. I'm Claire. I live in this house with my husband and our toddler, Ash. You'll be our guest for the next few days."

Erin shot a look at Mason that could only be disgust. She'd thought she'd climb right back in his bed? He wasn't that easy a catch. Liz should know.

"Well, I'll let you get settled." Liz took Avery's hand and guided her out of the kitchen and into the great room. "Want a story, too, Christopher?"

He already had the train set out in the corner and shook his head. Avery pulled away to pick a book from the nearby case then jumped onto the leather sofa and patted the spot beside her.

Liz obliged, sliding her arm around the little girl's shoulder and opening the book with her other hand. She read aloud, her ears trained to other activities as Mason carried a huge suitcase into the bedroom wing and the voices faded.

"See you tomorrow, Liz!" called Chelsea as she and Keanan bundled up to head across the farm to their cozy house.

Liz glanced up and waved then refocused on the story and the child snuggled against her. Soft footsteps caught her attention just as Mason's faded jeans crossed her line of vision beyond the book. The sofa shifted as he lowered himself on the other side of Avery. Liz poured enthusiasm into the closing pages of the story.

"Another one, Miss Liz?" Avery looked up at her with pleading eyes.

"Not tonight, princess. Put the book away and play with your brother for a minute. We're going home soon."

"And my mommy is staying here?"

Mason nodded.

"Okay." Avery slid off the sofa, clutching the book to her chest. "My mommy doesn't read stories," she said to Liz, lower lip full and pouty.

"I'm sorry to hear that." And she was. No matter how complicated Mason was, the twins were innocent. The thought of Erin breaking Avery's heart? Shattering. She caught Avery's hand. "I love reading. I love pretending to be someone else and having fun adventures while staying warm and safe." Hopefully that wasn't a statement on her whole life. Pretending to be someone else. Someone who hadn't made stupid decisions and gotten deeply hurt.

"Me, too!" Avery looked at her dad then back. "But Daddy said no more stories tonight."

"That's okay. We'll read another time. Maybe we can start on a chapter book, and we can read a bit every day. Would you like a long-ago story about a little girl, or an adventure in a make-believe land?"

Avery screwed up her face as she thought. "Long ago."

"Okay. We'll start Wednesday when you come after school."

"Yay!" The child bounced over to put the book away. "Did you hear that, Christopher? I get a grown-up book."

Mason chuckled. "You've made a friend for life."

What a loaded comment. Liz glanced at him, aware of the child-sized space between them. "How is it going?"

He leaned onto his knees, hands buried in his hair. "It's going to be a really long week is all I can say."

Liz could barely hear him, but that was okay. He couldn't want the kids to hear, and it gave her an excuse to shift a little closer and turn on the sofa so she could. "Do you—"

"Liz, I've made such a mess of my life." He groaned. "Well, you know."

"You told me once that God had forgiven you. You can't keep beating yourself up for it."

He angled his face to look up at her. "You really did have a come-to-Jesus moment in Des Moines."

She nodded.

"Erin is like another child. There's a negative one thousand percent chance we'll ever get back together."

Liz wasn't sure if her heart should thrill at that, but it did.

"Can you be patient with me a little bit longer?" He stretched his hand between them. "Give me a chance?"

Her fingers tangled with his. Her heart had been tangled for a long time, and her eyes wouldn't let go, either. "I think so."

Those clear blue eyes probed right through her, seeing into the depths of her being. His, too, hid nothing. This was Mason. The man he'd become through all the twists and turns of his life. The man redeemed by Jesus. The bad boy she'd been infatuated with as a teenager had become a man of God, and now she loved him.

"There's a lot of water under the bridge," she murmured. "But it's gone. Swept away."

Voices from the bedroom wing grew louder. Maybe just as well.

Mason squeezed her hand then pulled away, regret shining in his eyes. "Thanks. For everything."

Claire entered the room. "Our guest says to tell you goodnight. She's retiring now."

"Alrighty then." Mason stood. "Clean up the train, kids."

"Aw, Dad..." whined Christopher.

"You have school tomorrow, and it's already past your bedtime."

"I should go, too." Liz rose.

"Feel free to spend the day here if you like, Liz." Claire glanced between her and Mason. "It might do some good."

To get to know Erin a bit? It might not hurt, at that. The jealousy had dissipated after seeing Erin and Mason together. "Thanks." She crossed to the door as the twins raced past her.

The four of them left the straw bale house together. The children ran down the well-packed trail between the farms, lit with a few solar lights hanging from posts and trees.

Liz had never been more aware of Mason beside her as they strolled toward the division in the path, her hand clasped firmly in his. They stopped, and he turned her toward him.

"Thanks, Liz." His lips brushed across hers just once as his arms tightened around her. He released her with a grin and a shake of the head. "Soon." Then he turned and followed the twins down the path.

Snow drifted from the night sky, angling across the glow from the solar lights. The tingling warmth from her lips spread through her body, keeping the cold at bay.

If it took a bit more patience to get kisses that would curl her toes — and more — she could wait. But not too long.

Chapter 33 --

"*Y*ou wanted to talk?" Mason slid into the chair across from Kass at the bakery on his lunch break the next day. "Aren't you working?"

"Rylee agreed to cover my shift. She's been wanting more hours."

Man, Kass looked a mess, her green eyes rimmed with red. Was this his doing, too? He couldn't seem to come near a woman without causing problems.

Rylee set his sandwich and coffee in front of him. He took a sip. "So... what's up?"

"I'm leaving Galena Landing."

He stared at Kass in shock even as relief flowed through him. "You're what?"

"Going to Spokane. I told you about my grandparents' bakery downtown, I think. Well, they left it to my cousin and me. Hailey found a few people to invest money, and we're reopening it."

"Th-that's a terrific opportunity for you."

A shadow crossed her face, and she took a deep breath. "Yes, it is. There's more revitalization going on downtown. I think the bakery will go over well."

"I'm happy for you."

She flicked a glance at him then refocused on turning her

coffee cup round and round on the table. "I'm going to miss you and the twins."

"We'll miss you, too."

Kass shook her head. "But not enough."

Her meaning came through clearly. "I'm sorry." He could say he wished it could have been different, but he didn't. It wasn't Kass's fault he hadn't fallen in love with her. "You're terrific. You'll find someone else. Someone with less baggage. Someone who's just right for you."

"I don't know." She lifted her gaze to his. Regret shone from her green eyes.

"You will. You'll be glad you're not saddled with my kids' mother, at the very least."

She couldn't hide a slight grin. "Erin's a piece of work, isn't she?"

"She is that."

"But you don't love her." It was almost a question.

Mason shook his head and had a sip of coffee. "I don't. I don't think I ever did. We were two kids playing a game and ended up with children. She wanted the games to continue, and I didn't. She's still playing them." He lifted a shoulder. "Beats me what, though. All I can tell you is that I'm not playing. I've pledged to live my life for Jesus and raise those kids the best I can."

"I *will* miss Avery and Christopher. All the kids from their Sunday school class."

"They'll miss you, too. Do you know who's taking the class?"

"No. I'll call Ed Graysen this afternoon. I feel really badly about suddenly leaving him with no teacher."

Mason tilted his head. "Exactly when are you leaving?"

"That's the thing. Tomorrow."

"Whoa." How had he never guessed she had one foot out the door? "Good thing my freezer's full."

She gave him a lopsided grin. "You'll be fine. You have that whole Green Acres gang. Allison's all over the monthly meal prep thing. You don't need me for anything."

What could he say? She'd been a good friend, and he'd miss her. But need was a big word. Kass was right. He didn't *need* her.

"The twins need a woman, Mason. So do you."

Now she was on to giving him advice about his love life? He took a bite of his sandwich to mask the grin.

"Not Erin, though."

His mouth full, he nodded.

"Let me think."

"Don't worry about it. My mother's been doing a good enough job, as you well know. Besides..." He hesitated. "I'm not looking."

"The kids aren't getting any younger." Kass eyed him. "Neither are you."

"True."

"I think—"

"Kass?"

"Yeah?"

"I meant it. I'm not looking." He raised his eyebrows. Could he trust her with his secret?

"Ohhh." Her eyes widened as she leaned forward. "Liz."

"Everything has changed. She's rededicated her life to Jesus." He held up a cautionary hand. "First we have to get through Erin's visit, and then we'll see how it goes. I'm trying not to rush into things. We need to make sure."

Kass closed her eyes for a few seconds. "I'm happy for you, Mason."

"Are you?"

"Okay, I *will* be. Honestly. But it does make me feel better as I leave."

"Feel *better?*" Shouldn't this news break her heart?

"You guys need someone so much."

Mason would be offended if it weren't such a relief. He leaned back and crossed his arms, trying to give off a serious image. "We were only a project?"

"Well, at first. Kind of. I mean, I really like you, but..."

He chuckled. "It's okay. See? It's better this way." He took a bite of his sandwich and glanced at the clock. Not much longer until he had to be back at work.

"Thanks. I feel like a fool for throwing myself at you."

"No worries. Tell me about the bakery."

She straightened in the chair, eyes wide. "Oh, no! I forgot the twins' birthday. I promised them cakes."

"It's okay. I'll find a cake."

"No, Mason. I promised, and I can't do that to Avery or Christopher. Not after they spent so long telling me what kinds of cakes they wanted. I have time to make them this afternoon. Come by tomorrow and pick them up? They'll be fine in the freezer until their party Saturday."

"If you're sure."

"Totally. I'll run them through the till and pay for them today. My gift."

"Okay. Thanks." He leaned back in his chair. "You really are leaving tomorrow?"

"I am. Once I decide to do something, I don't usually wait around. It worked out fine here as Rylee is the owner's niece, but they didn't want to take my hours away for her. They've been great to me."

"Cool."

"It's been raining the past few days, so the highway should be in good shape. It might turn to snow again tomorrow. I don't want to wait."

"You've got good tires, don't you?"

She laughed. "Always the tire man. Yes, they're good."

Mason stood, wiping his mouth with the paper napkin. "Stay

safe, then. I wish you all the best. Keep in touch."

Kass came around the table and pecked his cheek. "Thanks for everything. And remember I make wedding cakes, too."

oOo

Liz glanced up as Keanan tromped into the straw bale house. Any break from the animal husbandry syllabus open in front of her was welcome. Claire puttered in the kitchen while Erin grouched from a stool at the peninsula.

"Everything coming back to you?"

Liz grinned over at him. "I'm learning stuff I didn't know. How are things in the barns?"

"It's raining." He flicked moisture from his nylon parka. "Looks like our first lamb is on the way."

"Really? It's not like them to give birth in the daytime. I seem to remember a lot of knocks on my door at two in the morning from my dad."

"We switched up the feeding schedule and hope that helps." He jerked his head toward the door. "Want to come see?"

Liz stretched. "I'd love to." Those middle of the night times with her dad had been the best. Even when they'd had to assist a difficult birth. Even on the rare occasion they'd lost the lamb.

"I'm coming, too."

Keanan looked past Liz. "Dress warm, and make sure to wear barn boots."

"Barn boots?" echoed Erin. "What are those?"

"They're not high-heeled leather, but something you can hose off."

"I guess I'll stay inside."

Liz shoved her feet into insulated rubber boots and, heeding Keanan's warning about the rain, grabbed a slicker from the hook. She followed him out onto the deck and glanced at the gray sky.

"Wow, it looks like it's going to rain forever."

"God promised Noah it wouldn't."

She chuckled. "Good to know."

A few minutes later she entered the dimly lit barn where the expectant sheep had been corralled at one end. She breathed in the pungent air and felt the tension Erin brought drift away. If she closed her eyes, she could be thirteen again, sitting on a bale over there, watching her dad shuffle through the flock as he murmured to them.

She belonged here. This farm held her roots through three generations. No wonder Zach had been tugged back. She was, too.

The man with her was Keanan, though, not Dad.

"Can you help me get this one into the solo pen?" He pointed at a ewe standing, head down.

Liz swung her leg over the corral. "Sure."

It only took a minute then Liz got water for the laboring animal.

"Shouldn't be long," Keanan murmured. "I caught a glimpse of hooves."

Gabe's quiet voice came from the shadows. "She'll be fine."

The ewe strained.

For a few seconds Liz saw tiny dark hooves and mucus that likely covered the lamb's nose, then the sheep relaxed.

A moment later she pushed again and, before Liz knew it, the lamb had been expelled in a rush of blood and liquid. The ewe struggled to her feet as Keanan knelt beside the wiggling lamb, wiping its nose with a handful of straw.

"She's got it, bro," said Gabe.

Keanan retreated to the planks where he leaned back between Liz and Gabe. "Wow."

A grin spread across Liz's face. "Amazing, isn't it?"

"It never gets old."

A shift in the air told Liz Gabe had walked away. Soon the

barn door opened and shut. Oh, no. He and Sierra couldn't have children. Even watching the birth of a lamb must bring pain.

"He's okay," said Keanan quietly. "Just tough sometimes."

Keanan would likely know. Their wives were sisters.

Liz swung her legs back out of the pen. "Thanks for getting me."

"Glad you came." His eyes crinkled as he smiled. "Just in case it didn't go so smoothly."

The ewe licked the lamb as the newborn struggled to stand.

New life.

Liz felt like she had new life, too, and a new direction. Green Acres was where she was meant to be.

o0o

"You know I can't stay long." Mason stood in his parents' doorway, coat still on. He'd dumped the boots in the entryway though. His mom would never stand for puddles.

"When will we meet Erin?"

The twins scuttled around the living room, putting toys away. Mason turned to the kitchen. "The party on Saturday?"

"But—"

"Mom, don't start. She's not staying. She's not a part of the family. She's a visitor with biological ties to my children. That's all."

"What's bi-bilogal?" Avery wrapped her arms around his waist.

Great. Mason gave his mother a significant look over Avery's head. "Biological. It means she's the person who gave birth to you." And that's all. But he couldn't say that.

"My mother."

He stroked her back, noticing she hadn't said *mommy* this time. "Are you done cleaning up?" The answer was clearly no from how many toys remained out.

Avery sighed, disengaged, and went back to help Christopher.

"Little pitchers have big ears," Mason said to his mother.

"You never come without them. When are you bringing Kass again?"

Mason held her gaze. He needed to tell the twins about the situation, not let them overhear Mom pick Kass's decision apart. "I'm not."

Mom sighed. "Mason, you—"

"Don't start." He held up a hand. "I'm twenty-eight years old, Mom. No more matchmaking from you. You're welcome to talk to God about it, but not me, and not anyone else. Please."

Her lips pressed into a tight line. "Fine."

He had no idea whether his mom would be happy about Liz or not, but today wasn't the day to find out. "Come on, you two. Let's get going. We're going to Green Acres for supper."

"But I—"

"Mom. Things are easier to diffuse with a dozen people around. Okay?" Especially when two of them weren't his parents.

She crossed her arms over her chest. "Fine."

"See you Saturday. Why don't you and Dad come for lunch? The party starts at two."

Chapter 34 --

*L*iz looked up as Avery, Christopher, and Finnley clattered in the door after school.

"That was so cool," yelled Christopher, putting his palms together and swishing them from side to side like a fish. "The bus went like this on the road. Whoosh. Whoosh."

Avery took off her boots. "It was scary."

Allison, who'd been working at the large plank table with Liz, crossed to look out the window. "When did it turn to snow again? No wonder the roads are a mess."

Erin turned from the stool at the peninsula. "Hi, kids."

Christopher ignored her, but Avery glanced over. "Hi." Then she came to Liz and slid her arm around Liz's neck. "Will you read to me?"

She'd been staring at the farm school notebooks long enough. Liz stood and stretched. "I'd love to, but maybe you kids would like a snack first."

"A snack! Yay!" Christopher ran over to the table and slid into a seat, Finnley beside him.

Allison laughed. "I'll get it, Liz. Today is Avery's turn to pick."

Christopher slumped and crossed his arms. "But I want cookies."

Avery looked at him. "Me, too."

The boys both brightened. "What kind is there?" asked Christopher.

"Oatmeal huckleberry."

Christopher scowled. "What?"

"Finnley, you remember, don't you?" asked Allison from the kitchen. "We picked lots of huckleberries on the mountain last summer. And then we dried some for cookies."

Finnley nodded. "They taste like raisins."

Erin made a gagging sound. "Sounds like a lot of work. Why not just buy raisins?"

Allison met Liz's gaze across the peninsula and table. "That's what we're all about here at Green Acres. Growing as much of our own food as we can."

Liz's parents had always had a large garden. Mom had canned fruit and frozen vegetables. They'd raised animals for meat. Lots of farmers didn't go to all that trouble anymore, but Liz was glad she'd experienced the full lifestyle as a kid. Going through the class material for the farm school had reignited her interest. "I'll pour milk. Want more tea, Erin?"

"Sure." Erin shrugged. "Going to all that extra work sounds silly when the stores have everything."

Allison said nothing but set a plate with two cookies beside Erin then brought a larger mound to the table.

Liz was right behind her with three glasses of milk. Then she topped off the chamomile tea for the women.

Christopher eyed the cookies. "How many can I have?"

"Two each," Allison said firmly. "See, they're big ones."

Avery nibbled the edge of hers. "This is so yummy, Aunt Allison."

Erin sighed. "That's another thing. She's not your aunt."

Wow. Someone was grouchy. Cabin fever already after only three days?

278

Allison turned a placid smile at Erin, but Liz could see the tension in her friend's eyes. "We are like a big family, and this is one way the children feel part of it. Having all these honorary aunts and uncles reminds them they belong, and there are many adults who care deeply about their wellbeing. Everyone needs a place to belong, Erin, and this system has been in place for years already. It works for us."

Erin opened her mouth and closed it again before biting her lip. Then she broke off a corner of a cookie and put it in her mouth.

Liz didn't miss the slight widening of Erin's eyes and the intensity with which she polished off the rest. Not that Erin seemed capable of giving a verbal compliment. Liz caught Allison's eye and gave her a quick nod and smile. Yep, good cookies.

Jo and Claire came in from a trip to town with their children. Claire set her keys on a hook then started stripping Ash's snowsuit off. "Nasty out there. I'm glad I don't have to go anywhere again for a few days. The rain didn't last long enough to melt off all the snow."

Jo set John free, and Ash toddled after him. Maddie ran to the table for a cookie.

Another storm was on its way according to the forecast, and the guys were stacking extra bales inside the barn to make feeding easier. Keanan had been testing a solar pump for the animals' water in case Mason's power went out again. Of course, the sun hadn't shone in days.

Liz glanced at the clock. It wasn't as late as it seemed from the dull sky. "Come on," she said to Avery. "I think we can read a couple of chapters of *Little House* before suppertime."

"What are we having today? It smells good."

"Roast beef, I think. Aunt Allison is today's cook." Liz turned to Maddie. "Do you want to listen, too?"

Maddie nodded and curled up against Liz's other side on the sofa. The same place she and Mason had talked briefly the other night. He'd asked for patience. Liz had agreed. Did he just mean because of Erin's visit, or was there more to it? Because this farm would never be a calm backdrop for quiet, romantic conversation. Yet somehow they'd managed during Christmas week.

"Miss Liz?" Avery tugged at her arm. "Here's the book."

Liz smiled down at the little girl. "Okay. I think we were on chapter seven."

oOo

Mason glanced in the window as he crossed the deck then came to a halt. The fireplace flickered, causing a golden glow on Liz's beautiful face and blond hair as she sat on the sofa facing it, a little girl wedged against her on either side. Maddie's brown curls tumbled across her face as Avery's hand traced a picture in the book they were reading. Liz's lips moved, her face full of expression, and then she turned the page.

His heart pounded erratically. How long should he wait to declare himself to Liz? He ached for a few minutes alone with her. He hadn't even kissed her properly yet.

Maddie slid off the sofa and ran out of view, probably to join the boys at play. She couldn't sit still long, that one. Liz looked down at Avery as they discussed something on the page. They shared a smile then Liz bent slightly and kissed Avery's hair.

"What's going on?" Brent came up the steps behind him.

Little pellets of ice flicked against Mason's face as he turned from the view. "Nothing."

Brent looked past him. "That doesn't look like nothing. It takes a special woman to love someone else's kids. I should know."

"You're right."

His friend poked his chin toward the window. "Question is, are you going to do something about it?"

"Yeah, I think I am. Soon."

"Good. Now let's see what's on the menu. I'm starving." Brent headed toward the door before glancing back. "You seen Zach?"

Mason shook his head. "He can't usually get the clinic locked up until closer to five-thirty, I think. He should be here anytime."

As one they turned and peered into the darkness. No headlights.

"He'll be fine. He's driven on worse." Brent opened the door and entered the house.

Mason followed, his gaze heading straight for Liz as though he hadn't just spent five minutes watching her. This time she glanced up and the smile she gave him sank deep into his heart, warming him.

Avery looked up even as she tugged on Liz's arm. "Hi, Daddy. Read more, Miss Liz."

Mason hung his coat. "Looks like we need more hooks behind this door," he said to Brent.

"Good call. I might not drive out to my build tomorrow. Maybe I'll carve some pegs instead."

"What's up?"

"Didn't you see how high the Galena River is? Made me a little nervous coming across the bridge tonight."

Mason frowned. "I didn't notice."

"I haven't lived here for many winters, but this is the most snow and rain I've seen yet. I looked it up, and it's breaking records all over the panhandle."

"Yeah, they were talking about that on the radio today. At least we're getting a good snow pack up high. That should keep the danger of forest fires down this summer."

"Always a good thing."

Mason glanced over at the kitchen. Erin perched on a stool at the counter, watching him. Not in a predatory way, but with a bit of panic. He could imagine how overwhelming this gang could get to the unsuspecting. He lifted his hand in greeting but turned to the scene in the great room. His kids needed a hug, and so did Liz.

Tonight. He'd find at least five minutes.

oOo

A cell buzzed, and the house fell silent. Liz glanced up. It wasn't her phone, for sure.

Jo looked out the window at the unrelenting darkness as it rang a second time then reached for hers. "Zach?"

They'd been waiting dinner on him for twenty minutes. Not that long in the great scheme of things, but the weather was ugly. Really ugly.

Jo's face paled. "Are you okay?" She sank into a chair, her knuckles white around the device. "Thank God you're okay. And your parents? ... Ed and Mona? Of course. No problem ... See you in a few." She lowered the phone and stared at it.

"Jo?" Sierra crouched beside Jo's chair and slid her arm around her shoulders. "What happened?"

"He'll be fine." Jo's voice choked.

"I'm glad. What happened with your parents? And the Graysens?"

Jo took a deep, shaky breath. "There was an avalanche on the south edge of town. Snow. Mud. Trees. Right behind Rosemary and Steve's house."

Liz shot to her feet. "Is it gone?" Her parents' retirement home. Mom's workroom where she sewed quilts for Romanian orphans. It couldn't be.

"No, but it could be if more comes down. Steve called Zach as he was locking up the clinic, so Zach said he'd bring them out to the farm for a few days until things settle."

"Of course." Claire rubbed circles on Jo's back. "We'll make room."

"Rosemary was worried about Mona and Ed. Their place backs that ravine, and the creek's rising. So Zach said he had room in the truck for them, too."

"My parents can stay with me." Liz crouched in front of Jo. "For that matter, so can Graysens. I have a sofa to sleep on."

"Zach could hear rumbling up the hill while he was loading a few things from his parents' house, so he didn't take time to call me then. He just wanted to get out of Galena Landing."

"Mama? You okay?" Maddie peered into her mom's face.

Jo gathered the little one tight. "Oh, baby. Yes, I'm okay. So are Daddy and Grandma and Grandpa." She glanced around the group, her gaze landing on Liz. "They're all right."

"Finish the story," suggested Claire, still soothing Jo.

"It all took longer than Zach thought. Finally they were on their way out to the farm. The river was high. He was almost across the bridge when he felt something slam into it. He gunned the motor and made it across, but the bridge is gone." Jo buried her face in Maddie's curls. "So close."

Headlights angled down Thompson Road. The crowd in the straw bale house surged for the door. Liz reached for Jo but too many bodies came between.

Strong arms surrounded her. Mason. She turned and clung to him, tears streaming down her face. "I can't believe I almost lost them. Just when I've let them back in."

"They're safe, sweetheart." He folded her against his chest and rested his cheek on the top of her head.

His heart beat steadily through the Henley-style shirt, the waffle-weave soft against her cheek. Nothing could harm her when Mason held her close.

Avery wrapped her arms around both of them, her nose squishing against Liz's hip.

Of course. The little girl felt the mood in the room and needed assurance just as Maddie had. Liz loosened her grip on Mason and encircled Avery but, if anything, Mason held her even closer.

"I've waited all day for this," he murmured into her hair. "All week. I'm not letting go just yet."

Feet stomped on the deck outside. Cold, damp air swirled in from the open door. Liz tipped her face to look into Mason's and smiled at him. "You'll get more chances."

"You bet I will." Once again, his lips brushed hers with the intensity of promise. He pulled away, regret shining in his eyes. "Later."

As Liz turned toward the door, she caught Erin's gaze. The twins' mother still sat by the peninsula with a puzzled frown marring her once-pretty face. Erin wasn't that different from Vonnie. From Martha and Anne and the others at the soup kitchen in Des Moines. Down on her luck, needing a helping hand. Needing Jesus.

Could Liz extend that hand?

Chapter 35 --

"No school!" yelled Christopher. "The best birthday present ever!"

Mason groaned and rolled over in his bed. No work, either. That bridge linked the entire north panhandle to the rest of Idaho. News had reached the farm that the avalanche had taken out the road south of Galena Landing, too.

"Daddy, I turned the light on in the bathroom but nothing happened," came Avery's worried voice from his bedroom door.

He squinted at his bedside clock, but there were no numbers. Power out, too? All the folks at Green Acres needed were more refugees. They'd invited him to be part of the group, though. His heart warmed. Liz would be teaching this term. At least if the roads ever reopened so students could arrive.

"Daddy?"

Rain rattled against the windows. At least this time it wasn't thirty below. "Coming, princess. Give me a minute." He swung his feet onto the cold floorboards then yanked a sweatshirt on.

It didn't take long to confirm the power outage. A glance at his cell told him the communications tower hadn't sustained damage. Whew. They could get messages in and out, at least as long as batteries lasted. He shook his head, grinning. Next door had plenty of power for charging. Plenty for everything with all those solar panels. Although even they would eventually need sunshine.

"Get dressed, kids. We're going next door."

o0o

"How many people live on this side of the bridge? And are they all out of power?" asked Sierra. "I've never stopped to count."

Liz exchanged a look with her mom. "I'll get a pen and paper and we can make a list. Not that we have room for everyone." *We.* It felt good to be part of this group where she could do something positive for folks in need. For the community in which she'd grown up.

"There's the dorm above the farm school." Allison leaned against the counter, cup of herbal tea in hand. "Desks can be moved aside in the classrooms to accommodate more. There's a commercial kitchen and bathrooms. Folks can be pretty self-sufficient, really. They can bring whatever food they have on hand."

"Which won't be a lot, for some of them," said Claire. "They count on going out to eat or picking something up from Super One after work."

"Grocery trucks won't be getting into Galena Landing for a while, either," Sierra added. "My dad drove for them for years. Most grocery stores don't have a warehouse out back, so when the shelves get empty, that's it until the next truck."

The women looked at each other then Claire shook her head. "We can't do much about Galena Landing with the bridge out, but we can make a difference for our neighbors on this side. I hope all our vehicles have plenty of fuel. Who knows how long before they restore the road?"

Keanan and Noel entered. "Four new lambs overnight, and that heifer looks close to calving." Keanan nodded, looking satisfied. "And the solar pump at the barn is working brilliantly. Could use some sunshine, though."

"It can't make up its mind whether to rain or snow," added Noel. "I guess it's good that it's not too cold."

Christopher's excited voice filtered through the discussion.

Liz's pulse quickened. Mason! He was here, if she could only get to him. She slid the pen to her mother. Mom remembered where everyone lived better than she did, and Zach could help her. He knew every farmer in the valley.

Liz jammed her feet into boots and grabbed her jacket just as the door opened to Mason and his twins.

"Miss Liz!" Avery's arms wrapped around her.

"Were you on your way out?" asked Mason, stepping aside.

"It's a zoo in there."

He peered past her. "I see that. Want to walk?" A slow smile curved his lips.

"I'd love to." Liz tied her hood around her face then patted Avery's back. "You go on in. Maddie's in there somewhere. Have you had breakfast?"

The little girl shook her head and released her. Christopher rumbled past. Mason held out his hand, and she took it. The cacophony lessened as the door shut. Or maybe Mason's touch was a force field all its own.

Hand in hand, they strolled down the slushy driveway. She hardly knew what to say to this man, the one who had captured her heart, but it didn't seem words were necessary. Just being with him was enough, away from their friends, family, and all the strategizing going on.

"Guess we're stranded," Mason said at last, turning to face her in the middle of Thompson Road. "I can't tell you how glad I am that we're both on the same side of the bridge collapse."

"I'm glad Zach got through with my parents." Liz still shuddered to think of the close call. "I'd be so worried about them in town, cut off on all sides."

Mason traced a finger down her cheek. "At least from here we can escape through Canada if we need to. But I don't want to be anywhere else." His blue eyes held hers from mere inches away. "Do you?"

His words held so many layers of meaning. "This is where I want to be," she whispered back. "Now and for always."

He leaned the tiny space between them and covered her mouth with his. This was no whisper. No passing brush of lips. This was the kiss of a man claiming the woman he loved.

Liz wrapped her arms around his neck and accepted his silent proclamation. Tasted his love and offered hers back to him. "Mason," she murmured when they came up for air.

"I love you, Liz. I love you more than I'll ever be able to tell you." His lips caught hers again, tasting, exploring.

She might never breathe again. Surely air was over-rated. "You're doing a good job," she said when she could.

"Of what?" He nibbled her lip.

"Telling me without words."

He trailed kisses across her nose, across her cheeks, across her closed eyelids. "Words are good, too," he whispered against her temple. "I love you."

Liz leaned back just enough to get his attention.

His kisses stilled as he looked deeply into her eyes.

She memorized his face. The angular jaw wearing a day's worth of stubble. The straight nose. The blue eyes, clear as a mountain lake. The lips that made her insides turn to mush.

"What is it, Liz?"

"I love you, Mason Waterman. Thank you for being patient with me. For coming to find me." *For being everything I need.* But she couldn't say those words. Not yet.

"If we're going to start with that..." His thumbs caressed her cheeks. "Thank you for forgiving me. For offering me another chance. I will never hurt you again. You have my solemn promise."

"I know I'm safe with you. All that is water under the bridge." She touched his lips and quirked a grin. "And the bridge has been swept away, just like ours. The past isn't here anymore."

"Only the future remains." He kissed her finger, but his eyes never left hers.

The future. She held his face between both her hands and touched his lips with hers, not wavering from the intensity in his gaze until he slanted his head and deepened the kiss.

oOo

A horn blared, reminding Mason he stood in the middle of a country road kissing his beloved. Not exactly a private place. He released her with a rueful grin and glanced at the big black truck looming beside him.

"Yo, Waterman! Anything you want to tell me?" Zach leaned from the open window.

Arms wrapped around Mason, Liz sidestepped toward the edge of the road, dragging him with her, like some kind of dance.

Not that he was reluctant. He kissed her again as they shifted.

The truck stayed parked. "Sorry to interrupt," Zach said drily.

"He's lying," whispered Liz. "He's not sorry at all."

"The county is in some kind of crisis situation," Mason murmured back.

"Are we supposed to care?"

"I think so. I think that's what this is all about."

"Sometimes I hate being a responsible adult."

"I hear you." He kissed her upturned nose.

Liz sighed and turned to face her brother. "What do you want, Zach?"

He jumped from the cab and strode over, jerking his chin toward the old farmhouse. "Christopher says you're out of power, too?"

Still holding Liz's hand, Mason nodded

"As near as we can figure out, the slide south of town took it all out. We've already had a few phone calls from people in panic about being cut off. No power, no water, and little food." He shook his head. "I'm glad I filled the truck's fuel tank yesterday. I'm headed out to every house on this side of the river to see how we can help."

Mason pressed a kiss to Liz's temple. "Duty calls."

"I know." She sighed, glaring at her brother. "Are you going with Zach?"

"If I can be of help."

Zach nodded. "I'd like that." A grin twitched on his face. "And on the way, I can grill you about your intentions toward my sister."

"All honorable." Mason held up both hands.

"Men." Liz shook her head and shoved her hands in her coat pockets. "I guess I'll go help cook up a storm. I'm sure we'll need a pile of food."

Mason caught her, twirled her around once, and gave her a quick kiss. "To be continued. I promise." He climbed into the truck as Liz made her way back to the farm.

Zach put the truck in gear. "I can't wait to hear the story."

oOo

"He loves you, doesn't he?" Erin's voice was flat.

Allison had assigned Liz and Erin to preparing the dorm rooms for an influx of guests, as though Liz wanted to spend time alone with the mother of Mason's children. A sharp glance at Allison had been met with a firm nod. Fine. It was probably overdue.

290

"He does." Liz pointed at the next door in the long corridor. "Want to check that one?"

Erin crossed her arms and leaned against the wall. "He's changed."

Guess they were in for a heart-to-heart right here, right now. At least they could be comfortable. Liz pushed the door open and crossed the small space to sit at the desk. "God changed him."

Erin followed her in and perched on the edge of the bed. "I don't understand."

"We've all sinned and disobeyed God."

"You mean like the ten commandments?"

"Yeah, like those. The Bible explains those and more. None of us can keep all the rules."

Erin's shoulders slumped. "I've tried to do good stuff. It's hard."

Could this woman be ready to hear what Jesus had done for her? Liz's heart stilled. What if Erin gave her heart to Jesus and wanted to be a proper mom to Avery and Christopher? A wife to Mason? She closed her eyes for an instant, remembering their kisses of only an hour before. Wouldn't it be best if Mason married Erin? But not if he didn't love her. He loved Liz. He'd told her so. He wouldn't turn his back on her now.

Erin's sins are scarlet. Jesus wants to make her white as snow.

Liz took a long, shaky breath. She had no right to withhold the story of redemption from this needy woman. *God, I trust You. I can't believe You'd give me Mason just to take him away again. But if You do, help me to remember that You are enough.*

"Death is the result of sin, Erin. God made a way to remove our sin so that we could be new creatures. He sent His only Son, Jesus, as a little baby to grow up in our dark world. Jesus didn't do anything wrong, but He was killed anyway. When He died, He accepted our sin and paid our penalty so that we can have for-giveness from God. God changes us when we accept that forgiveness. It means we want to please Him because we are so thankful."

Erin stood, her face twisted in distress. "That's easy for you to say. You're not me. You haven't lived my life."

"I've lived my own, and it hasn't been pretty."

"You?"

"Oh, yes. Trust me. God has a lot of work to do in my life. He's only now beginning because I'm finally letting Him do it."

Erin shook her head.

So Liz seemed like she had it all together? If only Erin knew. But maybe Liz didn't need to go into the whole story, at least right now. "You know what a mess Mason was."

"Yeah."

"God made him into a new person. He changed him from the inside out. You've been around for a few days now. Surely you've seen the difference."

"He does seem different. He was already different in Billings before I moved out. I didn't think it would last."

"God's power is strong in Mason's life. He meant it when he gave his life to God."

Erin shrugged, shaking her head. "I don't know. I've been messed up for a long time now. Drinking. Drugs. You name it. I'm trying to keep clean now though." Her hands rested on her belly.

Wait a minute. Liz's gaze narrowed. "Are you pregnant?"

"Yeah. Again." Erin peered at her between her lashes. "I didn't want to be. Nearly got an abortion, but a friend of mine had hers botched, and it scared me."

Mason wasn't the father this time. He'd been in Galena Landing for a couple of years. Liz dared to breathe. "There are lots of people who want babies and can't have them. Adoption is a better answer than abortion. It isn't the baby's fault they were conceived."

"I know. I just don't even know what to do. I wanted to see Avery and Christopher to remind myself that life was better. I hoped Mason..." Her voice trailed off.

Would what, take Erin back? Take the baby off her hands? A thought began to poke at the back of Liz's mind. "If you got your life straightened around, would you want to keep the baby?"

Erin shook her head. "I don't have a job or any training to get one. I don't have a home. I was living with Landon, but he kicked me out when he found out I was pregnant. That's no life for a baby."

Liz's heart went out to the hurting woman. She crossed the small room and wrapped her arms around Erin. "I know what it's like to have no home and no prospects. Without God, I would still have nothing."

"Really?" Erin sniffled into Liz's shoulder.

"Really." Liz's mind buzzed. "I have some ideas, but first I need to know if you really really want help."

"Yes." Erin's voice caught on a sob.

"And if you are open to a loving home for your baby."

Erin pulled back. "You?"

"No, not me. But will you tell your story later when I ask you to?"

Erin's brown eyes begged Liz. "Okay. If you think it can help."

"I do. For sure." Liz hesitated. "And one more thing. Can I give you a Bible? My friend underlined a whole bunch of verses that helped me understand how much God loves me. Maybe it will help you, too."

"You'd give me a Bible?"

"Absolutely."

Erin covered her face with both hands. "No wonder Mason loves you. You're so kind."

Chapter 36 --

*W*ho knew what was going on in Liz's mind this time? Mason allowed himself to be dragged over to where Sierra and Gabe stood by the door, ready to leave the melee in the straw bale house, no doubt craving some peace and quiet.

With no power next door and the temperature dipping below freezing again, he was as homeless as the three dozen other people who found themselves guests at Green Acres Farm. Avery was delighted to stay at Zach and Jo's with Maddie, while Christopher yearned for any excuse to sleep over with Finnley. That left Mason free to take one of the dorm rooms. It was noisy over there, too.

"Hey!" Liz caught Sierra's sleeve. "Can we come over and visit for a bit?"

Gabe and Sierra exchanged a glance then Sierra nodded. "Sure. I'll put on a pot of tea."

"We're bringing Erin with us."

Mason pulled back, his surprise mirrored on Sierra's face. "We are?" Not what he'd had in mind at all.

"Yes, we are." Liz's voice left no room for argument.

Not that he ever wanted to fight with her again, but he'd already cozied up to the idea of spending a quiet evening, two on two.

"Okay." Sierra glanced between them then went out the door, Gabe behind her.

"Liz? Why Erin?" Didn't she know he wanted to spend time with *her*, not with his ex?

Her eyes danced. "Trust me."

She was up to something, but he had no idea what. He raised his eyebrows. "Trust? That's a high order."

"You can do it." Liz glanced around the great room. "Wait here. I'm going to find Erin."

Mason sighed as Liz wove between the many visitors to where Erin sat alone by the window. Erin looked up, and her lips moved in response to Liz, then she nodded and followed Liz toward him.

Curiouser and curiouser.

He held the door as both women preceded him then took Liz's hand. Best to make sure Erin understood where his loyalties lay.

"I have something to tell you, Mason."

Liz's fingers squeezed his at Erin's words. How did she know he needed the reassurance?

"What's that?"

"Liz is wonderful. You're lucky to have her."

"I know." He swallowed hard.

"She'll be good for the children. And for you."

Emotion clogged his throat. What those words must have cost. "Thanks."

Liz reached out and tapped Sierra and Gabe's door, and it swung open. "Come on in, and let me take your coats." Gabe's gaze rested on Erin. "In all the crazy since you arrived, I don't believe we've properly met. I'm Gabe Rubachuk, and this is my wife, Sierra."

"Pleased to meet you," Erin murmured.

Mason narrowed his eyes at the glance she exchanged with Liz. Good thing Erin had expressed her blessing outside, or he'd be in a world of panic about now.

A few minutes later they sat around the small living room, a cup of tea beside each of them. Liz sat beside Mason and rested her hand on his thigh.

He just wanted to kiss her. Why were they here?

"Thanks for letting us invade your space," Liz began. "Erin has a story she'd like to tell you."

Sierra and Gabe exchanged a glance. "Okay," said Gabe.

Mason only wished he had someone to exchange a glance with. Liz looked like the proverbial cat with a canary in her mouth. Like a mama proud of her offspring. Wait a minute. He looked at Erin then back at Liz. Hmm.

"I don't know how much you know about me," began Erin, casting a glance in his direction.

Mason closed his fingers over Liz's. "They know about the time we spent together."

Erin nodded. "Okay. I left when the twins were about a year old. I didn't want to be tied down. I was partying and drinking and sleeping around, and Mason refused to join me anymore."

Liz turned her hand and interlaced her fingers with his. Her arm and thigh pressed tight against his, and he gained what comfort he could from her support.

"I was careful not to get pregnant, though. I hated being fat, and they couldn't give me strong enough drugs to get through childbirth. But one night a few months ago—" Erin's gaze caught on Mason's "—it happened anyway."

He could see the white of Sierra's knuckles as she crushed Gabe's hand on the other loveseat.

Erin looked down. "I nearly got an abortion, but a friend of mine had one and they really muddled it up. She's a mess. I didn't want that either. That's when I called you, Mason."

Mason cleared his throat, trying to get past the lump. "I'm glad you did." He was. Having her here had provided a good sense of closure, and maybe even more good would come of it yet. He breathed a prayer.

"My boyfriend kicked me out when I said *no* to the abortion. I needed to get away from Billings. I needed to see the kids. To know that going through this again would be worthwhile, somehow. I didn't know what to do."

Guarded hope shone in Gabe's eyes. Sierra bit her lip so hard Mason was sure she'd pierce it. She stared straight at Erin.

"I've made such a mess of everything. Liz told me today that God loves me. I don't see how." She touched her belly. "But all I know right now is this baby deserves better than I can give her. And Liz said there was no one who deserved a baby more than you." Erin raised her eyes to Sierra. "Can you give her a home?"

"It's a girl?" asked Gabe in a strangled voice.

"I don't know." Erin shook her head. "It's too early to find out, I think. Anyway, I can't afford the tests and stuff. I just think it's a girl."

Sierra leaned forward. "Erin, are you sure? Absolutely positively sure you want to give this baby up?"

Erin rubbed her belly. "Yeah. Even if I got things together right now, I have nothing. No education, no job, no place to live. I can't do this by myself."

"We can help with some of that," Gabe said. "If you're sure."

"A doctor," added Sierra. "Prenatal care."

"Really?" Erin blinked back tears.

Mason found his voice. "I'll call Pastor Dan in Billings if you like, Erin. He helped me so much when I was getting clean. I know he'll help you, too."

"I'm not sure I'm ready for a church guy." Erin glanced at Liz. "Though some of what Liz said today was intriguing. Maybe I'll give it a try."

Mason was so proud of Liz he felt his shirt buttons could pop any second. If he'd needed any more proof that she'd regained her faith, this was it. To offer hope and a future to someone she could have seen as a rival.

"When is the baby due?" asked Sierra softly.

"Late July, best as I can figure out."

Liz leaned closer to Mason, if that were even possible. "I think we should go," she whispered.

He dropped a kiss to her lips. "Good idea." He pulled her to her feet. "Liz and I are headed out now. You guys can take it from here without us, right?"

Moisture gleamed in all three pairs of eyes staring back. *Thank you*, mouthed Sierra to Liz.

"Thank you," Mason said out loud as the door closed behind them. "No wonder Erin thinks you're awesome. So do I."

For the moment, it was quiet outside on the farm. The temperature might be dropping and the rain turning to snow, but he wouldn't let that bother him.

He gathered her close and kissed her.

o0o

"I wanted my friends from kindergarten to come to my party." Avery crossed her arms and scowled. "Plus Miss Kass promised me a pink birthday cake with berries on top and she's not even here."

Liz couldn't help grinning. This crowd of invaders at Green Acres had affected everyone down to the youngest members. They were jammed to the corners with neighbors and friends.

"Miss Kass is in Spokane," Mason said patiently, glancing at Liz. "She has a new job there."

"But she didn't even say goodbye."

"No, but your daddy showed me the surprise she left you."

"A surprise?" A lilt of hope caught Avery's voice.

"A pink surprise. Want to see?"

At Mason's nod, Liz took Avery's hand and led her through the kitchen and larder to the walk-in fridge. Shelves were emptying in both sections, but two covered plates stood on a low shelf. Liz crouched and tipped one of the lids.

"Ohhh," breathed Avery, eyes shining. "It's pink. But where's the berries?"

"What kind of berries are you looking for, child?"

Liz turned to see Mona Graysen standing in the cooler doorway.

"I wanted strawberries."

"You know we can't drive to Super One to buy berries with the bridge out," Liz said. "And even if we could, they don't have any fresh food coming in, either. I bet someone already bought the last of the strawberries."

Avery frowned. "But Miss Kass promised."

"You know, I like strawberries myself, child. I was at Super One on Wednesday afternoon and I picked up a couple of baskets of them." Mona lowered her voice and glanced between Liz and Avery. "Shhh. Now don't go telling these local fooders that I buy out-of-season berries."

"I hope they were delicious," said Liz.

"Were?" Mona shook her head. "They were white on the tips yet. Not even ripe enough to eat. But I did bring them along when we cleaned out the fridge when your brother came to pick us up."

Avery's face brightened. "Really, Mrs. Graysen? You have strawberries right here?"

"I do, little one." Mona shuffled in and pointed at a high shelf with *Graysen* taped to the edge. "Right here." She lifted two small baskets down and held them out to Avery.

"Ohhh." Avery's gaze darted between the berries and Mona's face. "For my birthday party?"

"Sure, child. Maybe that's why the good Lord had me pick them up."

The good Lord. The words reminded Liz of Linda in Des Moines. The good Lord had led her back home, sure enough. Given her a way to make a difference right here. For precious Avery and Christopher. For Erin, Sierra, and Gabe.

The berries on top of the children's birthday cakes would be just that. The crowning touch. Could she be any happier? She could. The day she married Mason. That day was coming.

Epilogue --

The May morning dawned bright and clear and warm. Once again, Green Acres Farm swarmed with extra people — not refugees from the February storm, but guests gathered for a wedding.

Liz stretched in her bed in the duplex for the last time. Later today she and Mason would be off on their honeymoon, and when they returned, she'd be living in the renovated farmhouse with him and the twins.

Mason had gone to work for Brent in spring and lovingly handled every bit of Liz's childhood home, including all the parts that hadn't been there before, like the solar panels on the roof and the bank of storage batteries. The next power outage would see them snug in their own house.

She'd chosen the cabinetry, the flooring, and the paint colors. Maybe someday the little bedroom under the eaves where she'd spent her childhood would be home to a baby.

Erin had arrived yesterday and was ensconced in Sierra and Gabe's spare room in the other half of the duplex. The baby girl — they knew for sure, now — would love the pink room when she made her appearance in two short months. Erin looked radiant. Though she hadn't made a decision for Jesus, she'd been meeting with Pastor Dan and his wife and was taking a bookkeeping course through the local college with Gabe and Sierra's help.

"Hey, Liz! Aren't you awake yet?" Cindy tapped on her bedroom door. "Time's awastin'!"

Both her older sisters were here with their husbands and kids. A true family reunion, and the first time Liz had met some of her nieces and nephews. "I'm awake. Just thinking."

"Well, come out here and have some breakfast while you think."

There wouldn't be another minute of silence until she and Mason were headed for the hotel in Spokane later this evening. Suddenly she couldn't wait to get started.

o0o

Mason stood at the front of the farm's pole barn, Zach and Christopher beside him. Off to the side, Keanan nodded with the beat of his guitar as he shifted to the processional music. Brent escorted Mason's mom down the aisle while his father trailed behind. Mom caught his eye and smiled.

Noel brought Rosemary to her seat near the front. Then Jo, wearing a turquoise sheath and carrying a bundle of spring flowers, rounded the back of the gathering and started up the aisle, her gaze locked with Zach's.

Zach nudged Mason's back. "I got me a gorgeous girl, didn't I?"

Mason grinned but kept his gaze fixed forward.

Waiting.

Avery and Maddie, wearing matching puffy dresses, sprinkled tulip petals on the gravel path. After the long winter and late spring, the roses weren't up yet, but tulips made a great stand-in. Avery beamed up at him, and Mason bent to accept a kiss from his beautiful daughter. She joined Maddie and Jo a few feet away, leaving just enough room for Liz between them.

His bride.

Mason caught his breath.

She came down the path slower than any other bride he'd ever seen, not that he'd been to a ton of weddings. Not that he was impatiently waiting. No, she paced herself for Steve, who'd been determined to walk the aisle without a cane.

It gave Mason longer to feast his eyes. Liz's hair had been swept into some kind of knot on her head and held in place with a wisp of lace. Her gown hugged her curves and swished as she strolled toward him.

If he did nothing the rest of his life but gaze upon her sweet face, he'd die a happy man.

"Who gives this woman to be married to this man?"

Steve looked straight into Mason's eyes. Straight into his heart. "Her mother and I do." Steve bowed his head and prayed a blessing over Liz and Mason.

This. This was what forgiveness looked like. This was beyond acceptance. Beyond what he could ask or think.

Steve pressed Liz's hand into his. "I love you both," he murmured then turned and shuffled to Rosemary's side.

Mason turned to face his bride. This moment, indeed, was the berry on top.

The End

Recipe for Berry Platz ----------

There are likely as many recipes for 'platz' as there are Mennonite cooks. A platz is a baked fruit dessert that consists of a base, a fruit layer, and a crumb topping. While the base may vary from sponge cake to pastry, the version I'm sharing here has a short crust, meaning it contains baking powder.

Makes one 9x13 pan

Bottom Crust
1/2 cup butter
1/2 cup sugar
1 3/4 cup flour
1 egg
1 1/2 teaspoon baking powder

Blend the butter and sugar thoroughly then add the remaining ingredients. Mix together to form a soft dough and pat it into the bottom of a 9x13 cake pan.

Fruit Layer
1 cup of fresh* or frozen** fruit, spread evenly across the bottom crust.
Flour** or sugar*** as needed.

Crumb Topping
1 cup flour
3/4 cup sugar
1/4 cup butter
Dash cinnamon

Crumb the flour, sugar, cinnamon, and butter together and sprinkle over the fruit layer.

Bake at 350 degrees for about 20 minutes, until the fruit is hot and bubbly and the crumbs are golden brown. Best served warm. Try it with a dollop of whipped cream and, of course, a berry on top!

*Like many recipes from the Old Country, platz is infinitely adaptable to fruit in season. Try it with any of these or a combination of two or more: rhubarb, cherries, raspberries, blueberries, huckleberries, peaches, plums, etc. Our favorites are cherries, berries, or plums.

**Frozen fruit has a lot of moisture in it and may cause the bottom crust to become soggy. You can stir the frozen fruit pieces in several tablespoons of flour to coat them before spreading them in the pan to help soak up the juices. There's no exact science, though. If the bottom crust is soggy, it will be a delicious kind of soggy.

***If you're using a tart fruit such as rhubarb, you may wish to sprinkle 1/4 cup of sugar over the fruit before adding the crumb topping. For pitted sweet cherries, no additional sugar is needed. For berries and other fruits that land in between on the sweetness-scale, use your own judgment.

Dear Reader

Do you share my passion for locally grown real food? No, I'm not as fanatical or fixated as our friends from Green Acres, but farming, gardening, and food processing comprise a large part of my non-writing life.

Whether you're new to the concept or a long-time advocate, I invite you to my website and blog at www.valeriecomer.com to explore God's thoughts on the junction of food and faith.

Please sign up for my monthly newsletter while you're there! My gift to all subscribers is *Peppermint Kisses: A (short) Farm Fresh Romance* that follows *Wild Mint Tea* in chronology. Joining my list is the best way to keep tabs on my food/farm life as well as contests, cover reveals, deals, and news about upcoming books. I welcome you!

Enjoy this Book?

Please leave a review at any online retailer or reader site. Letting other readers know what you think about *Berry on Top: A Farm Fresh Romance* helps them make a decision and means a lot to me. Thank you!

If you haven't read the previous books in the series, beginning with *Raspberries and Vinegar,* I hope you will.

Keep reading for the first chapter of *Secrets of Sunbeams,* the first book in my brand new Urban Farm Fresh Romances, a spin-off of this series.

Also, please join my email list to read *Peppermint Kisses,* a short story that takes place at Claire and Noel's wedding.

Secrets of Sunbeams

An Urban Farm Fresh Romance
Book 1

Valerie Comer

GreenWords Media

Chapter 1 --

*E*den Andrusek stopped so suddenly the screen door slammed her backside. Where was Pansy? Eden shaded her eyes and glanced around the backyard. No way. She'd only been inside a minute.

"Pansy!" she yelled, jogging down the three steps to the barren yard. "Where are you?"

The answer seemed to be... nowhere. Eden's gut clenched. *No, no. No, no, no. This can't be happening.*

The gate at the side of the small house was definitely closed. The backyard was completely fenced with no hiding places. Except...

Eden's pulse quickened at the sight of a vertical board in the side fence hanging slightly askew. She ran across the yard, nearly tripping over the metal bucket Pansy had been playing with, and pushed at the errant board. It swung aside. That was definitely enough room for the escape artist.

She crouched and peered through the gap into the neatly mowed lawn of the Victorian next door. A side table with a glass of something clear and red sat beside an empty deck chair facing...

"Pansy! No!"

The goat only glanced over as she chewed the paper dangling from her mouth.

"Drop it, Pansy!" Like that would help. Dogs might be trainable. Goats? Not so much. Eden yanked at the board, but she wasn't as skinny as the Nigerian dwarf. No way was she fitting through that gap. And at eight feet high, she definitely wasn't going over without a ladder.

Eden dropped the board and bolted through the gate and around to the house next door. Man, they didn't even *have* a side gate. She pounded on the door while jabbing the doorbell. Wasn't there a new renter? Surely someone was home. Somebody had to have left the nearly-full glass out there, to say nothing of the papers.

The papers that were being devoured in present time.

She pounded again. "Let me in!"

No voice. No footsteps.

Eden twisted the doorknob, and it gave beneath her fingers. She hesitated for an instant. Should she do this? Was it breaking in if the door was unlocked? Maybe she should go back to her yard, grab a hammer and remove another board or two. That had to be better than entering someone's house uninvited.

She pushed just a little further. Was there a clear path to the back door from here? Maybe she could scoot through with no one the wiser. After all, if someone were home, they'd surely have come to the door by now.

A set of patio doors was clearly visible past the dimly lit interior. On the other side, Pansy knocked the glass onto the deck chair and began to lap up the liquid.

"Hello?" called Eden, gaze locked on Pansy.

"Hey!" a male voice exploded. "Get out of my yard!"

A guy Eden had never seen before wrenched the glass door open and ran onto the patio, his tanned arms flailing.

Whoa. No wonder they called those things muscle shirts. She shouldn't be staring, but she couldn't help herself as he grabbed the remains of the papers off the side table and began to whack Pansy with them.

That did it. No one was going to smack Pansy but her. Not that the goat didn't deserve it. Eden dashed through the house and out onto the back deck, skidding to a stop beside the guy.

"Don't hit her! That's my goat!"

The guy pivoted, hand still holding the sheaf of paper high in the air. His blue eyes blazed at her from beneath damp blond hair that stuck out all over, like he'd been toweling it dry when duty called. "Who are you?"

He was cute. Eden gulped. He was also stinkin' angry, and he had a right to be. She grabbed Pansy's halter and wrenched the slobbery paper fragments from the goat's mouth. She closed her eyes for one brief moment, then straightened and looked the guy in the eye. Although his eyes were much higher than hers.

"My name is Eden Andrusek, and this is Pansy. We, um, we live next door." She pointed. "She broke through the fence. I'm really sorry. I—" she hesitated, glancing at the remaining papers "—I hope this wasn't anything important."

His eyebrows shot up. "Sorry is a good start, but your hope is misguided." He smacked the sheaf against the table, and Eden jumped. He scrubbed a palm against his forehead and shook his head. "You have no idea."

"Is there anything I can do to help?" Eden ventured. She glanced at an architectural drawing on the top page. "Maybe not."

"All you can do is get that stupid animal out of here and fix your fence. I should call the bylaw officer on you."

Was this where she told him she worked in the City of Spokane's animal department? Probably not the best timing. Besides, if he reported her, she might even lose her job. Bylaw officers didn't get as much grace as other residents.

Eden dragged Pansy back a step. "Please don't. It won't happen again. I'll fix that board and check all the other ones, too. Promise."

He took a deep breath and let it out slowly. "I don't know how

I'll get this report done before the meeting on Tuesday now."

"I'm really sorry." Yeah, she knew it didn't help.

He flipped through the papers and chewed on his bottom lip. "Some of it I can reprint. But some were longhand notes to go with the sketches I was doodling. I'd just figured out how to mount the panels on the roof."

Eden frowned. "The what on what roof?"

He tossed her an irritated look. "This project is my chance to prove I know what I'm doing with solar energy. Not that easy when the community center is wedged in the middle of the block and doesn't get much sunshine. It even faces north."

Eden clapped her hand over her mouth. She'd been at the neighborhood meeting that agreed to hire him, but she'd thought he was probably some old guy. What was his name? "Jacob?"

He blinked. "Yes. Have we met?" He looked her up and down, his narrowed gaze lingering on the tattoos on her left arm. "I'm sure I'd remember if we had."

She lifted her chin. Another person who thought they knew everything about her because of her artistic choices. Well, she wouldn't explain a thing to him as long as he wore that sneer on his face. "No, we haven't met. I heard you'd been hired. I didn't know we were neighbors." Just her luck. Cute guy neighbor, into environmental stuff, but stuck up.

She hoisted Pansy into her arms and eyed the path past him to the back door. "I should be going."

"Wait. How did you get back here?" Jacob crossed his arms.

Heat flared across her face. "I came through your house," she mumbled. "Sorry. I heard you yelling at Pansy, and I didn't think. I just ran through."

He shook his head. "Let me escort you back the way you came." He gestured at the open patio door. "After you. And don't let her loose in the house."

oOo

Bang. Thud, thud, bang.

Jacob glared at the fence just ten feet away. The whole structure seemed to vibrate as Eden attacked it with a hammer. At least, he assumed that's what she was doing.

He could just imagine her crouched in the grass on the other side, biting her lip in concentration as she tried to pound the nails in to secure the loose board. Maybe the goat nibbled at her blond-with-a-tinge-of-strawberry ponytail.

A goat in the city.

He'd heard the bleating a few times in the two weeks since he'd moved in next door with his buddy, Grady. They'd looked up the animal bylaws and found that Spokane did, indeed, allow goats and other livestock in this neighborhood near the downtown core. So long as they were well contained, of course.

If Jacob hadn't been hired to outfit the new community center three blocks away with solar panels, he'd have already been looking for a new rental. His gut soured as he stared at the remains of his report, due in just three days. The fence had looked solid, but he hadn't walked the length of it and poked every board. Apparently he should have.

Thud. Bang.

Sounded like Eden was missing the nail more often than hitting it. Didn't she know that screws would hold the board tighter?

Thud. Thwack.

"Ow! Ow, ow, ow."

Good to hear his neighbor wasn't one for cursing. Jacob stared at the barricade. Man, he wasn't going to get any peace unless he went over there and fixed it himself.

"Pan-zeeee!" yelled Eden.

That did it. Jacob surged to his feet, scooped the papers off the patio table — who knew if that goat was going to escape again? — and strode into the house. The drill was in the hall closet, right where it belonged. A quick trigger-pull proved it had plenty of juice. He selected a bag of screws from the bin then marched out the front door, around to the side gate next door, and right in without so much as a knock.

The goat bleated and side-hopped toward him.

Eden whirled and dropped her hammer. "Ouch!" she yelped, rubbing her foot. "You scared me."

"Sorry I didn't knock." Jacob reached behind him for the gate latch. Maybe he shouldn't assume she wanted help. But, no. He was doing it to make sure that menace didn't get back into his space. It wasn't to help Eden so much, and certainly not to get a closer look at her... or her tattoos.

She had dirt on her arms, hair pulling out of its ponytail, and clothes obviously chosen for yard work not glamour. Somehow she managed to be pretty despite the mess, her eyes wild as she retrieved the hammer and stood facing him.

Jacob held up the drill. "I thought maybe you could use a hand."

Her gaze flicked to the fence then back at him as a pinkish tinge crept up her face. "I can manage."

"It's no trouble." Actually, it was, but that was beside the point. He wasn't going to get anything done while listening to her pound the board rather than the nail... or worse, smash her thumb again. "Please. Let me help." He took a few steps closer, trying to keep his eyes on her face, but... roses? Why would she have a ring of roses around her bicep?

Eden crossed her arms and widened her stance.

Guess he hadn't done a good enough job of blanking his expression. "I only want to be neighborly. It sounds like you could use a hand. I have the tools and the ability to use them." Unlike her.

She sighed. "I guess I should be thankful. I prayed for help, so I shouldn't be too picky who God sends my way."

"Am I that bad?" Jacob narrowed his eyes. "You don't even know me." Then the rest of her words caught up to him. "Did you say you prayed?"

She lifted her chin slightly. "I did. I pray about nearly everything, but it seems God sometimes has a sense of humor in how He answers."

"What do you mean by that?" He might not like the answer, but he had to know.

"I pray about everything because God hears and cares about me and my troubles."

Jacob waved a hand. "No, I meant about the humor."

"Huh?"

"You said—"

"I know what I said. Are you telling me you're not making fun of the fact that I pray?"

"Why would I? I pray all the time myself, only I never really thought about God laughing at me when He answers." He'd also never thought about a tattooed woman praying.

"Not laughing, exactly." The goat leaned against Eden's leg, and she crouched down to rub the scruffy head. "Just I was so embarrassed about Pansy getting in your yard and eating your papers. Why couldn't God have sent an answer that didn't make me feel even more stupid and inept?"

Was there supposed to be a valid reply to that? "I'm pretty sure God sent me." It suddenly seemed clear, anyway. "You wouldn't want to tell God you didn't like His answer, would you?"

"I didn't say..." Her words faded away and her face took on a brighter hue. "Never mind."

Interesting. But he didn't have all day. "Let me at that fence?"

She nodded and backed up a few steps, granting him access.

A quick glance at the boards in the vicinity of the loose one indicated that any one of them might work its way loose next. He might as well plan on doing the whole side, just to keep his yard secure.

The goat butted his leg, and Jacob winced. That could leave a bruise. Why would anyone want to own a goat, anyway?

"How can I help?"

"Keep her out of my way." He spied an enclosure farther back, where several hens scratched in the dirt. "Like in there." Man, she had a veritable farm.

"I don't think so." Eden's hands found her hips. "She spends enough time locked up when I'm at work."

Jacob frowned, pointing his drill at the fence. "Isn't that what led to the problem in the first place? She's an animal. Put her in the pen."

"No." Eden leaned a little closer, brown eyes sparking. "She's my family. She'll be fine in the yard."

He could think of all kinds of things to say about someone who looked at a goat as a family member. Her eyes dared him to say them.

Just then, Pansy picked up a metal bucket and tossed it over her shoulder, missing his leg by mere inches. The goat lowered her head and stared at him.

Seemed both females in the space trusted him equally. *Excellent start, Riehl. Excellent start.*

Secrets of Sunbeams
is available where you purchased *Berry on Top*.

Author Biography

Valerie Comer lives where food meets faith in her real life, her fiction, and on her blog and website. She and her husband of over 30 years farm, garden, and keep bees on a small farm in Western Canada, where they grow and preserve much of their own food.

Valerie has always been interested in real food from scratch, but her conviction has increased dramatically since God blessed her with three delightful granddaughters. In this world of rampant disease and pollution, she is compelled to do what she can to make these little girls' lives the best she can. She helps supply healthy food — local food, organic food, seasonal food — to grow strong bodies and minds.

Her experience has planted seeds for many stories rooted in the local-food movement, in both the Farm Fresh Romance series and the new Urban Farm Fresh Romance series, as well as in the Riverbend Romance novellas.

To find out more, visit her website at www.valeriecomer.com, where you can read her blog, explore her many links, and sign up for her email newsletter to download the free short story: *Peppermint Kisses: A (short) Farm Fresh Romance 2.5.* You can also use this QR code to access the newsletter sign-up.

Made in the USA
Monee, IL
11 June 2021